NARROWLY

ARNO BOHLMEIJER

Narrowly

Edited by Peter Wright

Published in North America and Europe by Running Wild Press. Visit Running Wild Press at www.runningwildpublishing.com. Educators, librarians, book clubs (as well as the eternally curious), go to www.runningwildpublishing.com.

Paperback ISBN: 978-1-963869-48-4
eBook ISBN: 978-1-963869-47-7

"The line between wrong and right
is the thread from a spider's web."
Katie Melua

"Sometimes I believe in fate,
but the chances we create, always seem to ring more true."
Mike Batt

To Florian, Fenna, Elias,
taking me far
across mental borders,
and warming my heart.

To Lisa and Peter,
seeing this delicate story,
giving readers the chance to witness
how culprits and victims can meet and heal.

1
THE SLICING OF TIME

<>

They have left the baby alone in the house, at first only for a sprint to a neighbor or the nearest store, always highly responsible and aware of time or safety.

Now they collect his sister Dilli from pre-school by bike. A chat on the sidewalk is kept brief, ended politely or abruptly. The habit and trust have grown on them slowly: they've never had a flat tire or an accident, and there's been no reason to fret about burglars, a fire, or sudden illness.

Mom Nomi loves her work as an honest and modest estate agent, including the moments with baby Art joining her for some exploring and minor chores.

This regular Thursday afternoon of good spirits, Nomi goes to buy groceries with Art and Dilli, who are so intense and perceptive, each of them seems to count for two outstanding handfuls.

They're at ease in the cargo-bike seats, facing each other, and on the way back Nomi has just enough energy left to stop at bike shops, hoist them out, and look at a two-wheeler for Dilli.

It's difficult to find the right size, due to her short legs and an amount of uncertainty that clashes with her passion for adventure and investigation. Disillusioned in two shops, Dilli's meekness is in tragi-comic contrast with the way she entered them.

Parking the bike outside the third store, in a friendly and calm street, they gather their last courage but find that Art has fallen asleep among the many if mild and humming outdoor sounds. Nomi doubts, peaking in. It would be a shame to disturb Art's healthy sleep, and Dilli has been so good about it all...

They agree, "We can give it one more go, just hop in and see – without him."

By the large windows, their bike must be visible from inside. There's no sunlight on Art's face, no draught or funny flurries of wind... "OK, Dil, he's fine here, we'll watch him and be back in a minute."

Nomi checks Art's firm seat belt, she locks the bike and holds the key, for a sense of quickness and security. They go in and leave the door wide open, so should Art wake up crying, for some crazy or usual reason, she'd hear him and be there in a second. They're really in the same breathing space, aren't they?

Dilli drifts between excitement and resignation, but when they spot the perfect sky-blue bike with the low step, her joy is heart-stealing. Nomi peers out the window, where a bunch of big bikes diminish her view. She squints, it's all quiet, and the stillness of Dilli's anticipation draws her eye and mind back inside, with a blurring twist of space and time.

Used to moderation all around, Dilli is afraid to believe this luck, and Nomi pauses a moment to watch her and take that happiness in.

Life has not stopped, it pretends to go fast. With careful purpose, Dilli is riding around the shop, and during some haste or delay at the till, she won't part with the bike, which is needed for the barcode. Normally she keeps away from strangers, as Nomi has made her promise ten times, but now she stays close to the busy man and holds on to the bike.

Once or twice, Mom says, "Just a sec" and Dilli knows the difference between a sec and "later". Sometimes that helps to be patient and wait.

Then she steers out without swaying or crossing the street, which is not allowed, either. Her new bike seems as grand as the one out here, standing solid and silent, but the cozy, two-seat cargo box is so very empty that she can feel more than here and now, in her tummy and legs.

<>

"Never switch your microphone or camera off!" is the creed of a good producer, for any live or recorded interview.

Journalist Anne Hoaver finished college with Honors and big expectations, not only because her work was far above average.

In her early days as a freelancer, before stumbling into motherhood, Anne phoned a prominent newspaper's editor and said, "What about an interview with David Grossman?"

"What's the journalistic urgency?" the editor said, catching her off-guard.

"Well, I admire his work..." Anne began, instead of, "His books are sold by the millions worldwide; the man is a treasure that I'll fathom. Buy me a cheap ticket, I'll stay in a hostel and roam around for two days and nights, like his most original characters."

The proposal was rejected, but a few weeks later the same paper featured a page-size interview with David Grossman. After more examples of such "coincidence" in Anne's life, her innocence grew grim.

As a consolation or passionate investment, it was her own initiative to translate a part of a Spanish novel, a hidden gem.

"Not commercial enough," said the publisher on second thoughts, but six months later the book was turned into a major feature film – and translated by someone who'd heard *that* news before Anne did.

Through fate or synchronicity or absurdity her best ideas tended to end up with somebody else. It drove her mad, but she ignored that here and buried it there. There was work enough left.

Her journalistic writings had as much feeling as pluck, depth and a special style that dazzled many good editors, who were keen on her spontaneity, but they warned her for inflammable impulsivity, "Use your head, Anne!"

"What did I say?" Someone sighed when Anne's baby was not planned, certainly not by the father.

She interviews authors, athletes, politicians, and she loves writing her pungent, enchanting columns for weekly NUNA, even with baby Reg at her feet in his rocking seat or play pen.

Anne takes her anxiety medication, brings the monitor into the garden, pressing the volume buttons, and moving it with her everywhere. She always washes her hands and checks the windows, her watch, and the stove burners.

Very soon she loves Reggie deeply, he's a dream kid who doesn't seem troubled by the trials of life like stomach cramps or a diaper that's too tight.

"Yeah, he's on a cloud," Anne says with mocking concern, when Reg is called a bouncing boy again. "He's so easy-going, no ounce of bother to anyone."

"Wake up, woman, he'll be teething; his fangs will catch up!"

He's a bit late in that respect, which does disconcert her. Silly jokes about "an ancient soul" upset her disproportionally.

On the whole she withdraws more and more, content in a brittle or little peace of mind, fortunate with work that can be done from home, even her interviews, so neatly and adequately that everybody is pleased.

Anne will keep sufficient contacts and incomes for someone whose lifestyle is voluntarily moderate. In case of an outdoor interview or an editorial meeting, she can afford day care for Reg, and sometimes she leaves him – only a minute – for instance, to mail a letter that can't be emailed, or a signed contract.

She loves taking Reg with her, but now and then he's in such a sound sleep that a sense of confidence lets her go a tad further, like ten minutes to a store and get something important or a treat, when a humble celebration is in order.

She always checks every possible risk and has a big note in the car as well as in her pocket, with her name and address – *baby Reg is asleep upstairs!* – in case something worse than a flat tire were to happen.

On her return he can be exactly as she left him, not having blinked an eye, or he looks around curiously and smiles to her, all of which confirm her good faith. They always embrace gratefully, bonding placidly.

"Intuition is the blend of reason and feeling," says her wise and kind doctor.

"So," she thinks out loud, "when it feels alright in the brain and guts, can Reg be home alone for a minute?

"I agree."

"Five minutes?"

"Hm," Doc says. "Yes."

"And fifteen or twenty?"

"Ah, good question, the eternal boundaries..."

He reflects hard and the jury is still out.

The family doctor, Mullan, is a gray-haired, sympathetic man in a homely office. What human person can decide such matters?

Anne pledges not to skip medication, although her nervous inclination has been under control for years.

<>

Still on the broad sidewalk, clasping the handlebars of her brand-new bike, Dilli is torn between bliss – is it hers for real now? – and the discovery that the world has gone wrong, since Art can't walk or climb yet. Ready to cycle home as a grown-up, she's waiting for Mom and Art.

Her stare at the bike box is seen from behind by Nomi, who gets nauseous in her whole body. She doesn't want to move another inch, knowing too much already, but her senses cover ground all over the place, and the limbs try to follow through glue. She glares around, checks the bike blindly, trips and turns, afraid to see Dilli and afraid to take her eyes off her. She clutches her head and stumbles over nothing, gawking at people walking by, accosting them without a voice or an "excuse me."

"Where's my son? Have you seen someone with a little boy? Six months... Have you seen a baby in a green jacket, right here or nearby?"

Splinters of time can be life-deciding, but they're slipping through fingers, hitting her, swelling her throat. Will she rush and look for Art, or phone for help first? How long before that would arrive and confront her with reality?

She scurries against the wind and her better judgment, not getting far.

"Wait here, Dil, stay put."

Which Dilli always does, before crossing streets and everything.

The sunlight is knife-sharp in Nomi's eyes, when she finds her phone and wipes her brow, dialing, in and out of a daze. She lifts Dilli with her little wheels and all into the safe cargo-bike, and a police voice asks for the street name.

So they take her seriously? This is no frantic and inhuman prank of some television kind?

It's a scalpel of reality, which grows and misshapes.

On the bike that's cumbersome now, they plod between the shops and cars, past pedestrians, traffic poles, flower pots, market stands with colorful products.

While Nomi's head fills up with mucus, now burning, then ice-cold, she gets off the strong bike, which just stops and stands here on its three wheels, and she reels into a shop to throw a glance at God knows what, red in the face and sweating, panting. But a scrap of her brain is working sardonically: watch it, next thing, Dilli could be gone too.

With a hand on her bright-blue bike, Dilli sits up and helps, calling out Art's name shyly, knowing better, too. She'd recognize his voice anywhere, so he's still asleep, must be.

"Can I go to Granddad?" she says hoarsely. "Let's call him."

<>

Bernard Bloomsdale, a young granddad and famous but amiable and timid author, may be outdoors, writing on paper in ample concentration, his phone turned off, deliberately or by accident.

He could also be with an editor and journalist, discussing a book title and cover design or review, holding a glass during a festive book presentation with microphones and cameras. At such gatherings he might catch glimpses of Anne Hoaver, but they don't know each other and both try to avoid the crowds, although networking becomes horribly essential.

About Bernard's first novel an eminent critic said, "If Bloomsdale did not experience this himself, he has an incredible ability to enter a person's mind and feelings. If he did go through it himself, he merits big praise as a writer."

The book's blurb mentioned its "authenticity and intimacy." What marketing expert had thought of that ambiguity?

At the time, well-known literary radio journalist John Gallen requested an interview and visited Bernard's former house on the old picturesque street, to record their conversation for a broadcast in the evening.

Pleasantly nervous, Bernard answered the door, shook Gallen's hand and saw the man's eyes running down his legs to the feet, floating back up – curious or insecure? Bernard didn't stop to think further then. With supple and tough steps he preceded Gallen up the quite steep stairs, to his study with two antique armchairs.

The recorder and microphone were tested and planted between them.

"No problem?" Gallen said.

"Only making me self-conscious."

"Never mind, that will pass. We'll be very busy with your book."

"And," Bernard worried, "what if you find a technical defect tonight?"

"Ha! I'll hurry back here or make up all sorts myself."

Bernard laughed at the bold joke, that would be dangerously true coming from some journalists, and it was the friendly or defiant start of a discussion about the young man who undergoes a leg amputation at age seventeen. He fights with the doctors and life, with the prosthetic leg and himself, the novel's protagonist.

At a given moment both awkward and thoughtful, Gallen asked, "How is your handicap now?"

It should have been live television: each second of Bernard's struggle was observed by Gallen, whose eagerness and sympathy didn't match his reputation.

"I um..." Bernard began.

A fraction of silence on the radio can be as fatal as a general power cut. Fully aware of that, Bernard forgot that a recording could be edited by experts. "Actually, you know..."

His humor and brain and big breakable heart were battling outside of time: *handicap* – do you mean my tender spot for melancholy? Sensitivity? Over-sized honesty or naivety? My ego or impatience? The fear of pain and war and sea-level rise. Not death itself but some ways of dying or what may precede it, such as a slowness and saying goodbye.

His mouth formed parts of words. "Y'mean..."

Why didn't the idiot pick up a thread and give it a clever, witty and above all sincere twist?

Bernard's eyes noted the microphone and Gallen's despair: wasn't it autobiographic then, the leg amputation?

Irreversibly Gallen turned the machine off. The finest compliment a writer can receive – the reader's belief that it's a true story – was erased unused.

After some clarification and raw disappointment on both sides, Gallen began anew and asked the same questions, but, taken aback by the man's lack of inspiration, Bernard became pre-occupied, toneless, unable to make a smart suggestion: do edit and use the first take, it's revealing and only human, a fascinating opportunity for great journalism!

Yeah, exposing my incompetence! Gallen would say.

Bernard would receive numerous more media requests, but he grew reticent, sometimes torn between honor, morals and special chances.

<>

During interviews for the radio or an article, Anne Hoaver never switches her devices off, she makes sure there's no need to, and when a colleague of Bernard's requests to see the text of her article before publication, no offence is taken. "The piece will benefit."

At work in the living-room, Anne checks the baby monitor, opens the door to the hallway and listens there.

On principle she honors and sticks to the spoken words of her guests, but so far she's refused to print some trends or deterioration of language: 'the person *that...*' replacing 'the person *who...*' or 'less' used for 'fewer', even on The News and in official statements.

At the invitation of quality journal NUNA, she writes a series of unusual columns called *Denoting*, in which a degree of humor and mildness tackles little or big public disgraces, to shake people awake. As NUNA has sworn that her alias will remain intact, she'll be direct and truthfully to the point –

SEX

Is it characteristic, this ignorance of men who pee standing up? Can they help it that a squirt flares out capriciously and shows the boundaries of a toilet? After all, a penis may not be steered easily.

The fact that urine is a sticky stuff can't be blamed on gentlemen, either. It's just bad luck for the woman who cleans or comes next.

Benevolently she pins up a polite note: MEN, HAVE A SEAT, PLEASE.

But will civil decency or basic respect be learned? A man has so many duties as it is. Thanks, Creator (M/F), for the genius fact that an erection blocks the pee way.

. . .

Up to a year ago Anne lived with Evan. He had a mellow and attractive side, but another part of him sneered when she mentioned the toilet, and that was the foolish beginning of worse. As to their unborn child, Evan suggested a termination and was vexed when she refused.

He may have had his unmentioned reasons.

Did she see him through bad glasses?

Each of them was out of reach to the other. Two years of intimacy with success and attempts ended in a synopsis: he gave her the cottage and made a clean sweep, to which she agreed. That seemed to buy or pay off the baby with all the work and responsibility.

After her consent, the resoluteness of his departure gave her a shock with a fear of the future that never faded: Reg could be a crybaby or might have a nasty disease, defying her abilities. But she would not think of that anymore. Every day she'd be thankful for their health and happiness.

Once in a while, people called her unstable, or a mean person would say: "Is it the monthly bitch again? Go see a doctor and ask for pills. Your moods are a liability!"

If her mental sensitivity had been a point for 'not having kids', Anne might have agreed, but the pregnancy went very well, including the emotions and moods, as if she got into a natural balance.

The father missed the most part of that. Dreading complications of second thoughts or grudges, they didn't keep in touch, although for some time she expected him back on the doorstep again, bashfully sad and mad, begging to see his son and take him out for a day to the zoo or Fair or Formula II.

Look, she'd say, we can't be lost between the past and present, I won't have it!

Or would she be happy to give it a go? Thrilled to give them both a second chance?

. . .

Today Anne wants to go into town, but Reg sleeps long. She never wakes him and now she's afraid to leave him. Silly misgivings can be corny or right.

Both indoors and out in the garden, the batteries of the best monitor are always charged to the utmost. It enables her to work a stretch in concentration, and the silences (what's 'long' anyway?) don't trouble her exceedingly or constantly – that's what he's like – except today.

A vague uneasiness can be exaggerated or eerily right.

In the garden, musing about an audacious and true column, she tries to pull weeds with their roots and all. She relishes a coffee break but glances at her watch in doubt: let Reg sleep now, in order to skip a nap later and give him an early night?

She hates making choices that have too many consequences. Can something go wrong because she's frightened of it, or is it the other way round? *If only* caused angst: *if only I'd been alert one minute earlier... Please, can I start from scratch?* But she doesn't want to be hysterical.

When a doctor talks about instincts, it sounds feasible and interesting. But how to turn them into wisdom and practice?

Such thoughts can drive her crazy again. She won't think at all since little things would become heavy. She needs the bathroom, the coffee is funny on her stomach, or it's just a bit of histrionic sickness because she forgot to eat.

So, girl, she admonishes herself, you sit and breathe, and read what you've written. You can soon be active and practical again when Reg is awake. He loves the home-making bustle.

When or *if* he's awake... Other languages have one word for both, so in those countries people don't need to choose. Or they do even more! We always have to choose. But why the heck stop and think about simple words?

That's my passion and profession: compelling and boundless. It's a nuisance, though, to be so maddeningly conscious of details, for instance when shallow celebs are crowding TV land, and their language becomes the standard crap.

Can she hear Reg crying now or is it *her* fear? He never seeks attention, and for all she knows, he may have been waiting for ages. But hold on, crying could also be a good thing; at least that would not be worrying.

She climbs the stairs and there's no need to go on tiptoes. With a song she'd like to let him know that she's coming, but what on earth is wrong with her lungs? Halfway up the stairs she can't breathe, needs to pause, wants to call out: your mom is here, on her way!

Whatever she learned before, it's no use anymore: take a breath and sigh, press your feet on the floor, sweep your arms or rest the hands on your head. Her throat and chest are frozen. This can't melt, only break; it's like brain freeze on a full-body scale. But the pain around her heart is worse, while the stairs are a wintery hill, a slope of ice where she slides down. It would take all spring or summer for this ice to melt.

Up in Reg's room she crouches, then shuffles and crawls to his crib. Shaking her head, she carries him, sits on the floor and rocks back and forth, going numb, just mumbling "No" countless times.

She lies down and rests him on her chest, his head on her neck, so close that his lack of breathing is felt in her flesh. Her eyes fade as well, while the world has gone still.

2
FORTY-EIGHT HOURS

<>

In the books that made Bernard a well-known author, the death of a loved one played a main part, and he found it hard that 'great success' was based on tragedy. How to receive the compliments, how to celebrate reprints and prizes?

At the parties he felt uncomfortable, but that was also due to the buzz of those who found themselves important. The letter from a sublime poet, expressing moving gratitude for his novel *The Lee*, does not feature in her big biography. He never showed it to media people.

When he was invited several times to appear on national television, he would have liked the publicity as an author, but not via his fragile books on death, despite the sympathy of a journalist. He declined even thirty minutes on a major talk-show at a location of Bernard's choice, although he did hesitate for days.

Reluctant to write another true and intimate story, he can't wait to invent his heart out for an immensely exciting and romantic adventure, that will keep the readers awake at night and make them late for work. Then the media can ask him all the cheeky or stereotype questions –

"How did you get the idea?"

"With a spark that started a life of its own."

"Such as?"

"The woman's fall down the escalator. To be terribly honest... I get annoyed by people standing still in the middle of an escalator, for example at the train station, blocking the way when I'm in a hurry."

And the devil's advocate says, "It's only twenty seconds!"

"In which all or nothing can happen."

"How do you mean?"

"In seconds we can make a decision, that may set a chain in motion and turn life upside down."

"For a catastrophe?"

"Or a miracle," Bernard says.

"With a special encounter?"

"Or something like that."

"And then?"

"The manuscript was finished and promptly I read this in the newspaper: *Injuries after pushing on escalator*."

"Oh, do you believe in such coincidence?"

Bernard obliges. "Coincidence is an instance without meaning or purpose. And whether this did mean anything..."

"What do you call it otherwise?"

"Oh dear... Destiny?"

"*It's meant to be?*" the journalist fishes.

"Yes, I believe in that very much."

"Or you're pulling the legs of fools."

"Why would I do that?" Bernard asks.

"For marketing and promotion! Do you ever tempt or defy fate?"

"No, I do prefer to call it destiny."

The prosaic phone disturbs Bernard's wayward reverie, and he wavers before answering.

It's his son-in-law, Mark, who is not fond of social calls, and he asks with a stammer, "Can you come over?"

"Oh? Now?"

"Please."

"Um, yes, what's wrong?"

"I'll explain later."

"No, Mark, it's a twenty-minute drive; tell me now."

"But... Art is gone. Missing."

Bernard puts a thumb and finger on his eye sockets. Hang on, son, this can't be, that happens to others only, rich or famous or notorious, and in the crime series we like on TV, so this must be a misunderstanding, since the four of you are kind, normal and honest people.

"How long?"

"An hour, but I'm on the phone because it's serious."

Bernard looks up and around, shaking his head. "Where's Nomi?"

"Here, home, she can't speak."

"And Dilli?"

"Just... Sorry."

"Have you called the police?"

"Yes," Mark says. "They're on their way."

"So am I."

<>

Anne is losing her mind, but she knows that cot death happens to babies in lovely and safe beds, used or new, even last week in broad daylight, in a care center among other children and sweet staff, trained and experienced.

As to Reg, she only knows the other phrase: he's gone.

From his cozy and quiet room with tender colors on the first floor of this warm and good cottage, where he was protected even from sharp lights.

At the same time, he looks as peaceful as ever, his face serene, because he's there where you don't need to say goodbye. Who claims that a heaven is far away?

True, he's been *too* good for the world, there's nothing to keep him here. It's alright, he has no sense of place or time or regret. She'd better bury what's left behind, return the remains to dust as the Bible says, because it's supposed to be that way, apparently, as a matter that speaks for itself – predestined by higher or lower powers? Who keep their mouths shut tight. Cowards!?

The stony coldness in her limbs could be over. All she needs to do is dig something relatively small, but in a shielded corner of the garden she works herself into a mad sweat, encouraged by the whole place, telling her in loud and clear polyphony: you can plant a beautiful tree here! Not for camouflage, you don't need that in the secluded country garden of this detached old little cottage. No, it's an homage and image: in winter a tree just *looks* dead, but right through the rugged wood the softest leaf will grow again, and ethereal petals will bloom. By the time the foliage gets dark and heavy, all will fall off again, for another fresh start. What more can you wish for?

Even afterwards there's no wish to eat, she drinks profusely, takes a loud shower without end, rubbing and scrubbing as if her hands and nails have toiled in the soil themselves.

Before rush hour she cycles mechanically toward Garden Center, where they have a young and white-flowering fruit tree, which can be delivered tomorrow.

The area is a mixture of lively, carefree and colorful, and here's a shopping street full of character. Without imposing, the wide sidewalks and porches look hospitable, appealing, and a kid-cargo bike fits well, waiting for someone to take care of the lost baby, outside the bike store.

She can park her own bike just yards away – around this corner – steady and ready – and with calm quickness it's no effort or time to click the safety belt open and lift him in one soundless go, all natural again. "Here's my darling good boy, it hasn't been too long now, has it."

Look: our carrying sling, straight from our bag, since life is gliding back into place, isn't it.

"Right, Reg, high time: you must be thirsty. We're on our way home, you can cradle in the big sling, and your bottle is waiting for you. We'll be there in a minute."

What are you gazing at with your big eyes? Mommy will never leave you like that again, all by yourself out there, except in your own cozy room, and in the garden. Or, later, you might enjoy the nice house with other children, for a morning or two. We explored last week, remember, and you found it quite interesting.

"Oh, you've got the sun in your eyes?"

Just keep low in your snug hole, as Mommy needs to steer and focus. We'll take the quiet road and the bike track. Never mind the police car, there's no siren on, because nothing is wrong. They protect us against mean people, or they deal with traffic when there's been an accident.

Ah, it's a bit scary after all? OK, here's a short-cut, leaving town. Comes with the weather, everybody goes out, and you are lucky to have a mom working freelance, available!

I'll sing to you, but hold on, people don't see you in your deep sling, so they'd think I'm bonkers when I sing a nursery rhyme.

Oh, you want to look around and see those people? First you need your bottle and we'll cut your hair, or else they won't know you anymore. It's grown so much and all, with the peace and good food. Fancy more fruit already? We'll go easy on the strawberries, though. Your tummy doesn't like these pips in them.

"There, we're back, see?"

As practical as usual, she puts him in the play pen – he's hardly protesting – and she boils water for the bottle that's been ready on the kitchen board, thoroughly rinsed and dried earlier. No bacteria and no leak! Add the exact amount of cold water, better lukewarm than too hot.

She lifts him up. "Ho, are you greedy today!"

As soon as he sees the bottle, he almost jumps off her arms, crying blue murder, but they reach the couch safely.

"Easy... Goodness, as if you've had no food or drink for days. How long have we been in the fresh air? Wait, better sit properly, or else I'll have a sore arm, remember?"

He swallows the wrong way and quickly she pulls the bottle back, putting him upright. "Well, you're so impatient..." She tries a smaller hole of the bottle top, which has opposite effects.

My my, you're growing like anything. And you're right, we'll find new clothes; these don't fit anymore, we'll get rid of them straightaway, for something completely new!

"Hey, Reg, watch it, we don't want the hiccups now, do we."

His eyes are probing. A hand slides along the bottle and stops to hold her thumb. He's drinking more calmly, yet she makes him pause a few times, although he thinks two seconds will do.

"Yes, love runs through the tummy, I know."

Decisive, she changes his diaper and clothes.

After that she cuts his hair deftly, as if all of that was due, and they cuddle until he smiles. "No tickling, I agree, you can really trust me. Ten minutes play time? Fine, I'll send a message to my boss and tell her to have a little patience. I can do with a nap too, frankly."

Gently she lays him in the pen again.

Inconspicuously his old clothes are wrapped in plastic and dropped in the outside can, and how long was that, leaving him out of sight: one minute?

<>

Mark is an active and handy dad, who tackles complications well as long as something can be *done*: the dishes, cook dinner, feed a kid, take them to bed. He can do Art's bottle in forty seconds.

On the dining table most food is untouched, in spite of encouragements, "Let's try and stay fit, with a clear mind. For when Art comes back."

And they keep picturing that moment ahead. But it's hard to say his name. One doesn't very often, really, not in general? The use of 'she' and 'he' is a habit when you have a girl and a boy. But even the word "have" becomes difficult now.

Art's bottle has recently been scalded, along with the new top. It was tough to find the right one. For his age he's extremely attached to what's familiar, like the color and shape or size of things – and people? Is he devoted to everything and everyone around him, or is he spoilt? Some strictness will be effective.

"I don't want to sleep," Dilli tells Mark upstairs.

"But you're very tired," he tries.

"No, the police must go away."

"The police are good people. Maybe you can sit in their car one day."

"Now?" she asks. "To steer?"

"No, they've come to help now, looking for Art."

"I want to look too, but not in the bike."

With the lightest pressure Mark makes her undress. "First go to sleep, Dil. Tomorrow, you can help."

"No, tomorrow he's back. Then I can skip school."

"We'll see," says the Dad.

"Or we don't see him. Will he sleep too?"

She's scrutinizing Mark's face and he turns away, rubbing his brow. "Yes, Art is going to bed too."

"Outside? At the farm?"

Mark's hand covers his mouth and his eyes close a second.

"At school?" Dilli asks.

"No."

"Where's the bike?"

"In the yard, by the shed."

"But Art is gone. Can he sleep then? He can come in my bed."

Mark clears his throat. "I think... he's deep asleep in a nice cot."

"At Granddad's? No, Granddad is downstairs. Is he a good finder, far away? Me too, behind the street."

"Dil, I can see in your eyes how sleepy you are."

While she reflects on that, her arms and legs have slipped into the pajamas. "Will you sing to me?"

As Mark does his best, Dilli is cuddling Toy Cat for two, and it's fairly flexible.

In the tasteful and large living-room with its current function of Incident Room, which ought to be for a short while, detective Hattum says, "A team of officers have been to all the stores in that street, canvassing and patroling."

The state of affairs is a mere outline: they've searched all the trash cans and more, men and women have been seen with babies, but nobody looked suspicious, there was no deviant behavior, and no baby was crying, which can be a good or a bad sign.

"We've released Art's picture and description, and we're paying visits to previous offenders in this field."

They don't ask for specifics of the latter.

Radiant six-month old boy, dark-blue eyes, brown hair with little curls in the neck. Grass-green jacket, beige trousers, blue slippers – like a million kids throughout the country or abroad, and some vanish mysteriously for horrible or harmless reasons, wounded or miraculously unscathed. Or dead. Is *never found* the heaviest outcome?

Hattum and his sergeant Ingram have asked many questions, most of them to the parents or Bernard, and some to each other with the eyes or aside at a distance.

"Who is your family doctor?"

Mark gets a piece of paper.

"Our apologies for delicate questions; we *have* to ask them – it's all standard procedure. How long was Art alone? Out of sight?"

"A few minutes. I don't know exactly."

Did she often leave him behind? Has she suffered from post-natal depression? How is their relationship?

"Mark, where were you when Art went missing?"

Sad as well as bitter, he says, "At work."

Here and there, with witnesses for corroboration, if needed.

The police are not flesh-and-blood humans yet, but nondescript strangers, asking from their routine list, "Do you have any enemies at work or elsewhere?"

"No."

As if all this is anything deliberate, criminal, instead of a grotesque misunderstanding.

But they have to investigate.

"Is there a colleague or client you've crossed, caused grief?"

"No, we're a good agency."

"Forgive us, anything personal and seemingly rude or absurd, could be important – in a roundabout way."

"Any mental illness in the extended family?" Ingram asks.

He can't have been over forty, but his hair is gray.

"No," says Mark. "Nor a crazy burn-out."

"How's contact with the neighbors?"

"Good, neutral. No wars or beefs over noise, a tree, a fence."

Is that all weirdly easy?

In exchange for Art, they would have gruesome fights with everybody.

Neither Nomi nor Mark or Bernard can tell something to help

the investigation. They are in genuine shock, but to a sharp detective even that can be deceptive, sick, charming, and hiding anything. From the start the police need to keep very open minds, be ready for extremes and new insights. Disturbed people can be geniuses.

Hattum might be a family man, mellowing, and how does *he* combine that with work of this kind? Alright, if he's about fifty, children of his would be grown up.

"Sorry," Hattum explains, "please understand that each little factor, physical or mental, has to be looked at, either to rule something out or create a lead."

"Yes," Mark says.

And yet the conversation runs on parallel roads that never cross.

"Given some recent tragedies..." Ingram begins, not finishing: like the kid found in the car boot after years of undernourishment and abuse, or bodies found in the oddest places, even close to home.

"But after confusion," Hattum hastens to take over, "the smallest or oddest detail can also lead to miracles."

"Yes," Bernard says, "you're doing your job – the more thorough the better."

Without knowing if it's anyone's fault that there's no lead or clue.

Nomi is a shadow in her own house, gray-faced on a table chair, afraid to look at someone, answering questions with a nod or a single word, and often she can only shake her head. "Sorry that I don't understand."

To a stranger like Ingram, it might seem she's aloof, while her daze must be a form of self-protection, concentration, in a state of shock. Lost in thought, she drinks the juice that Bernard gives her, taking timid and careful sips to prevent throwing up.

In a certain way it might help to turn or empty the stomach and lose a burden, but she doesn't want to. Each image and feeling of every moment with Art needs to stay in.

Her eyelids are sagging and her fingers push them open, as if to keep them alive and active. Most of what's unbearable would be seen with closed eyes. Her hands rub the temples, eyebrows and cheeks.

Nomi stands up and walks to listen in the hallway. For a long time she leans on the banisters and sits on a step of the stairs, heaving and fighting sickness.

Through Dilli's bedroom door on the third floor comes her voice, talking and singing, "Left, right, back."

Nomi crawls up the stairs, but on the second-floor landing she sits motionless again, her feet one step down, until Dilli calls out softly, stretching the vowels. "Mommy... Granddad..."

As it sounds tentative instead of whining, Nomi wants to go and answer all the more, and her will appears to provide energy for the next steps. Children notice more than most people think or want to know, and every day Nomi is surprised by all the things Dilli perceives.

Out of breath she stops by Dilli's closed door, hearing her legs brushing restlessly – against what?

The very instant Nomi opens the door, Dilli springs up. "Hi!"

"Hi, Dil."

Nomi sinks on the floor beside the bed, and Dilli climbs onto her lap, holding Cuddly Cat, nestling and sucking her thumb hard. Cat may serve as a lifebuoy in the big world, but occasionally it needs repairing.

Suddenly Nomi is felled by sleep like an anesthetic, impossible to fight. One more minute of standing or sitting would snap something in her head. And she mutters, "Let's get in bed."

Dilli is quietly thrilled and curls up to share the lair. Helpless, Nomi sleeps immediately.

<>

"Well, Reg, it's really time for bed now," Anne tells him with gentle authority, but when he sees the cot, he cries.

"No no, your belly is full, you've got a clean diaper... Sshh. Are you *too* tired? I know, it's been some intense day! Or are you teething after all?"

With a finger she tries to feel inside his mouth, but he flounders. As he's crying, she can go ahead yet and find bulges and white tips – are they? "In that case, my boy, there's not much Mom can do! Nature is cruel. Hush, here's your Bear and the music. Sshh, better listen then."

She turns him on his side, but he rolls back already and pushes Bear away. Anne pulls Bear's rope and Art is caught off guard by the cheerful Mozart tune. While his big wet eyes look up, he seems to recoil.

"Good, sweetheart, now lie on your side, close to Bear in the corner, and sleep tight. See you tomorrow, or sometime in the night, that's OK too."

Anne pulls the thin rope again, as far as possible without breaking it. She rushes out of the room and heaves a sigh on the landing.

Halfway down the stairs she can hear him again, but it's alright for babies to cry themselves to sleep. Besides, the phone rings. Everybody assumes that he's in bed by seven, all content and everything.

Before answering, her eyes close a sec and she bites her lip. "Hi, Mom."

"Oh, girl, you're panting!"

"Yeah, coming from upstairs. I think Reg is teething now."

"Well, be grateful that he's home safe. Or haven't you heard and seen?"

"What?"

"A boy the same age is missing, from your area, and I believe he even looks like Reg! But OK, I'm having Alzheimer's, you keep telling me that I overreact, and my eyes are deteriorating, but still... Annie? Are you there?"

"Sorry, just listening if he's crying."

"As I said, count yourself lucky he's there at all."

"Ah, well, don't stop to think so much."

"True, Anne, wise, but this feels close by, and of course the two of you are always on my mind. How are you?"

"Fine, as usual, if not for long, I suppose, with Reg's teeth and molars coming up."

"Have you bought these soothing meds? And the cream for his bottom?"

"Yes, Mom."

"Because you won't know what's hitting you. That bottom of his will be on fire, like real burns! Strange, how fast things can change. Do remember: as long as they're crying, nothing can be very wrong. But um, you seem too absent. Are you truly alright?"

Anne has taken the phone to the kitchen, putting things ready for dinner. She also checks the baby-monitor and listens in the doorway again. Back in the room, she turns the television on, switches the News off and clicks to sports. "Just a lot on my mind, sorry, about an interview."

"The one with Bernard Bloomsdale?"

"Nah, that's been cancelled or postponed."

"Oh, why?" Wil asks.

"Don't know, a vague message came at the last moment, *until further notice*."

"I hope it's nothing personal."

"Between the boss and me?

"Or on Bloomsdale's part," Mom Wil says. "Work will be hard anyway, when Reg is more and more awake."

"That's why I need each hour."

"Sorry, Anne. It's too damn sad that I live far away."

"Well, it could be worse."

"Sure, like overseas, for a warm winter. But I'll come over, for a day or two? It's been weeks!"

"No need, Mom."

"But I'd love to help out! So you can sleep late, as a treat, and go out, do some work without interruption, or keep in touch with friends... You're always crying that your hands are tied, no time or energy..."

"Nah, I never say that."

"Not complaining!" Wil cries. "I know how happy you are these days. But in the long run... I miss you too, Annie. And you know I'll never impose, we go about our own ways. Don't be considerate for my sake."

"Sweet, Mom. Look, we'll see how it goes, with work and Reg. First of all I have to be selective and focus. It's manageable now and we've got our habits, rituals... Do come when it's more urgent."

There's a polite hush, until Reg's granny says, "Sure, if you know what's best. Bye, love, talk again. Call me, please, when you feel like it. Even a single day could be done. We can be spontaneous and improvise, right? We're always open and honest. So never hesitate, even at a short notice. In ten minutes I'd pack a bag with a thick book, for the train, and with you. Did you read Bloomsdale yet?"

"Mom..."

"Sorry, I'll shut up, you go on and have a good evening. Give Reg a hug for me!"

"Thanks. Have a good evening, too."

Anne can hear him crying upstairs again, but the editor phones with a PS, "Do not contact Bloomsdale."

"Oh, give me some credit."

"Yes, you're a dynamic, enterprising journalist, who has been known to act independently or recklessly."

"OK, point taken."

"Your work is first class, Anne, that's why I like giving you some space, usually, but this is off limits now."

"And how long will you keep me in the mysterious dark?"

The editor says, "I would not heighten the tension, if I could help it. Hope to talk again soon."

"With something extra nice, yes?" Anne pleads with a wink in her voice.

There's a lightness in her head, and her legs are trembling, so she'd better eat something. She hurries to cook an easy, savory rice meal with sauce and burgers – not the kind that causes cancer, as someone on TV tried to frighten her.

Meanwhile it's quiet. Even so, she goes up for a glance in his room.

He's crosswise but comfy in the cot – the sides are cloth-lined – and she retreats again, reassured. He tends to sleep so deeply that she doesn't need to keep her voice and feet down. Yet her moves are hesitant and she's aware of each sound. It's ridiculous, paradoxical, how happy she can be with a sound he makes.

Dinner is perfect now. She takes her plate to the couch and TV, for something light, no realistic mystery.

<>

At the table Bernard is choosing more pictures of Art, for the media: recent and clear and characteristic. A grave or laughing Art? He may not have many reasons to be happy now, so people will possibly recognize him from a solemn photo. Bernard dreads involving Nomi in this. Even for him it's difficult to get a grip and look at Art in a striking close-up: as full of spirit as he is.

For days they roamed parks and skirted the lake on foot or by bike. They fed the animals and found feathers, went for a paddle. They sheltered in the shade or cherished the warmth for a nap.

When Art's tummy cramps were so bad that only the uppermost distraction would help, Bernard tilted the pram or stroller and rode it on two wheels. He'd push or pull it, depending on the wind and sun. He ran and sang, until people were staring.

With the 'freedom' or 'solitude' of Bernard's profession it's just as well that he dislikes driving, otherwise he'd go and help out too often.

With one assistant Nomi and Mark run a quirky estate agency. It occurs that they work till nine pm, also the weekends, but they can be flexible and available at home, the phone at hand.

"Are you here tomorrow," Mark asks Bernard.

"If you want me to? I can help, of course."

Mark explains, "I have an appointment at ten a.m. It's the third and decisive viewing of a special cottage. We've put lots of work in it, and provision would be a two-month income."

But what does that matter if Art is lacking? And who'd care about money if he's back?

Detective Hattum looks closely at Mark, more surprised than understanding.

Bernard tries to stay neutral. "You haven't cancelled?"

"No, that's tricky or impossible. I mean... The viewers have come over from France, and our colleague doesn't speak French. They're deciding between two properties, so postponement could be fatal."

That's the wrong word today, which he swallows under the eyes of Bernard, who says, "What does Nomi think?"

"I haven't asked her yet. When you are here, and one or two detectives, I'm useless, fretting." He gives Hattum a pleading look. "This is a rare opportunity. One big sale will lead to another. And for Art..."

Defensive and apologetic, he watches Hattum again, who says, "Tomorrow there could be leads – there should be – with new questions, also emotional ones. Do you want to leave that to Nomi?"

"And Bernard, a couple of hours. He's totally at home here, he knows Nomi and Dilli and Art as well as I do."

"If differently, for a part?"

Mark's tone drops. "I'm away a lot, and now this... You must be thinking."

"*Can* you appeal to Nomi for this?" Hattum wonders out loud.

"Do you mean if she's responsible enough?"

"No, can she make essential decisions on her own? Won't your client allow for an emergency?"

"Well," says Mark, "they wouldn't *blame* me, obviously, but I know how it works; we'd come second, literally. Tomorrow the deal could be closed, if I'm in form – I mean, considering."

He's taken aback himself: to be in form now, is that a betrayal to Art?

He has made up his innocent or guilty mind, while his hand makes an apologetic gesture of its own accord.

<>

Nomi wakes up after some fifteen minutes that feel like half a night. Lying beside Art or Dilli, she's never at ease: a limb of theirs can get pressed or crushed, and something worse could happen. The other day she watched a crime film in which an exhausted mother breast-fed her baby, lying down on the couch. She fell asleep and smothered him. The father found them and wanted to save his wife from a guilt trauma. He took the baby, buried him in the woods and told the police a story they believed. The film was a little corny but realistic enough to show Nomi these hazards again.

The numerous abductions on television are intriguing or even exciting. They don't always end well, but viewers relax with drinks and snacks.

Nomi can't switch off her thoughts anymore. Moaning from stiffness, she stumbles up to the landing and stops there. At the top of the stairs there's no safety gate for kids – between the risk ages of Dilli and Art. Nimble and confident, Dilli walks up and down on the broad sides of the steps, even holding toys. But for the hasty Art it's probably a very different story.

Parents can't forever watch each inch of the kids' movements.

The door to his room is open. Nomi goes in, gently draws the curtains and turns the lights on. In his cot she arranges the covers and his cuddly rabbit. "Ready for his return." She leaves the rest as it is, including the empty diaper bucket; she only loosens the lid.

She slips down the stairs into the living room, trying to avoid these detectives' eyes, that seem to expect a miracle from her, something illogical or merciful that would turn the whole day into a mistake, to be erased or reversed. Her mind is going its own way and wonders: how many people deserve that sort of pardon? First, no doubt, the ten thousands in areas of natural catastrophe, who had no chance to prevent it. They're not to blame in any way.

Hattum goes over to her and asks, "Would you like us to call your doctor?"

"No, thank you."

"You don't want something to help you sleep, to calm the nerves?"

"No, I want to keep a clear head."

To know and feel every detail, or else it's like letting Art down – once more.

"OK." Hattum is a tad chubby but fit enough, with patience, tact and experience. "But do take enough rest and keep your strength up. It may be a while."

And the longer it is, chances will shrink.

"Do you think it's about ransom?" Mark asks. "A thick or false mistake?"

"That's one possibility. Your landline is now connected to the station, so better keep it free."

"Would a ransom attempt be a good thing?" Bernard asks.

"Maybe, if they fail and leave a trace."

But that could also cause a panic with tragic results.

"We have no money," Mark says.

"Does anybody *think* you're wealthy?"

Surprised, Mark shakes his head.

"Have there been any large transactions at work that went bad? With angry or aggressive clients?"

Mark thinks. "We've never bungled up or anything. There's been some bad luck, sure, and a wrong estimate can always be a human error. But if anything, it's been a client who played a nasty trick on us."

Hattum gives a little nod. "And do you get on with your assistant?"

"Certainly."

"Nomi, what's your field?"

"I keep the books and..."

As her voice falters, she thinks of the work that enabled her to bring Art along, for a productive and playful time, grateful.

"The books are always correct," Mark says with a hurt smile on stiff lips. "No need to call the police."

The two of those here are not amused by his attempt at a joke or panicky distraction.

"And mainly," Bernard hurries to add or repair, "Nomi does the creative part of the business: photos, the shop windows, brochures, flyers, ads..."

Mark is proud of her despite the situation; she needs his defense or support more than ever. "It's the personal touch. Nomi makes our style and reputation, original and inviting."

"If you combine that with homemaking," Ingram says to her, "you have a double responsibility!"

His note-making hand is as thin and sinewy as the rest of him – with a sharp brain making him a valuable detective?

"Well," Nomi says in her shelter, "there's good variation, and Mark takes his big share in everything."

"But," Ingram looks around the room, "you're working from home a lot. Don't you want to go out more?"

Mark wrings his hands, Bernard drinks water, and Nomi clings to herself, saying, "For the photo or video work and more, I get out enough."

"And I'm fine here too, in all my elements. Too perfect to be true?"

"By yourself?" Ingram checks.

"Or with Art and Dilly. That's a f..."

Her voice cracks again, and she cringes like a hedgehog without pins.

Mark takes over rather fiercely. "That's always good and safe! Art loves the motion and action. Nomi can do two things at the same time, better than I can, and the children come first. It's a great combination!"

Ingram taps his fingers on the table, *except this morning*, but he stops himself.

"It's true," Bernard says, "objectively. Anyone for coffee or tea?"

"Sorry to push and be inquisitive," Hattum says. "But we need a full picture of your lives; it can matter in unexpected ways."

As in life or death? Nobody says.

"So we want each aspect of the situation, also what's painful or trivial."

And confrontational, in any necessary way.

Despite himself Mark is getting sarcastic. "You forget to mention that we're close night and day, privately and professionally. That's unhealthy, right? It produces mad reactions."

"Actually," Hattum tells Bernard, "I would like some coffee."

And Ingram nods expressly.

"You take care of that?" Bernard asks Mark. "I'll get the tea. Any treats in the house?"

Thus, for a second, he forgot that this is no social visit.

<>

Anne has no website or blog or any trendy media on which Reg would shine. She dislikes the massive private prancing. There's no need to post pictures of mother and son.

She's trying out a column for *Denoting*, about the degrading insipidity of tickling the kids – for dumb fun – when the phone rings. It's Doctor Mullan.

"Just tell me that all's well, Anne."

"Absolutely."

"Because, you see, there's an Amber Alert out, most doctors are connected, and it's for a boy Reg's age. I hope that's not upsetting you excessively?"

"What I don't understand," Anne says, "the Alert system is named after the girl Amber, who was brutally killed, so that's no good connotation."

"I see, no. The point is that Amber might have been saved with the help of many civilians."

"OK, if it works."

"Yes," doctor Mullan says, "directly or indirectly. Can you shield yourself from it all?"

"Or else I'll lose my marbles again, will I?"

"Hey, easy on the self-mockery, please. Never play with fate! But you sound steady enough."

"Not phobic and unstable then? So you'll stop worrying about me?"

Her tone has turned friendly and serious again.

"Alright," Mullan says.

"And I appreciate your concern, you're a good family doctor."

"You're welcome, Anne. I admire your perseverance. So you won't hesitate to call me, not even for something crazy or creepy?"

"Nah, thanks."

She can picture him smiling, because well, how many *serial* abductors can there be around here? There's no need for her or him to get nervous. Yet she's pleased that she never put Reg or herself on Facebook.

<>

After an anxious pause Hattum asks Nomi, “Art is not in day care?”

“No, we’ve tried. He needs a lot of sleep, and he’s a light sleeper, so that can be tricky in a group.”

Ingram grins. “I wouldn’t like it either.”

“We have applied for something new – in September, all being well.”

A common phrase.

She turns pale again, but it’s not really noticed, because Mark has come in with coffee and slices of cake, which he puts down insecurely. Some cups are rattling on the tray.

“Art loves the outings with Nomi,” Bernard says.

No comment is passing Ingram’s lean lips.

“And he’s got a granddad from heaven,” Mark says.

“But he’s not being spoiled, mind.”

The present tense is going on and on, drawing more and more attention from those who are then startled by the doorbell.

Ingram looks out the window. “Let me.”

He and Hattum came in his own car, since a police unit would betray this address to the press. The vultures will discover it soon enough anyhow, without keeping a decent distance. With the days growing longer, it’s unpleasant to draw the curtains early, which would make people wary too.

It’s neighbor Lara at the door. “Sorry, usually I pop in around the back, but I saw Nome and Dil come home this afternoon, and something appeared to be wrong. Now the News...”

In short and calm terms, Ingram explains what’s going on, and he says, “You didn’t notice or suspect anything before?”

“No, in what sense?”

“For example, was Nomi out of sorts? Burdened?”

“No, never!” Lara says.

“You met regularly?”

"Well, as it goes between neighbors with hectic lives. I mean busy in a positive way."

"Right. I don't think Nomi or Mark want any company just now, no matter how supportive, but I'll tell them you came by, and they can get in touch when it suits them."

"Sure," Lara says. "For anything I can do, God knows what, let them call me, even in the middle of the night. But they know that. We have one another's house keys, and we water the plants in vacations."

There, says her face, is that sufficient evidence to rule out anything horrible?

Mark's parents and brother have been informed before the Amber Alert has spread. On the phone they offer help and feel worthless, trying to say something optimistic, "It will all turn out to be a ridiculous mix-up. You'll be OK. Art steals everybody's heart. Somebody will bring him back to you."

Hattum suggests to send a general message to all friends and contacts, with a request to wait and see without communication. Mark and Nomi are given a police phone for private calls, but it's not used much yet.

Bernard types an email draft for them, which is approved by all and sent by Mark as a 'newsletter.' They decide to do that from time to time.

"The digital media may be dominant and mean," Bernard says, "but now they can do good things."

"Loads of people will be in the loop," Hattum says, "keeping eyes open for Art."

Kids go missing every day, nearly all of them are traced and found alive. But most of them "only" ran away or strayed by themselves, and such happy endings don't apply to babies who can't walk.

Mark knows that Amber Alerts go out in cases of imminent danger. Even babies are abused. Without a ransom demand there will be no contact, no possibility to plead and beg, nor to persuade or outsmart the perp with any detective tricks.

By ten pm Nomi knows there won't be any ransom call. The facts are too callous and public: the police find no usable forensic prints, door-to-door canvassing with an occasional 'witness' gives them nothing either, and time is the primary enemy of a taken child. Nobody utters the icy other thoughts: after abuse the victim is often killed or dumped in a deserted area or in deep water.

No suspicious people have been seen around the house and no relatives have received threats. The detectives have discussed, followed up and eliminated or saved the options ranging from logical to far-fetched: there's no surrogate mother or post-adoption parent with regrets, nor a deranged stepfather or some religious and radical family honor clash.

In many cases hundreds of 'tips' yield at least one lead, but here there are just a few phone calls from cranks and sensation seekers. No psychic has come in.

At eleven, Hattum says, "Would you like someone in the house for the night, from Victim Support? Our family liaison officer can camp on the couch..."

But 'victim' is a word that lingers and grows, hitting Nomi in the knees. To keep herself going, she wants the house to remain the same, if possible. A personal world can delay or filter the truth, or keep it out.

The spare room on the first floor is used for breaks with privacy, or for daytime work, but Art can sleep there too, in a camping cot, when the kids tend to wake each other up in their adjacent rooms on the other floor.

Two children are much more than one plus one: the mental intensity can be a quadrate. "The one complex kid is a piece of cake," they said half in jest lately, when the other one was away for a morning or day.

"I've brought a toothbrush," Bernard says. "Or do you want me to come back tomorrow? I've cancelled a journalist."

"Thanks, Dad, tomorrow please, if you don't mind driving up and down. Was the interview important?"

"Nothing is more important than Art now, of course. What counts is what matters to you. Tell me what you want, and all's well."

That's a catch-phrase of his, with or without irony, but many a light and common expression becomes heavy.

On his way out, Bernard gets a short hug from Nomi and a shoulder pat with "Thank you" from Mark, who seems to go on thinking meekly about his work appointment, which is not mentioned again by anyone. It shows that his brain and feelings can function separately. Also how much it costs to keep them together.

<>

At five thirty a.m., in the first daylight, Nomi is woken by a door click, sounding so nearby in the silence that she sits up and gasps from expectancy, like more times this night. But nothing happens. With biting disappointment she realizes that it's Dilli, one floor up.

Hush, Dil, think of Art! is her first instinctive thought – from an innocent past with minor worries.

Groggy, she needs to reach Dilli, before Dil wakes up more and starts playing noisy games. As if that would matter now! Nomi slips out of bed and scrambles upstairs, where Dilli is looking 'guilty' outside Art's room, saying, "I can't?"

Don't wake or disturb him!

It causes a flashback with a bang: the other early morning she got very angry when Dilli entered Art's room and acted as if it was eight o'clock, while Art slept an extended spell at last, for once – a craved breather for the parents.

Nomi explained and apologized for her vehement reaction. Over ice-cream the next day, Bernard would hear that Mom threw precious toy Cat out the window, onto the roof. Luckily the gutter caught it, and all was fine after Dad climbed and almost broke his neck, using a bad word.

Now Dilli points to Art's room and says, "The lights are on, is that alright? Oohh, he's still gone. But we are quiet! Can we go pick him up? At Granddad's?"

Nomi kneels to Dilli's height, who says, "I can see in your eyes that you're tired."

Her own are piercing the silence, until Nomi comes round and says, "It's still night, sweetheart. Will you doze in bed, nice and cozy?"

"Or play?"

"OK."

"No need for quiet?"

"No, my love, not today."

For the rest of my life I'll whisper and tiptoe around the house, I'll never let anything bang or rattle or clink again, if it helps, if that's what it takes for a life-size cause, a divine intervention or second chance. No need to pray for that? Because it's deserved or not? Which is long known in this timeless dimension beyond the human mind?

Dilli's bed becomes a friendly zoo with plenty of care and comfort going on.

Nomi is restless beside the sleeping Mark. Tender rather than titillating, his naked arm lies toward her in a free curve, the muscles relaxed in the stretching, soft light. Some other time she'd kiss the tiny hairs or the inside of his elbow, drifting to the wrist and fingertips. Now she's crying, partly because these are sensual thoughts in spite of everything, and she'd like to be stroked herself, but like a child after a fall off her bike, that narrowly ended well.

She's kept her robe on in bed.

After a long and hot shower she slowly eats a cracker and fruit, peeling with eerie precision. Shocked, she finds that it tastes good. She wants to stay healthy at any cost, as fit and sharp and perceptive as can be – for two – with a retroactive or amending strength.

However, she's afraid that someone will come and request her part in a public appeal, with cameras and microphones and glaring eyes. The prospect freezes her over in advance, presuming what people will think of her. The worst thing is the near certainty that a media performance is pointless. It resembles leaving him in the lurch.

She needs to get groceries. Outside the supermarket is a sizeable toy plane that rocks and throbs and flies when fed by a coin – which lasts a minute? In a near future she can see Art falling in love with it and begging for a spin again and again. How to explain that it's not about money when she says no after one go? Or two then.

She pictures him aged nine or ten months: beaming away in the plane, that's fed with coin after coin. But between him and herself in that wishful image, a group of reporters and equipment are gathering, bombarding her head with questions:

How many turns for Art in the plane in exchange for your redemption: a hundred? How long will you be watching here and staying patient in the bustle or heat, with a big list of errands to run: fifty hours for his return? Did you leave him then and will you again? Did you leave him behind and abandon him? Would five hundred rides buy his return? OK, maybe here's feasible: how many if you could see and hold him again one more day... A hundred?

What number to do that fatal day all over again?

Or the one single second.

After watching a number of rounds, her joy over Art's elation is fading, and the voices of that scene continue until they must be temporal in her sound mind: Yesterday's mishap mess, was it ruthless fate or loony you? Are you blaming a God whose omni-power could have stopped everything, or caused it for a devilish and secret purpose? Who can forgive who now? Yeah, if love is unconditional...

<>

At eleven pm and four thirty a.m. Anne has fed him a bottle. "OK, now you'll sleep late, won't you?"

And he does till eight.

"Well well, with your teeth and all you're a completely new person!"

Who explores new borders eagerly, first in his pen and then on the carpet, when the phone rings. A friend invites her to a shopping spree, to help her get an outfit for a smart work party.

"Sorry, Fran, I'm stuck here between work and Reg. He's teething seriously after all. I don't know what's happening to us."

"Oh, I haven't seen him for ages! You're insulating yourself, girl. Bring him along!"

On the carpet between dining and living parts of the modest one room, he's giving cheerful shrieks, growing very conscious of his voice and its power. He rolls his hips athletically and acts as if he's moving mighty far. Who can tell?

"Hold on, Fran, the doorbell. Sorry, back in a sec."

With a wondering frown, Anne checks the clock, but five past nine is not as early as she thought.

At the door, Doctor Mullan is apologetic from the start. "I don't want to impose at all, it's a spur of the moment, I finished early a few streets away. Sorry, just one more question."

Involuntarily, Anne steps back. "I can't leave Reg alone."

"Oh, is he up? Look, a little head around the corner."

And seen through Mullan's eyes at a distance, the boy looks exactly like the missing kid, would you believe, even if the hair is different, as far as he can tell from here. Thank God Reg Hoaver is at home, because the mother would sink into a psychosis if he were gone one day.

Doctor Mullan wipes his shoes thoroughly – invited?

Crawling away, the baby's hands cross the edge of the carpet and his lips are tasting the materials difference.

"I see," Mullan says, "you can eat off the floor here."

Anne steers Mullan to the other end of the room, by the dining table, and she explains, "Reg is awfully shy with strangers, I mean... I suppose it's his age! So let's not disturb his play."

And ruin the rest of the day?

"Certainly, I won't grab and toss him, like stupid adults do the first minute, as if children are objects! Look, he's turning his back on me – bright boy. No, you and I, we don't get hold of each other either, do we? You can write a column about this, and expose a mass dysfunction!"

Anne stands there, not knowing where to put her hands: fold them firmly? "Sorry, I can't offer tea or coffee. Reg really needs a bath and his bed. He gets only short whiles out of the pen, or else he'll be spoiled with too much freedom."

"True, they pick that up quickly. But forgive me," Mullan says, "I've come to ask if you're taking your meds."

"Yes, cutting down slowly, as agreed."

"Very slowly indeed?"

She gives him a comedic smile.

"Good," Mullan says. "In times of stress this medication remains extra important. Is Reg giving you some rest at night?"

"More and more."

"Have you never heard of the father again? Even now?"

"No, why?"

"Well, with a baby gone missing like this, he may realize that it might have been his son."

Silent, Anne is gazing at the phone in her hands.

Mullan walks back to the front door and says, "Incidentally, have you been to the health center – I mean with Reg?"

"Yes. All his check-up scores are about average or above. He's shy there too, with a bunch of strangers, but they find him funny – in the good sense – and ready to learn. Or did they say he's curious? Anyway, he has carrots for dinner now, truly interested, smacking his lips."

"And the vaccinations?"

Anne glances at her watch. "Definitely, we'll do them all! I won't take any risks, no matter what they say about the dicey side effects of these cocktails, in the long run."

"Good, I'm proud of you. And should there be any complication after all, call me, will you? Always! I'm so old and wise that I don't need to work for money anymore, merely for the pleasure and fulfillment of it."

Anne has moved to the door. "Thank you."

Out in the radiant air, Mullan adds casually, "Beware of the sunshine, although Vitamin D is important. But he's growing less blond, isn't he?"

"Hi Fran, you're still home?"

"No, I've dreamt away."

"It was doctor Mullan, remember, the guardian angel. Of course I didn't want to get rid of him."

"Don't worry."

"And," Anne says, "I've got bad news, I can't join you, so sorry. Shopping with Reg around is no good, and going without him is tricky now."

"What about your sitter?"

"Yes... I need her for work occasions. And Mullan tells me about the abduction, so I'll keep Reg close to me."

"Well, I'll come and look after Reg when you take a day off, you'd do me a big favor, and the two of us will have a town spree some other day, like the old days, for instance when your mom is there for Reg. About time too! For us, I mean. Then you'll buy yourself something gorgeous your old size, yeah? How are the belly exercises? Loads of cute men fall for 'lonely woman and child'. That makes them think they are the heroes."

"Sorry, Fran, I've got to go before he's bringing the house down. See you!"

"Yeah, you'd better."

With a frown that might have been heard in her voice.

Anne puts him in the low seat with a rattle in his hand, that appeals to him considerably. She cooks an apple, mashes a banana through it and sits next to him on the floor. Fascinated, he tastes it, but by accident he sweeps the spoon out of her hand.

"Reg, what's this: you love your fruit!"

The splashes of the valuable food are on her clothes and the floor.

"I've just told everyone what a big boy you are!" And, apprehensive, she tries a new spoonful. "It's neither cold nor hot, only soft and sweet, come on..." His mouth is shut tight, and she pushes the spoon against his lips. "Do give it a try, please. At least you'll know how good it is." And she shows him that with emphatic mm sounds. "See? Delicious."

As she's convinced that he will love it, she presses the spoon some more. "Come on, sweetie, have a taste. Don't be silly and stubborn for no reason, please."

But he bends away and cries.

<>

For some fresh air, Bernard has his muesli in the garden, where the blackbirds have been busy for a long time. Their nest by the back-door is boldly close in the laurel bush. They have been lucky with a cool and wet spring; Bernard has not been under their feet very much.

The mother soars past his head, to show him how vigilant she is. Once the parents know that he's harmless, they fly to and fro again with juicy worms and more proteins – after cracking a snail shell?

The hungry squeaking chicks in the laurel can be heard, but they're drowned out by the father's sharp alarm shrieks when a magpie lands ominously on the shed roof and starts a nerve war right above them.

Perspective can be a bitch. The magpie is a large bird of prey now, whereas yesterday it was chased from the acacia by a crow. The blackbird looks tiny, but its defense is fierce and its counter-attack is helped by the piercing squeals, like David's sling against Goliath. The same throat can produce the heavenly songs at other hours.

The impertinent assailant could rob or kill with one bite or blow, but it rears and tarries in menacing circles.

The alarm noise is driving Bernard nuts and he gets up force-fully. The magpie with its dazzling colors and proud posture leaves at once, and the blackbirds resume their food transport. They are giants now, beside the sparrows and tits, and they have to be, should the magpie return when Bernard is gone all day.

<>

"Should Dilli go to school?" Mark asks between the bedroom and shower.

Nomi has been in doubt about that for a while. She'd like to keep her close by, but that wish is caused by a fear that can undermine everything. Dreading the emptiness, she wants to be busy and useful without having to think. There's work to be done for the agency, but the beginning and end of her life are missing. She needs a clear and urgent purpose.

"What's best for Dilli?"

"School," Mark says. "Tomorrow it's the weekend, she likes the social contact, and there's turmoil here. Heavy tension affects her a lot, don't you think?"

"Too much?"

"No. We could have taken her... I mean, she can stay with Bernard or Lara, but we're not shutting her out. That would hurt more."

At the breakfast table with an empty high chair, Dilli is opposite Nomi on her knees in a grown-up seat. Lost in thought, Nomi puts a lovely bowl of peeled fresh fruit in front of Art's chair. Dilli was waiting for the bowl to come her way, and she looks up at Nomi with big eyes. It's a few seconds before Nomi sees what she did. Two more before she recovers and moves the bowl to Dilli.

Mark takes a sip of tea that seems to cause a little cough. "I need to know now, what to do about our viewers this morning."

"Oh, are you sure they can't wait a day, if they know why?"

As if a day would erase that reason, Mark doesn't say.

"No, I'm not telling them. It would scare them off."

Dilli listens and pecks away at the best bits of food, unnoticed.

Nomi asks, "Can you honestly go as if nothing is wrong?"

"Well, no, I'll need to block it all out – for an hour or two."

"And then?"

"I could finish the paperwork, the pre-contract. I'm not sure if I can manage, and if you have a better idea... Tell me. Bernard will be here, and Hattum or his colleague. I know it's insane, I want to go and find Art, run or cycle, drive, shout everywhere... But it's no use."

Nomi knows that anger will stand in the way of grief for as long as possible, as a form of self-protection. She's surprised by Mark's teary and helpless outburst. Art's name came out of his mouth, but his hands cover his face, like a child who thinks that no one can see him this way.

Neither of them gives Dilli a cheap smile of 'reassurance'. Mark turns away to get a tissue and Nomi won't touch him, shielding herself. Wild and rugged, he wipes his eyes and nose.

He stays beside her around the corner of the table, watched by Dilli, but his gaze is blank and he's holding the tissue, saying, "I'll be in the way here, I'd go mental, but please, tell me what you think, truly."

Nomi gets up and folds herself around him. He crouches and creeps in her shell.

At first Dilli wonders, then she stands on her chair and bends over the table to throw herself on both of them – since this appears to be done? – with a smile and closed eyes.

"No school now?" Dilli asks, back on her feet.

"Yes, today is a school day. Jo will be there too."

"Mom goes to work?"

"No, love. I'll pick you up later."

"Art is playing?"

Only her eyes ask how or where and more. There's no answer

yet and Dilli continues her probing reflections. "Art is too little for school."

Nomi nods. She doesn't want to choke Dilli with her emotions, she's trying to butter a slice of bread, and the syrup should be equal and smooth, but it won't stick on the butter very well, and the bread becomes messy.

Her hand rests on her chest.

Eventually the lunch box for school is ready to go neatly into the cool rucksack. Art has a similar box with his name on it.

"Finish your milk, Dil."

She does so without much resistance, and Nomi is glad, because if a mom's natural authority fails in hard times, a child will grow insecure.

The cargo bike is out in the same spot as before, and the rain cover is off, but Nomi gets her other bike from the shed, with a kid seat on the back, where she puts Dilli with a bit of trouble balancing the bike.

"Art can almost sit now, can he?"

"Yes, I think he's learning."

Nomi navigates the bike fairly straight, past pieces of glass and some dog poop, dodging cars parked badly, while Dilli calls out about all that's changed or stayed the same: flags and clouds, a lorry, a Mini, and is that a crow or a jackdaw?

Although they're not so close to the bike shop, a couple of streets look longer than before, cold here and stifling there, drawing more attention. Most shops are closed at this hour, which catches the eye today.

Dilli's former baby seat on the handlebars is kept in the shed, but for Art they've looked at a new model. The nicest and safest one seems very expensive, by comparison. Is there a good reason for that price?

"By comparison" resounds obtrusively.

In the bike shop Mark tried out a handlebar-seat with Art and smiled. "He might as well wear a helmet! See? Next thing, he'll make motor sounds!"

Nomi did say that one day she would miss the 'care bike', as Dilli calls the cargo bike, even though it's so heavy to maneuver that it gives her pains in the hips.

Now it feels as if her whole body is disjointed by an abnormal headwind, or it's distorted by the question: what would you pay for a bike seat if Art could be in it? With a windscreen for him on the handlebars, all comfy between your arms, close to your heart... A million dollars or two weeks without food, and a life without grumbling? Ten million, if it could be paid back in a lifetime?

People with fortunes like that do exist: oil tycoons in corrupt countries, the young men who invented lucrative media as if we have nothing better to do, a movie star who gets twenty million per film, the young heiress who is so empty that a gen-manipulated lap chimp is her fashion accessory.

Those people can donate or organize a fundraiser: ten thousand for a dinner seat. That's also how elections work in a democracy or a dictator's nation. They could easily write a cheque for the life of a person, couldn't they? An awesome reward for the finder, or a good lead!

When does adoption come down to trafficking? The purchase of a baby can be legal. TV shows on the subject are announced before commercials with juicy entertainment. How far then should we go to find our existing child?

In the TV guide:

A new couple arrive in the real-life series called *The Surrogate Moms*: Erica and Max travel to India. The procedures in an Indian clinic prove to be a true ordeal.

An embryo is re-planted in surrogate Joletta's womb. But Joletta is tormented by doubt as well as by the supplementary hormones necessary for this pregnancy.

Joletta will have twins. The trio want a caesarian, to make separation less gruesome, but suddenly labor sets in.

Some fervent sprints and climbs are going on in the large yard of Dilli's school. Curious or frightened, siblings are looking around, behind big and little persons.

A father shakes Nomi's hand silently. Most parents have not prepared themselves for seeing her here today – or any day soon for that matter. A mother nods to her and mutters, "Good luck. I mean, have strength."

Dilli's friend Jess asks, "Is Art stealed?"

"Yes," Dilli says, as if she follows the News too.

"Can you go in a police car?"

"Yes."

"And the fire car? Can I go to your home?"

"Yes, Mom?"

Dilli looks at Nomi, who says, "I think so, but I'm not sure when exactly."

"Tomorrow?"

"I can't say yet. It would be great, and we will try."

Unsentimentally, Jess's mom puts a hand on Nomi's shoulder. "It goes without saying that Dilli is always welcome with us. Call me any time, for anything."

As if the situation will be ages?

Everybody hates to say the wrong things. Nobody knows if they're supposed to "act normal", and what the hell does that mean here? They may see that Nomi had rather be left alone, but on the other hand it could make her feel lonely if they kept their distance.

Other parents haven't heard yet.

Dilli's teacher is as busy as usual, but she hugs Dilli and Nomi, who says goodbye soberly and leaves. Dil and Jess are playing ardently already.

<>

On some occasions when Art was sound asleep, Nomi left him home alone for fifteen minutes, or a few more, to take Dilli to school or collect her. She's never asked anyone how they solve that. Bernard told her that they used to do it as well. A healthy sleep shouldn't be disturbed, should it, only to plant the kid on a bike into crowded places?

Cot death can also occur when Mom or Dad is downstairs and dozes off on the couch or makes a long phone call, cooks dinner, plays music, talks to a neighbor across the hedge – about a celebration or a death in the family.

But what about fires or burglaries? Check the locks and burners, don't forget your phone and keys, leave a note! Bad people can watch your house and see you leave. But then, if we want to be on guard for calamities all the time, what kind of life do we lead?

Returning home, Nomi always went up to have a look through his door window. Did she take it for granted that he slept peacefully, or was she relieved? What would relief indicate: a lack of faith or a sense of guilt or the awareness of danger along with the fact that happiness is no matter of course?

She knows a mother whose nasal organ (or a brain function?) is defective: who can't smell a poop diaper or anything singeing or burning. That woman is never warned. Each time she puts a pot on the stove, she needs to check if any crumbs or fluffs are sticking to the bottom that may cause a fire.

Cot death can't be seen through a door pane.

Close to the house Nomi's heart is pounding so madly that it makes her dizzy. In fact, she doesn't want to go on. The sun stings from behind a roof edge. She gets off her bike and walks a stretch, taking small steps.

"Keep moving," doctors urge patients in certain cases. "Come on, keep awake, stay with me, what's your favorite color? Do you like books? What are you reading at the moment?"

Anything to prevent losing them.

On her street there's a bunch of media people, the grief chasers, who may be important now. They could even save Art's life, which increases her nausea.

The coarse loudness of a group or crowd can lame her on any day. She likes intimacy, quiet creativity and some depth. Her inspiration and enthusiasm are fed by a strong intuition, but that let her go into the bike shop without Art, so now she's gravely lost faith and bearings.

It's not as if she knows in hindsight that it didn't feel good. No undercurrent of a fear or warning was disregarded. Her instinct is often strong and on time, they've seldom failed each other.

Nomi can sneak into the house around the back along a winding alley between houses of another street. For how long will this work and be necessary? Those people showing up here, means that Art must have a chance. They wouldn't be staying and waiting if he were dead, would they! Or to witness the family's mourning?

A funeral needs a dead body.

As reporters are focused on the house, it seems less empty, but in a deeper way it's made double empty.

Mark is wearing his best suit, he gets his things and says, "Hattum called."

Nomi's head jerks toward him. She did have her phone on her, so any important news would have reached her sooner, but her heart jumps and she sags against the wall.

"Sorry, sorry!" Mark holds her and hurries to explain, "I meant, he just called to say that Detective Ingram will come over. I think Hattum worked all night."

"Because of leads they have?"

"The entire investigation, I assume."

"Without results?"

"It seems."

"What can they do here, anyway?" Nomi says, gazing over his shoulder.

"Don't know. Keep the press at bay. And there could still be a vital phone call."

Nomi can guess what it's like to have an officer around the house. Six months ago the maternity help sat on her bed and chatted about vacation plans and TV shows. She must have thought that Nomi had few visitors, looked lonely, while Nomi relished each moment of peace.

She says, "I'd like to go about my own way, do chores, keep myself rested and ready..."

"For Art, yes. You could still go your ways, though. The officer would be downstairs, only to be on the safe side."

"And you? And Bernard? The four of us would be hovering around Dilli. As if that's good for her."

Is she supposed to do what's done in the movies? Hang on the couch with a drink or a smoke and pull at her hair, or stare at the phone and bite her nails? She hates that weakness even on the screen.

"You want to do some work too," she says, "but not for the sake of work, apart from this cottage."

"No, I'd prefer to knock on a thousand doors, with the odds of one in a million. Art could be anywhere, overseas, or else I'd stop at every house in town."

All the terminals and border routes have received Art's details and picture – as if a baby is not easily disguised. Besides, all babies look alike to strangers. What are 'distinguishing features'? The teeth change them so much that we don't recognize them anymore.

<>

Feeling foolish, Mark pulls a cap down to his eyebrows and makes a detour toward the car. Driving off, he needs to keep his head, as his searching eyes tend to be everywhere but on the road since Art could be on somebody's arm or in a buggy just like that, contrary to Mark's common sense after all, which cries out that nobody would be that stupid.

Other voices whisper to differ and undermine his right mind with intelligent bluff. In this all-revealing and blatantly beautiful morning he perceives each little boy. He bends left and right and looks over his shoulders, until a perilous moment at a crosswalk warns him: next thing you'll hit and kill a kid.

Outside the driveway of the property for sale, he parks his car and calms down. There's time to inspect the garden and first impression of the cottage once more: no litter, no bird poop on the windowsill or fresh cobwebs in the doorway, only a couple of blown-off branches on the gravel. Due to the sound of friction under walking feet, he doesn't like gravel, but for the rest his great enthusiasm about this house is all too real.

Inside, the country-grace mood has remained intact as well.

There's one flaw, that could be a point of discussion: the magnificent back garden borders a day-care center for grown-ups with mental and physical restrictions, with boisterous moments in peculiar ways, outside. On days with commotion in the air, some of the residents may react like wild kids, with funny roars and shrieks, but that's not the reason the house is for sale. It would be worth it to see the light side of it all: "It's a country estate with a tropical garden, exotic birds!"

"The adjacent ground serves a good and pleasant cause," Mark finished his tour with previous viewers. "If you had a brother or sister like those people with severe disabilities, or a child growing up, you'd be grateful for such care in a lovely place, wouldn't you?"

At any rate this is better than barking dogs of shouting masters, a sports field with violence, a steel drill or seeping levee, or thundering freight liners day and night.

Once in his early agency days, long before they had kid plans of their own, Mark said tactlessly, "Anything is better than loud kids."

This has been one of their favorite projects, not only for the large provision. The flowers in subtle spots of the house were carefully arranged by Nomi and Art, since first impressions go a long way.

Twenty-four hours ago Nomi called Mark, but she could not speak.

On one side of the house he opens a window – no draft! In corners of shade he lights a few safe scent candles, attentively selected by Nomi.

A big expensive car arrives and is parked less modestly than Mark would like: in front of the door. The middle-aged couple with their sons and a daughter-in-law shake his hand tensely.

"Can I get you a drink?" Mark asks without emphasis.

"No, thank you."

"Would you like to walk and look around by yourselves?"

My controlled praise of the house is no longer needed.

"Yes, please, thank you."

Mark sits at the table in the lounge by the garden, with brochures, papers and iPad in front of him. There are business matters he wants to glance at, from contractors and barristers, but his concentration is lost. The past days and six Art-months are waves of a storm. It makes the trees bend and he crouches.

Times are shuffled like cards – never dealt – and he's nowhere when the clients are back in the room, waiting politely. None of them gives away if they're even more enchanted by the premise than before, or awed by Mark's introverted 'absence' – calm and full of confidence?

He'd never ask about children and grandchildren anyhow, not without research beforehand: what if a kid in the family has a serious disease or handicap?

He's on his feet and addresses the parents reflectively. "The garden?"

"Thank you."

Mark opens the French doors and smiles to himself: do these French-speaking people know that English phrase? He walks out after them but hesitates on the threshold without knowing why. This is nothing to do with politeness or strategy; he's helplessly waiting for some kind of guidance.

"Is there a license to chop trees here?" Mr. Roumière says.

Seemingly Mark hasn't spoken French for years, but he has prepared issues that may be decisive. "Yes. These permits are tricky and notorious everywhere, but the green parts offer privacy, shelter."

"Do we need that here?"

Mark looks around with a see-for-yourself gesture. "That's always a personal matter, but bushes and small trees can be removed as you wish."

"And the building of the disabled people? That's closed at night and the weekends?"

"Yes, each weekday they leave at five. You can always have dinner outdoors, no problem, so it's the perks of peace and space, not found easily elsewhere."

"It's no hang spot with weed smokers and secret bonfires, is it, here in the bushes?"

"No," Mark says, "the Council have a strong youth policy, and should it ever..."

Suddenly he's bewildered by human 'tropical birdcalls' coming from the center, invisible behind a lot of greens. It's a blend of lament and primal cries, of rawness and rapture. Or it sounds like pleading. The air is tight with it, and countless tree leaves are trembling against the blue sky. Ordinary real birds hold their tongues. Everyone could hear that it might be a child, but is it a happy or sad voice?

Mark is motionless, while all the fluids in his head are running to his eyes.

<>

A creature of grace may have conveyed to Anne that she really needs to mash the fruit for the baby, not just crush it with a fork. And after an hour's sleep he's given that delicious dish of fruit, with her loving grumbling. "You're ruining a fine time-table, you know that? But OK, we're flexible and we'll improvise away."

At the right moment his mouth opens, and he observes her – with affection in his eyes? All previous fuss is forgiven and forgotten?

Next she puts him and his favorite toys on the blanket in a secluded part of the back garden. "There, Reggie, wear your sunhat, and nobody can see you here in this corner, so don't be scared of unexpected strangers."

She answers the request from a regional librarian: would she like to coordinate the area rounds of the national Read-Out-Loud competition? There's no fee, but it would be good for new contacts in the network of press and publishers.

"Sorry, usually that's a festive honor, but the upcoming months are filled with work and Reg."

"Don't you have a sitter or nanny?"

"Well, sadly, that's expensive – given my earnings. And Reg is too sensitive, sensory, for regular day care..."

"Oh," tries the librarian, "why don't you bring him along? That's lovely for everybody!"

Anne's laugh is charming. "As if he's got a rhythm with naps and everything. He's not adjusting to circumstances! I always wait and see if we can leave, go out at all. After one minute of sleep in the car, he won't shut an eye for hours at home."

"But he'll meet other kids here."

"And... to be terribly frank, I can take on paid work only now, as time is more and more limited. Day hours are a clutter, with the multiple chores and all. Mind, it's no complaint!"

"Oh, what a shame, Anne. Good luck!"
Sounding like: So glad I'm not in your shoes!

Writing reviews is time-consuming and badly paid. Sometimes she reads the first and last chapter of a book and knows enough, keeping her report civilized. If only there came an invitation to be the ghostwriter for a wealthy big shot. So long as it's no mafia boss...

Her columns are very personal and candid, gaining fame among women, alongside a fascination from the men, who pick up the magazine for its striking style with the topics of body and fitness, natural health, sports, food, and family.

Lasting bangs and blasts

When military and police people are killed in action or the line of duty, their funerals are large and solemn ceremonies, including the beautiful uniforms and music, with rituals following tradition and discipline.

One of these protocols is the series of salute shots, fired by rifles or heavy guns, painfully loud and sometimes numerous. Most of the officers were killed in some kind of shooting. Why repeat that emphatically, if it reminds the families and rubs it in to the marrow?

<>

Art's warm jacket is still on a peg in the hallway, after wistful service on cold spring mornings. His stroller is by the front door, still in the way a bit, under heavy feet, yet cherished like a sacred and breakable object.

Some of his clothes are in the corners of the stair steps, to be taken up to his room or the laundry. Nomi leaves them here and wants to preserve their scent, but she's not stopping to smell them now; no self-torture of that kind.

This morning no fruit or vegetables need peeling and cleaning – for him. There is a wash to be done and the machine sounds fill the house. Noises from outside still worry her too, but there's no need to mind a sleeping child.

Normally a day flies by, with the variation of Art and work, housekeeping, taking him for a walk, buying groceries. Now the main occupation is aimless.

Detective Ingram has no more questions or information, and he leaves with Nomi's blessing.

Nobody in the entire country has seen an abandoned baby, dead or alive. No family seems to have a 'new or extra kid' out of the blue. It's no use waiting for a ransom demand anymore. The media return to sports, a divorce in Hollywood or other Royalty, quarrels in Whitehall, rates from Wall Street and The City, where the Sugar Trade spends billions on lobbyists versus those who know what sugar does to the teeth and vital organs, particularly of little kids – if they live.

"You haven't heard from Mark yet?" Bernard asks. "Do you want me to pick up Dilli?"

"Yes, I don't know what's keeping Mark."

"Have you tried the office? And you won't call him during a viewing?"

"Only in case of an emergency."

And when exactly would that be?

Could an 'emergency' include a lucky escape?

Bernard says, "It's a good sign, though, isn't it, that he's away this long?"

"Yes, could be."

And his tad of gladness or hope regarding the sale, is something so separate from Art's gone missing that Nomi can also feel it, but it hints that this could be a glimpse of her life ahead, in which Art will be out of her thoughts frequently, inevitably, which could be necessary for Dilli and Mark and herself. Who knows for Art as well, if the mind knows no limits of time and place, as they say.

Ultimately – after how long? – it would be good for him if she let go, but 'let go' is a trendy phrase, either cheap or deep.

How long before memories of six months are gone?

She's been so busy and intense that in order to 'survive' she had to block out certain thoughts and perceptions. One hears this often, right: after feeds in the evenings and nights, you take a baby back to bed as quickly as possible. Worn out, you can be relieved each moment you don't hear him, thankful for one day without him, then profoundly happy again.

Is 'love you to death' a general phrase?

Nomi prefers, "I'll hug you to bits."

She could "eat him up", that's the sort of child he is.

What would be the first emotion to fade away? There are days when their first month together seems far away now, unreal. Eventually it's hard to say whether a picture in the mind is a true memory or an image lingering from a photo.

Nomi is a passionate business and family photographer. The properties inside and out with telling vistas, creating space and atmosphere. Series of the kids, to be sternly selected. Both have their own albums.

Despite her strict criteria, half of Art's big book is already full, and the remaining empty pages could be filled with her second choices, for new chances. "I'd kill for some of those," is a common expression.

If this part of Art's album will prove to be a lifetime of its own, she'll lack the courage to open it for the time being. As if some of his vibrance would be lost each time, she'd shy from showing the book to others, who are not afraid and do ask to see it.

"Shall we open the curtains and switch the bell off?" Bernard says, almost pleading. "We could sit in the back."

Functional practicalities work well.

"Yes, but if somebody is at the door with..."

Information about Art could lead to new steps, to a moment of heavenly joy. That can be felt in advance, but she has to hold it off again and again –

Excuse me, are you Art's mom? I've just found him by the entrance of the hospital, in perfect health!

Look, somebody seems to have left him in my garden – don't ask me why!

Hattum wants her to identify a live-and-kicking boy, and he's quite sure it's Art.

It happens the other way round, too: parents are asked to identify a dead child, they prepare themselves and say goodbye inwardly, or they wear a mental armor, keep their distance, and then the child is not theirs.

"Alright," Bernard says, "the bell stays on. We can also sit in the back yard."

He takes a look there and sees Dilli's toys. When Art watches her, he's aching to participate, holding a sandbox toy for ages. The sun casts a sharp light on each object that's not been touched for some time.

"You go and sit in the garden?" Nomi says.

I don't feel like talking anyway. What's there to say?

"But Dad, don't move or tidy anything."

The air is so clear that she can hear kids' voices coming from behind the other houses, laughing or shrieking on bikes, dawdling for no reason.

"Except the plants and flowers?" Bernard checks. "If they're dry or withered?"

"Sorry, yes, of course. Do they need water?"

In the evenings Mark likes doing that, now perhaps more than ever, so Bernard restrains himself.

When Mark comes home, it's late, but Nomi can tell from his face that her anger or complaints would be out of place.

The viewing was long, they negotiated, conferred and signed. Mark doesn't know what factors were decisive in the end; he didn't ask. Where possible he's placed the SOLD signs and stickers right away. That will generate faith and draw new attention to their other projects, but his joy has already evaporated.

Their celebrations were always gratefully moderate, with a few close friends, a fine wine and meal, and especially the children, who love to understand it all. "Good work, house sold," Dilli always said on behalf of both.

"Pancakes or pizza?" Mark asks.

"All!"

Plus a tropical pool or a small amusement park, some grilled cheese, three turns each in the plane at the market, a big syrup waffle. "That won't make holes in teeth now," Dilli states. And she would give a piece to Art. "Chew! Or you will choke and Mom will shock."

She counts on some extra TV time thrown in. "But Art is too little, is he?"

She says that so often, eager to deny that he's growing fast elsewhere?

School is out and Dilli is pale from fatigue. There are four extra kids in her class, because another teacher is off sick.

In denial she tries, "No need to sleep, yes?"

"We'll cycle home first," Bernard says.

Better take no roundabout way today, their beloved route past the marina boats and large park with sharp, poisonous hogweed, and the pond with waterfalls or swans – to see how their chicks have grown, leaving the nest in which one egg was intact and abandoned.

The other day or week, Dilli and Bernard stole down closer to the wild pond, the edge with dense reeds, very careful indeed around a corner, scared to bump into the swan parents yet, who'd slap, blow and snap hard. But the big strong swans left, even crossing the street, and Bernard didn't know why. So they could go and see that one egg was cracked open, with stuff in it, and one was huge, smooth, heavy. Granddad took them both in a hurry, and he let her feel them too, at home.

"Allowed?" she checked.

"Yes, they're left behind."

Eating turkey or chicken is allowed, Jo says, if they've had a good life, so eggs can be eaten too, but the special perfect swan egg stays on the table.

"No chick will come out anymore? It's dead?"

It stays heavy, she can only hold it at the table, on the safe side, so careful with two hands. And next year? That exists! Because there's a next week too. Then we go to the beach, Mom said, with a tent for Art, to keep the wind or sun out. It was tried out on the grass, and she could go in with him, because Miss Ruby says: playing is sharing. And a teacher knows everything, except this: who is sharing Art?

<>

Even after the garden air, 'Reg' sleeps a short spell, and Anne adapts her schedule again. At eleven she feeds him a carrot and potato mash. "Mm, so tender, to melt on your tongue."

He rather likes it and tries to operate the spoon himself, with hands and feet.

"Alright, together then... Watch it, not in your nose."

He laughs and his body wriggles from top to toe. She's playing with his foot, and in no time his plate is finished. "OK, Reg, well done. Let me tidy up."

The badly needed cleaning cloth is on the kitchen counter, where she knocks over a pot by silly accident. The lid clatters with a racket on the stone floor, and his reaction reaching her from the room is heart-rending. She unbuckles him and lifts him in her arms. "Oh, my boy, your mom is so stupid. I hate the noise too, just horrible, but it's over now, can you hear? Hush, it made me jump too, out of my skin, that's only normal, and you were so close to the naughty floor!"

Swiftly she wipes the food mess off his face and hands. Then he can lie in her arms for a light and rocking walk around the room from window to window, so slowly that it's like a stroll to the park pond with the swans and chicks, one of their favorite spots, time allowed. If it's crowded, however, the new parents are bound to get aggressive.

He snivels a bit more. But at the front of the room the light catches his face, which makes him look out curiously, pointing and mumbling away.

"True, Reg, after a fright you're happier than ever. So long as the phone won't ring loud now, right?"

They sigh. She caresses his cheeks and removes the last tear, surprised by a passer-by on the sidewalk who waves a hand and smiles to them spontaneously.

"We don't even know that person! Come, let's go watch the birds on the other side. Look, a finch. I used to have one like that in a cage, but a garden is much better, isn't it? See how beautiful all the greens are. They do need pruning, though, or maybe not, actually. Look at the hazel and the box trees. We're snug and protected here."

It's a tranquil area with ample space between old little 'cottages', where mostly young people move to be creative or eccentric, tolerant yet busy with their own lives.

The doorbell rings and this time it's Anne to startle most, now that he's being so attentive, at peace.

At this fragile moment she doesn't want to put him in the pen, in sight of God knows who. They walk out into a corner of the back garden, where the bell won't be heard in the south wind. Hazel branches can be broken off by hand, which he likes tremendously, including the yellow snail that's taken to a spot with heaps of shrubs and weeds.

They pick a bunch of daisies, chasing the flies away, until it's certain that no one is at the door anymore, for charity or with a mail parcel for next door or a special offer for plastic window frames.

Nobody has been so rude as to walk around the back.

Anyway, in a clearance there's a pretty pear tree now.

"You know what, Reg, let's have a bath, you're all sweaty. Then you'll sleep extra well."

The phone rings, but she lets it be.

. . .

In the bath he floats on her arms and giggles when she covers him with little kisses, getting water-sprayed herself. He keeps moving so brusquely that she has to be focused each second, and, in her opinion, fifteen minutes is fine.

Being dressed, he's protesting. Next his bottle is lapped up, and when the cot comes in sight, he's bawling from disappointment.

"Hey, come on. There's a time for everything! Reg is tired, and Mom has piles of things to do. In fact, I could do with a nap too! Or do you want the soother? OK, that's good for the bulges in your mouth."

Downstairs, Anne would like to eat, catch up with some sleep and work all at the same time. She doesn't recognize the caller's number and stops to wonder, won't ring back, although it may have been a nice journalist's gig.

Over dinner she decides to turn the monitor off a minute and leave the hall door ajar. At one instant she needs to go upstairs, when he's lost the pacifier – the miracle emergency device.

Now her eyes fall shut and she lies on the couch, fairly relaxed, until the phone rings again: another unfamiliar number. But it turns out to be a well-known publisher, Simon Mills, who says, "I have your number from a mutual friend, Marcel, and he swore that I could call you with an exciting proposal. Can I?"

Anne laughs. "What proposal?"

The publisher readily joins her laughter. "Do you want to hear it now or do we make an appointment for lunch, a coffee?"

"Now, please."

She puts her fingers on her eyes, trying to relieve some pressure there, after the broken sleep.

Simon says, "I admire your interviews, and it must be your alias who writes the columns in weekly NUNA, of which I'm a fan – the columns."

There's no response from Anne except "Thank you", while she closes the door again, turns the monitor on, sits down at the work table. He proceeds. "We intend to publish a book with that sort of combination, column and interview. Would you care to write or compile it? Thematically or otherwise... If you have the time and fancy it."

"Yes, I do, if there's no haste, I hope?"

"Sadly, I'm always impatient," Simon admits, "from passion. And that doesn't work very well, so let's say asap. You have a baby?"

And no load-sharing man or nanny. How long will the torment of teeth and molars be? Many places and moments are suitable for column-writing. The interviews can take place in the evenings, even by phone and email. That works for shy as well as critical people. A project like this has been a soul wish of hers for years. The ideas and concentration will come of their own accord. In the long term she can be brave enough to invite her mother over – won't be able to stop her anymore! – or get an affordable sitter.

"With only the one child I've grown inventive enough, out of necessity."

"And I get the impression that your work pace is fast?"

"Yes, gaining time for ripeness and depth."

"Good," Simon cheers, "it's a pet project. You'll have an advance of twenty thousand, or more in the course of greatness. We are expecting a great deal."

"So am I."

Anne's eye strays between the future and her table with papers and the laptop. One hand holds the phone and the other arranges notes, pens of different colors, her tea cup. If the world is tidy, she can be on top of it and keep it intact, even when Simon's voice has been vague for a minute.

"Alright." He hesitates. "The contract will be straightforward. I'll email the sample first, and all can be discussed, of course. Or will each available hour go to a Special Person in the book now?"

"Yes, indeed. No restrictions to their professions or expertise?"

"No, a poet, baker, swindler, an actor who was famous and wild and now wants peace... Delight us with all kinds and with surprising links, of people and themes. You have the knack of making folks talk, open up, with anything original or secret, I mean sweet. You make them feel at ease. Am I right?"

"I have no schemes to that effect."

"Ah, see, that's what I mean: you're guileless! That's humorous and disarming, exactly what we're looking for. Stick to it, don't reflect on it. Who may I approach first, as a star or victim?"

Anne's laugh is rich. "*First,* I don't know yet, but high on my list are royalty in the shadows, of course, in exile for a very unusual story. Next Josh Gelder, and Bernard Bloomsdale. If you consent."

"Oh, Bloomsdale is not so conspicuous or mind-blowing, as far as I know, apart from his extraordinary qualities. But sometimes I know too little. No doubt you have a plan to *make* him blaze trails with you?"

"Let's say that I may have a hunch."

"Don't tell me: he leads a secret life as a criminal? With obscure and spooky connections? A second Boris Becker!"

"No," Anne grumbles. "You said *surprise us*, did you? So you don't want a list of candidates beforehand?"

"Well, since you're making me this curious, I don't mind thinking out loud. I did mean it about autonomy, but I like interaction and openness."

<>

On his way home in a gloomy mood, Bernard needs to stop at the supermarket, where it's just as crowded as he feared, with grabby and sassy kids of passive or permissive parents. He'd like to smack the latter and shake them awake from their weakness, but his bleak fatigue holds him back. Anger can keep something more difficult at bay only temporarily.

At the register he's trying to ban or postpone thoughts of Art. During a jam in the line before him, he blocks the whole world out – in vain.

Behind a special railing outside the exit, kids are begging for the gift packets of football pictures that customers receive with every fifteen dollar's worth of shopping.

Shall I keep mine for Dilli or Art for the long term? Even Dil is too young for them now.

Numb, Bernard walks on, ignoring their pleas, but a boy of about eight cries and runs away from the barrier, to hide behind a woman waiting at the bike racks.

To her he says, "Is it about the pictures?"

"Yes, my son is afraid to *ask*. He just waits."

Bernard puts his full bags down, gropes for a couple of packets between cartons of juice and yogurt and hands them to the mother, who passes them on. The boy reemerges partly with half a smile of disbelief and bliss.

"Do you live close by?" Bernard asks.

"Emrick Road," she says.

"Because I've got more at home. I'll bring them around. What number?"

"297. A funny number."

"But interesting too, 300 minus 3. A way for me to remember."

The boy stands and stares at Bernard as well as the packets, without opening them.

Bernard tells him, “I’m scared too. Maybe we can have a go together?”

He walks back to the railing pensively, where other kids gawk at him. The boy follows in tentative haste and joins Bernard when he squats nervously: as low as possible between restless legs and fumbling hands.

Customers leave the market, pushing loaded carts, and Bernard pleads politely, “If you don’t collect them, can we have your gift packets, please?”

Some kids and adults are baffled by this, including the boy.

“Sorry,” a woman answers. “We collect them too.”

With the next, he tells the boy, “Together.”

“Could we please have your football packets?”

“Nah, they’re for my neighbors.”

Bernard’s partner in courage takes over with a minor stammer – to receive a four-packet bull’s eye! That’s twenty pictures.

His back to the barrier, Bernard stays on his haunches another minute, he nods to the boy and witnesses more successes, realizing for the umpteenth time how relative or irrelevant time is.

Then he says, “You carry on? I’m off to cook dinner. Do you want my stack? OK, I’ll bring them over to 297. But not tonight. I’ll tell your mom you’re hanging on here.”

The boy has nodded once or twice.

“Now hoist me up, please. And look, a loaded cart freight is coming your way!”

At the back of his garden path lies a dead bird chick. It’s hardly more than a fetus, with delirious flies on it. This happens each spring and every time Bernard needs to conquer his cowardice in order to clear it with a scoop. Do other chicks drop in spots out of sight or are they always on the path to confront his weakness?

The scoop is hard but effective. With his hands he’d lack the courage to do this, even wearing gloves, because he'd feel their helplessness too much, which is exaggerated drama, he would admit.

He can't believe what a melodramatic day this is, while he knows too well that they do occur. Now what: at three or four feet from his backdoor, a blackbird fledgling sits at the foot of the laurel: a bulge of feathers with its head and beak up, the wondering eyes toward the sky or the nest where it flew and fell or was pushed out, doomed to die or simply dazed?

One thing that Bernard confesses when interviewers ask for his biggest act of cowardice, "When Nomi was about six, I sent her to a cool woman down the block, to have a lost creature put out of its misery the proper way: with a wrench of the neck."

Now he hopes for respite, promising to do better in the future, or know better.

His mind is tired, he's hungry and has a headache. Matching his mood, a thunderstorm skulks in the area, there's a weather warning out, but no one has closed a door or window yet, and delectable dinner smells float his way.

There's time left to open his own windows, and he has a few bites of cheese, which makes him feel better, getting busy with a meal of rice and a spicey, well-filled sauce and a fresh salad.

Back outside it's hotter than in the house. The air itself is eerily still; the acacia is rustling in a different dimension. And the young blackbird is gone. Bernard checks behind the flower pots and yellow nettles. He spots no feathers or blood, nor a cat in a corner.

The meal is very good.

Tolerant, if each in their own trees, the magpies and crows are waiting for what's to be. The swallows are coming lower and lower. It's growing pitch dark, but the pink-purple roses between lilac traveler's joy and yellow honeysuckle are luminous, in some lost light, it seems.

The grass should be mown before the rain, but he won't disturb this glory and his headache isn't over yet.

No finch or tit is venturing out anymore.

The heavy rain is slow, first the single and soft drops. Then he goes in, where the lights need to be on, but they're not shining on photos of loved ones. In the living-room he'll never have pictures of those he sees in daily life.

He keeps looking out, where the balsam leaves are trembling although they love water. Can they be shivering from pleasure?

This hour the day before yesterday, the sun came straight through the kitchen and touched each object as if it were the last time – with or without Art. Surely that will happen again one day, if it's the first time.

Generally, thunderstorms don't bother him.

What will Art look like in eight years' time: all meekness or eagerness outside a market exit, collecting the next generation of football heroes?

There may be baby photos of him in every room then, but not in the sunshine, because they would fade away.

<>

In Art's room, with all the space for a very good time, Dilli and Jess have played intensively, and at night Dilli is so tired that stair walking, and teeth brushing become too much.

Mark loses his patience and Nomi says, "A little leniency please. She must feel the tension too, swallowing a lot."

"Sure, if only she won't think this could be standard. They get used to routines quickly!"

And in the circumstances, the force of such phrases goes far, charged and disruptive. Nomi can't carry Dilli up the stairs. "But look, I put my hand on your back, here, and you're going almost by yourself. Just try and see, you in front. Can you feel?"

It works a miracle, they seem to be pushing and pulling each other up.

"Lights on for Art?" Dilli says on the landing, like an agreeable routine after weeks.

Nomi wants to keep fit, swimming and skating, but tonight she stays in, doing exercises in front of Art's heartwarming pictures, more and more fanatically, watching him hard, as if strength and effort and good intentions can be passed on or exchanged this way.

Some time ago she too joked that one kid was "no sweat".

Among the work emails read by Mark, there's one that he won't mention to Nomi. In a reflex he's almost deleted it immediately, but it might be important to the police.

"What were you thinking, leaving a baby out in the street? For a start, there could be a huge dog to jump onto that bike, to sniff or lick and bite! It could kill, if the child didn't have a heart attack first! At the play-farm I had a goat on my baby's buggy once. What would have happened if I'd not been there?"

. . .

The account is probably an alias for the occasion: worriedparents@gmail.com. Or is there in fact an organization like this? Doing good work too?

Mark forwards the email to Hattum before deleting it. In two minds, he grinds his teeth, he can't help agreeing with the sender's concerns, but he can't accept them either. All the same the message brings a flicker of hope in the sense that it could lead the police to the abductor, but the facts and lack of logic tear his life apart again. Mark loves Nomi deeply, as he realizes more than ever; he might well have done the same thing, the other day with Art. Caring and considerate, she puts the children first until she's beat. Fatigue makes you do freaky things.

In the middle of the night she talked to him in bed, in a choked and teary voice. "It was the third shop. Dilli stayed so good and grown-up about it. She didn't understand much anymore, but at last we saw the right bike. Deftly she rode around the shop and I was picturing all the things we could do, the three or four of us. We were happy, Art was comfy and asleep. For a minute nothing else existed, for instance how harsh life can be. But we had to wait at the counter... Why didn't I look out more? Forgive me, forgive me."

"Stop it, Nome, there's nothing to forgive!"

"All felt so peaceful or normal. And it was. How to know the hidden contrast? Do we need to watch out for deranged people constantly? Look who's talking!"

"No," Mark said, "never mind what you could have done."

But she went on. "If only I'd seen and checked more, it might all have been prevented. Or – much better, of course – if I'd unbuckled him... He would have woken up grumpy. But I thought we'd just walk in and out, like before, giving us a last chance. I wasn't thinking of sick people. He was sleeping so beautifully."

"You were a trusting person," Mark said, "*please*, you were being sweet, brave, positive. I love you, and remember: it's not your fault. Hear me? No need to mention it again, to anyone. You can speak your mind as often as you want, but not as a defense! Got it now?"

For one minute of a second chance, I'd carry the heaviest bike seat for the rest of my life, everywhere if needed.

<>

At some point it's unavoidable for the police to inform the media. So far most of them have complied with a forcible request to be ethical and keep their distance. The extended families, friends and neighbors receive Mark's emails – as if there were anything to report.

The police get messages to be forwarded to the parents, also words of support from strangers who are regarded as suspects first, to be on the safe side. Hattum calls and talks with Nomi about the possibility of a television appeal with a reconstruction by the shop. She's unable to consent or decline.

Time will heal no wounds for ages, while small doses of work, any kind, help more than talking. Doing nothing is a slow sword.

They barely watch television, because the news is a nightmare and entertainment is painful. There's no peace or interest for strong drama or a compelling book. Hattum can *still* call or drop by with developments or a spark of solution.

Through the monitor they can hear Dilli talking and singing.

At dusk the doorbell rings and for a second it sounds plain, but hope collides with fear again, both causing a sweat, bangs of the heart, nausea.

Who's got the nerve? Is there no physical or mental cordon?

Mark gets up with gestures in his arm and hand: do you want me to answer?

Nomi nods.

If Art has been found, healthy or dead, will they phone or come over?

There's a woman of about sixty at the door, slender, grey-haired but modern, serious and slightly insecure. "Sorry to disturb, my name is Liza Jacobs, and perhaps I can be of help, if you wish. Sorry, I mean, not like bringing Art back..."

Mark is disconcerted and torn, appalled by the woman's impertinence, yet fascinated by her natural and goodhearted openness. She doesn't look woolly-headed or sensationalistic, more like an experienced and wise grandmom of Bernard's youthful age, the best Gran lacking.

Bashful, Liza moves forward and blinks a sec, but she does look Mark in the eye and says, "I saw Art's picture and got this outspoken feeling."

She waits politely and Mark asks, "How do you mean?"

"It's a perception, a sense, not bound to place or time."

"Clairvoyant?"

"No, there are no images. I don't see places or people. You might call it clair-feeling, if you wish."

Staring, Mark swallows, Liza is also silent, and Nomi comes into the hallway, wondering what's keeping Mark – without anything mad happening? When he doesn't budge, Liza takes a step toward Nomi, introducing herself again with striking honesty, adding, "This feeling about Art lingers and it's so strong that I'd like you to know, but it's no solution or lead for the police. That's why I've come here first, almost reluctant. I'd hate to intrude."

Her dazzling sincerity removes a layer of resistance, and Nomi says, "Come in, please."

They shake hands, Liza follows through the hallway into the living-room, and Mark closes the door behind them pensively.

"Please, have a seat."

They take the couch opposite Liza, who says, "It's an ongoing sentiment that Art is alright, healthy, with benevolent people. A certain level of that life seems reasonably regular or happy. You must be sick from dismay, but I hope this can also console or reassure you, to some extent."

Nomi and Mark are gaping at her, until he says, "We don't want anything psychic or supernatural."

"And something extra-sensory?" Liza asks. "A sixth sense? Have you ever had premonitions or dreams that are linked to reality?" She pauses, but there's no reaction, so she goes on. "I'm nothing like a fortune teller. What I sense and say, tells an impression or comes from a truth in the present."

Without too much cynicism, Mark asks, "Does it always come true?"

"That's not how I put it. Often it's confirmed or recognized, sooner or later."

"Do you run a sort of practice?"

"No, I don't take money and don't appear in public, let alone in TV shows. This is the first time I've turned up uninvited. It was rule number one not to."

"Why this time?" Mark says.

"I don't really know. The feeling just lasted, persisted. The whole situation is exceptional because Art is doing well. Not the way he should be, of course. Does that make sense?"

Mark storms to the other end of the room, comes back and sits again, but his legs keep moving, up and down on the spot.

"Art is no victim?" Nomi says.

"Not of any violence. On the contrary."

They don't ask what the hell the opposite is. They've been telling themselves over and over: Art may be in a better place than millions of children far away and nearby.

"Is he cared for properly?" Nomi asks.

"Yes, with love."

"As if that's properly!" Mark cries.

"No, but the care in itself is, which I'm telling you only to lift some of the agony, if possible."

"As if that love is not insane!"

"Yes, disturbed."

"Do you know for what reason?" Nomi asks. "Is it anything to do with us?"

Liza sighs. Her eyes close an instant and a shiver runs down her shoulders. "No, it's a tragedy that stands on its own. I don't think there's any cause or guilt."

"No guilt?" Nomi says.

On which side?

"No, it's more like a melt-down of the mind or soul there, an extreme fit of anxiety."

"Temporary?"

"I don't know. I detect how it is now, but it's rather radical, sorry to say. Some absolute blockage."

Nomi rubs her brow hard. "Will you hold his clothes, or his cuddly rabbit?"

It's a burden to know that he doesn't have that now. Dilli used to be dependent on her toy Cat's presence, causing disproportionate drama, and they wanted to protect Art from that. It's a new rule that Rabbit can come along in a bag only, for 'emergencies'. This hurts Nomi like gastric acid in the chest.

"Up in his room?" Nomi asks.

"Yes, but don't count on a miracle, please, or anything concrete, like a solution."

"No." Nomi stands and says, "Will you go up alone?"

"If that's what you prefer."

Nomi nods. "Be my guest, please. I don't want to interfere. It's on the third floor."

"Where the beautiful light is on? I saw it from outside."

"Dilli sleeps in the room next to him... next to his, but there's no need to be very quiet. You don't mind the steep flights of stairs?"

Liza is a bit pre-occupied now, saying, "No, it's fine."

Is it? Or have they lost their mind? A stranger in the house: they wouldn't think of it 'before'. But nothing is normal anymore. Liza seems utterly safe and we shouldn't be too polite, or else Art is kept at a distance too.

Liza looks earnestly at Nomi and Mark both, who nod, and he smiles, more or less.

"Alright. Thank you."

Nomi closes the hall door behind her.

After a lull, she sits on the left side of Mark again and takes his hand. She rubs and kneads it, which keeps him quiet.

Finally he says, "She could be right, as long as you don't expect anything."

"No, yes, merely that it can help Art in any possible way, I mean, we can't let him down, as it were, by rejecting Liza before we know more."

Nomi has almost spoken in a hurry, out of breath already.

"OK," Mark says, "I'll be neutral."

"Yes, that's good, neutral is open. You go on and do something, if you want."

On second thought, he wants to google Liza Jacobs, or clairvoyance of any kind, because you never know, but there's no result. The first sites on clairvoyance are horribly bogus and sleazy – because the true psychics don't sell or show themselves commercially?

He says, "Dilli was supposed to stay over at Bernard's tomorrow. Is that still on?"

"I'm not sure it's a good idea," Nomi says.

"You mean for her or us?"

"Oh, there's a point."

Mark's thought dates from last week: a weekend with just Art, since "one kid is a holiday now." Until his first tooth. If Dilli no longer sleeps in the afternoon, the hours between three and six count double.

Now Mark says, "We don't want an empty house, but Dilli loves it at Bernard's, without..."

"Yes, of course."

Without Art getting under her feet.

"Do you want me to drive her?" Mark asks.

"Don't know yet. We'll see tomorrow, OK?"

There's a knock, and Nomi opens the hallway door.

Liza comes in but she won't sit down again. "Art has a wonderful room. All beauty and peace..." No other place can emulate that. "I didn't feel a big or peculiar contrast with Art's present whereabouts, I mean no clash or conflict regarding the atmosphere, as a reassurance or confirmation, if you wish."

"You don't have... any news?" Nomi asks.

"Except, it struck me... that Art must be relatively close by – in the literal and mental sense."

And you've never been mistaken? stays on Mark's lips.

"Thank you," Nomi says, wanting to ask so much more that her throat is blocked. She must not defy, challenge, test Liza or herself.

Liza moves to say goodbye. Mark's handshake is firm and short, and he says, "You won't take any fee at all?"

"No, imagine. I barged in here."

"Or um... if ever you're looking for a house?" he asks inadequately.

Liza and Nomi are equally in the dark, for different reasons.

"We might be able to help *you*," he explains.

"We're real estate agents," Nomi comes to the rescue of all. "And it's hard for him – and me – to accept this just like that, I mean to receive it in all respects. But I'm not sure myself," she goes on. "How grateful or confused he is right now."

With a brief broad smile, Mark says, "Not sure either. Both? Sorry, it just came out like that, the house-looking bit, so I meant it."

"Thank you," Liza says, with a modest smile of her own.

There seems to be some relief in the air, similar to the elation after a funeral, when something difficult is over and went well, with all the emotions of responsibility and togetherness. After a funeral there may be a new start.

At the front door Nomi says, "Many thanks for coming. You didn't phone ahead on purpose, I take it?"

"Yes, that can give the wrong impression."

"And if you perceive something again, a change, good or bad news, please let us know. It won't be uninvited anymore."

"Alright. Thank you."

"Can I give you a lift home?" Nomi offers.

"No, thanks, I like my bike, to freshen the mind, keep fit. And it's still dry."

"You don't live too far away? Sorry, I'm not prying."

Or should we ask more?

"No, I'll be home before the storm. Bye bye."

<>

"Are we going to report this to Hattum?" Mark asks in bed after a spell of rain and wind, with one theatrical thunderclap.

Other nights, they would have cuddled up and called this 'cozy'.

"No, it wouldn't help, would it?"

"I don't know what came over us, but then I think: we could have given her our card. Has she bewitched us?"

"Not me," Nomi says. "She's very human, almost humble."

"Unless that's a mask."

"Please, come on, Mark."

"But what if she's telling us what we want to hear?"

"Why?"

"A sick need of attention. Happens a lot."

Nomi seems to get rid of all misgivings.

"Stop it," she whispers, "don't. You're not thinking there's anything sinister behind it, are you? I'm serious!"

"Liza is no part of a conspiracy or something, like a wrong-footing scheme, leading us away from a real trail...."

They're lying on their backs, close, and his hand is on her upper leg, caressed lightly by her. He won't disturb that by turning on his side. Their eyes are lost in thought, with a lot to figure out.

Mark is musing along as a devil's advocate. "What would Hattum say: for all we know, she's a sly, calculating accomplice, and this act of hers is part of the smart plan, a red herring! I would have liked to ask her more, for example if she's qualified or registered."

"That's no vote of confidence," Nomi says.

"Just curious, truly."

And it almost slips out: *I wanted to show her the vile email.*

He says, "We should have asked if Art is in a family. No, of course he's not, he couldn't be with other kids. They would tell. With a woman or a man?"

"Liza doesn't know that sort of details, I think."

"Maybe she can interpret something."

"Well, interpretation is her specialty, isn't it?"

"Or association?" Mark says. "In the morning, all down-to-earth, we'll think it's baloney."

There's no row or drifting apart, as could happen when tragedies and doubts provoke us to the utmost. They're so close that before they know it, a consoling caress of the body can grow into something more, that used to be about 'having babies' for years, and they shy back with turbulent thoughts, as if Art could ever be replaced. As if they haven't considered 'the procedure' for Mark yet, since two kids are about right in this family, aren't they? At times, the pair of them are more than enough. Or do most young parents say that? "Ah, these years pass by and next thing you're longing for them."

Nomi doesn't want to think this, but it catches her off guard: there will never be a new Art. Another child might be possible after a long time, or would that accentuate who's missing?

<>

When Anne took him to bed, the air was still sticky, and in the night she's changed his thin cover for a warm one.

Now she knows that his bottle needs to be ready before he sees it, certainly in the morning, to prevent a fierce fuss. During diaper-changing and getting dressed he's such a keen and quick mover that she can't leave him for one moment, not even to fish a diaper from the drawer, let alone to take a step and grab his clothes from the chair.

The teeth-tummy-bottom disaster implies half a dozen poop-diaper changes a day, huge efforts with patience, determination and swift neatness. In both his room and the living, she has a set of tools and props within reach, and during the operation she keeps a hand on his strong, springy body permanently.

"Good, sweet boy. We need a stair gate. You'll crawl around like a baby tiger."

The skin of his bottom looks inflamed or whipped. Around the changing mat she stashes diversion objects that rattle or squeak, bend, open and close. She's bought piles of the softest and oiliest wet wipes without irritating perfume.

She smells and checks continually, before his skin could burn and break again. Still it occurs that he's trembling from pain and stress, lying on the mat and clutching a special object. But when the ointment is applied, he holds his breath and lies still – begins to remember that it helps?

Yes, new memories are essential, as old ones will fade.

After these comradely sessions, both are proud and pleased. His out-reaching hands are covered with her series of kisses, of relief and sympathy. Getting his clothes on seems easy then, his clever arms find the openings of sleeves by themselves.

"No tight shirts, right? Nah, I don't like them either. Mm, I could eat you, but oohh, you're putting your big new teeth into me!"

He should sleep through a good part of the morning, safely upstairs.

In high spirits, Anne sets to work at her laptop in the living-room, on the multi-tasking table, snug with the easing rain outside, and the monitor is never far away.

At a quarter to ten, the doorbell rings, and automatically she looks at the play pen, but he's been in bed for nearly an hour. A little social break might be alright, and cheerfully she answers the door, but her face collapses when it's Evan, her ex-boyfriend and Reg's father, without an umbrella, slightly bending forward – as if that helps. He's not too wet, coming out of a car that she hasn't heard?

When Anne is too astounded to react, he puts his collar up and stoops a bit more. "Sorry, this is very unexpected, but I did phone yesterday."

In a sharp flashback, Anne sees him smash a bunch of keys down and leave –

"I can't be a dad!"

"I can't have an abortion."

"So there's no us. Keep the house."

"In exchange for freedom: a good deal for who?"

That was over a year ago. Now Evan is waiting and facing her, growing more uneasy, while raindrops roll down his thick hair and over his face. It makes him look so tough as well as vulnerable, shockingly attractive and new. An entire past throws itself into right now.

While she's quavering from disbelief, he takes his hands out of his pockets and wrings them like a film star who needs to improvise.

"I don't want to impose, and some rain is drifting in, but I've changed. Sorry, are you very busy?"

As Anne steps back, the doormat is free, which he sees as an invitation to enter, and if that's in spite of herself, he can understand, meekly glad of the opportunity. He shakes his hair like a dog, takes his jacket off and shakes that out on the porch, saying, "Better not mess up the floor."

Fine wood, which used to be his too. He put it there with his own bare hands, not even that long ago. They fell in love with this cottage from the 1950s, affordable because there was no luxury, only the basics and its character.

"Sshh, Reg is asleep."

There's no hug or kiss. Anne gets his jacket and drapes it over the stroller. Evan takes his shoes off as well, which gives her goosebumps. After a glance up the stairs, she precedes him into the living room.

He looks around admiringly and his thumb rubs the playpen railing. "I'm sorry it's been... Well, the one year, but it's also a sort of lifetime. If it was definitive then, the break-up, I'm sorry. Have you coped all on your own?"

"You mean without a handsome, shining knight, to rescue me with riches and time."

"Hm, I've got a fair amount of both now."

Anne doesn't laugh, she asks, "Why suddenly now?"

"To be honest, I wanted to come before, but I needed a while to pull myself together, first to find the guts to see how dumb I'd been, then to change enough. I was scared, thinking you hated me too much, after my stupid and shameful exit. I didn't mean to leave you in the lurch."

"Oh," she tries hard not to be ironic *or* forgiving. "I did consent, didn't I, by taking the house, and I wouldn't know much difference anymore. It's all a blur. So why are you brave now: to confront me with failures?"

With a sigh, as if standing up takes too much, Evan finds the nearest chair at the table, opposite her work spot. "As I said, I've so changed, I'm not selfish and ignorant anymore. No sentimental smart-ass either. I have learned a lot and I would like to prove it. Make things right. That abduction has a weird or extra effect on me too, I guess. Have you followed it?"

"No."

"Just as well. It's made me gloomy, feeling guilty toward the two of you. Know what I mean? I don't get it myself, and I reckoned it would pass, but it won't let go, I keep thinking of you, wondering. Sorry, it sounds too corny! You must be yelling: find a therapist!"

Anne folds her paperwork on the table's work part and puts it in the cabinet. She saves a Word file, pushes the laptop aside, moves her chair backward and sits down, gazing at Evan and out the window and back at him. "I don't know what to yell or think – at you or me."

"Of course," he says. "I have no clue what to *say*, haven't *prepared* anything. I'm too young for a midlife crisis, right? Damn it."

"There's no wife or girlfriend or boyfriend?"

He grins. "Tried many, it's all over, and it wasn't all my fault."

"Only the sixty-hour workweeks, then down and out by the TV?"

"Yes, I'm truly ashamed of that period." He looks at the computer. "How's your work?"

"It's doing well," she says. "I'm also working on a book."

"How do you manage with a kid and all?"

"Well, basically I don't do much else, and that's fine."

"Wow." Evan's brow goes up. "There's been no man at all? Sorry, that comes out wrong. I won't pry!"

"You mean between pregnancy, stitches, breast feeding and stretch marks? Nope, no room for a man. But the publisher is nice and cool, generous, from the sophisticated city."

"So he won't change diapers."

"Nah," Anne smiles. "He wants to have lunch with me, he's got no idea about Reg or anything personal."

"Reg..."

He's tasting the name and seems moved, looking away to overcome the emotion, touching Anne in her tailbone.

It makes her restless. "Would you like a coffee?"

"Yes, very much, I mean, if I'm not disturbing?"

Anne gets up, bewildered by her conflicting feelings. "I'm having some myself, so... Milk and sugar?"

"Just milk now."

"Ah, changed indeed."

"Yep." He seems happy in defeat. "Sensible at last."

"I see," Anne says, "my advices didn't help."

"They did later, with interest! Now I'll stay young and fit."

Anne evades his eyes and walks to the semi-open kitchen. She doesn't know where to begin and needs to focus on the coffee: How many spoonfuls? It should be nice and strong. Don't drop the tin lid; Reg would hear that horrible noise and should definitely not wake up now! She's shaking, hasn't eaten properly yet, ought to have toast or a banana first, as she would otherwise. She can do as she likes, can't she? But then it would seem as if Evan was a part of her life. He doesn't even know Reg!

Concentrate.

Wait... As the coffee machine is on, it's not so quiet anymore that she hears herself. After a glimpse over her shoulder, seeing that Evan is walking around and looking at things, she cuts a few slices of ginger bread and has a bite already, while buttering them. Was anything too private lying there? The less company you have, the more mess you leave.

She eats another slice, also butters buns and rolls, and puts a plate of them on a tray. Tentative, she carries the big tray to the table and regrets this welcome display now that it's too late: Evan will draw the wrong conclusions.

Softly she closes the door to the hallway.

On the other side of the room he says, "There are no pictures!"

"Whose?"

"I don't see Reg or anyone!"

"Wait, I don't want to spill things."

She puts the two coffees in the right spots, the rest in the middle of the table, and she gets wooden plates from the closet. "No, it's funny, I'm not keen on photos in frames, like showing off, don't ask me why. And as to Reg..."

Evan comes and sits at the table again, attentive, shyly surprised by the food.

Anne says, "Remember my Mom? She's nagging my head off, she wants a new photo of Reg every day. But I don't have the time or energy to take any good ones. So I don't share them too much. It's hard to explain, like pride: I can't stand people bragging about their kids."

She sits and has a currant bun.

Gesturing to the rolls, he says, "I did not mean to be obtrusive. But I had a question." He pauses as if waiting for permission. "Is there anything I can do for you, or Reg? Maybe things you don't get around to, like taking pictures and making an album for Wil?"

Anne is gaping, which makes him say, "Sorry, I won't push it."

After a hesitation he takes a croissant. "Mm, now I wouldn't dare say how good this is."

Too much?

"Don't worry. My turn to say sorry, I forgot breakfast."

"And you have no weight problem, you're looking good."

"Oh? I burn piles of calories, I guess."

Anne has her eyes on the monitor.

He follows her eyes – why? – and looks at her again. "You're as slim as before."

She's blushing like a teenager and knows it, almost hoping for a beckoning sound from upstairs, and she blurts out, "We need a stair gate. But it's not urgent."

"Today? The weather is perfect for a job like that."

He takes a large bite with a gulp of coffee and makes ready to go.

"Oh, nah..." Anne says, plainly realizing the consequences. "You're making me self-conscious!"

"Because you haven't seen me for a year? That's my fault, let me make up for a day, and a stair gate is easier than a leaking gutter or long-horned beetles or a marten under the roof!"

All that house-owner's doom is realistic, and there's more work for which she needs people who cost fortunes, or a sympathetic neighbor, friend, relative...

Evan can see her thinking. He continues, "I'll go buy a stair gate, I'll install it and will be out of your hair again, unless you can do with a babysitter, now or later. Reg will be up and about all day, he'll creep into everything and mess it up, if he's anything like me."

Their eyes meet, measuring.

"Or is he in day care?" Evan asks. "That's expensive, isn't it? Shall I pay half or more? So you can write your great book. With famous people in it? Not about bad fathers, please?"

She can't hide a smile but doesn't reply.

He finishes his coffee and makes for the door, taking a slice of cake. "Do you want a specific brand or shape or material?"

In this manner she had two good years with him, and he may have grown up indeed – like herself. She says, "The safest and easiest, please. Go check out the top of the stairs, but hush!"

Fortunately he took his shoes off, so thoughtful and pleasant.

When he's in form, she helplessly likes his bubble, that annuls the rudeness. And if his 'wild or bad side' has truly changed... In hindsight it may not have been that bad, and she's learned a lot as well, about the black and white sides of things.

He doesn't ask for shopping money and she fails to offer.

<>

For sleepovers at Bernard's, Dilli is usually picked up by him, but today she's brought by Nomi, who stops for one soda and half a cookie.

Her stomach doesn't respond very well to these, as if she's taking a major exam or finding that she's late for it. Are the detectives working all weekend? What's left to do for Art?

With Dilli around she can't talk about Liza, and on the phone she won't either, but Bernard is the only suitable person. Anyone else who hasn't met Liza would say, "Have you lost your mind? Despair makes you susceptible to such nonsense, a prey to borderliners or psychopaths."

She has told herself that, or tried. She 'forgot' to ask for a phone number or address, didn't she. Why was Liza unable to say if it will end well with Art? Because her gift is limited to the present, and that's what makes it so real and plausible. It's remarkable enough, a gift from heaven, to know that Art is healthy or even happy.

If ever she knew how, she might believe that his lasting absence could be bearable to her someday – would have to be, first of all for Dilli's sake. The other day she read something in a waiting room that touches her more now, "The one who loves, can set free." Or was it "Who loves, does let go"? They may be trendy lifestyle words, but still...

If she could see for herself just once that Art is alright, would she in the long run be able to accept it? Or this is a frail start of a life sentence. Less difficult than a child's death? It's not fair to compare! There are too many cruel deaths per day that could reduce this tribulation to something bearable.

Such insights or whatever they are, last a couple of minutes. Then her mind and feelings can't grasp the meaning anymore. But maybe, if she dared say something like that out loud to a special person, would it be more true or helpful?

<>

Here's a dauntingly narrow dam bridge across a brook, with a railing on one side only, and Bernard clutches Dil's hand, but the water can take them like a slide without end: until she slips out of the world like Art.

"Ooh," Bernard mutters. "Hold on, step by step, careful."

They venture three runs of excitement, back and forth on the bridge. "Come, Dil, we're off again."

"Or," she pleads, pointing to the water basin below the mini waterfall. "Wait until it's full!"

But they do move on and he's not explaining how some things can run forever.

Meanwhile, not madly far away, a gusty wind has chased the rain. The nerve endings in Anne's arms and legs are itching and pricking. No more coffee today! Father and son exist in different worlds: one out and one inside of her. They put her off balance, she's close to the person of about two years ago again.

Evan will be back in a minute and Reg will wake up, but fair enough, he does need to meet people. All is going well. As a mom and woman united, she can take care that it stays that way. It's normal to be busy, so long as you know the limits of yourself and others on time.

She rearranges books and papers, toys, magazines, she tidies the table, washes the dishes, changes and puts on make-up.

She can hear Reg as expected. He's exploring the reach of his voice, going from a scream to this mumbling that resembles "Mom." When he bumps his head it's only logical that he cries. Then she hurries up to him.

As soon as his door makes the least sound, he turns and looks at her, smiles and calls out, reaching and toppling from pleasure.

"Yes, here I am, hi, sweet, and you are so big and active, lifting your strong arms! Had a good sleep?"

She carries him to the window and shows all the motion in the sky. "Look, that cloud is hauling the sun along. See how blue some parts are? They're so bright it hurts the eyes, but you have a cool cap, we'll try it, yes? I think Evan will like it too. Or you prefer a sunhat with a broad edge? Sorry, we have to change diapers first, you're totally right, we don't need that Evan fuss."

Or we do: he'll flee again!

And the possibility makes her smile with a taste of doubt and pain, because it would be sad-ish again too.

Evan comes around the back now, but that door is accidentally locked, which Anne hurries to explain with an apology. "Only when I'm upstairs! But I forget."

Evan brings the package into the room, where he sees a busy boy in the playpen, exploring each centimeter of himself and surroundings.

"Hey, great baseball cap!"

For an instance the cap catches more attention than the son himself, and confident, Anne says, "Yes, we're testing it for outdoors. I'd like him to get used to it; there's so much UV radiation these days..."

"Good idea. Looking smart too."

"Also, for his eyes; the light must be so tiring for a baby."

"Oh." After his tiny frown: "Yes, I don't think people give it much thought."

"Besides," Anne says, "I know a toddler who's got sun allergy because he was sun-burnt once."

"Does Reg have light skin?" Evan says, bending over to look under the cap. "That's one thing he hasn't got from me."

"Reg could be pretty blond, but he doesn't have much hair yet, so it's hard to tell. Careful, he's over-sensitive with new people."

"OK. Is that the age or his character? I mean, the shyness is nothing personal about me, is it?"

"Ah," says Anne, "grant him a minute of space, a chance to get used to somebody."

"Well," Evan tells him and her. "That's perfectly natural, if it's not my fault. As a kid I was the same, so... It can change! You know what, Reg, I'll do your gate, and then you can ramble your legs off up there, let your mom get some work done in peace and quiet. How's that? See you."

To Anne he says, "OK?"

"Yes, I guess, but it's strange."

"Because you have no tools for me to use?"

She grins with a prickle of recognition: it's typical of him all over again that his charm and ease or directness can cover up anything. So attractive, it's precarious. But hey, I'm aware of it and can be balanced now! No saint before myself, so give him a chance!

He used the tools often before here. As if skipping a year, he finds his box in the hallway closet. She's watching aside, the way you let a kid go ahead when he's out of reach anyhow, counting on a better moment to connect, even though the question is for what and who.

If Evan has only come to see his son, it could be either good or menacing. He'll want to take him out for rides by bike or car, he'll take photos and show them to friends or relatives. And if he offers to 'babysit' again, many a problem could be solved, or would arise.

After a picnic in the glorious full summer fields, Bernard and Dilli are cycling along paths among waving grasses as tall as the handlebars! Humming a nursery song, she is now behind, then in front, queen of the east wind, and so close to the greens, they can touch and tickle her, making her laugh. She used to be scared of them ages ago – like last week with Art?

Once or twice she swerves, but Bernard is not worried sick. "Whoa, that's a sharp bend! Don't capsize."

She steers back to the safe part of the path and says, "It's a soft bend now. Good?"

Finishing the stair gate upstairs, flushed and sweaty and pleased, although it was "nothing at all", Evan's eye is caught by the bathroom, which he patched up last year. He undresses and hops in for a lush and carefree shower, heard by Anne downstairs, who pops over to stop in the hallway, to listen and 'imagine' or remember other times with a smile and a shake of the head. Will she go up for a polite peek around a corner?

She can visualize his clothes in a clutter on the floor, and how he's turning, spluttering, splashing innocently. He never fished a towel from the closet until he'd soaked the mat.

This time, or henceforth, will his clothes go in the laundry or stay scattered on the wet floor forever again?

At eleven-thirty Evan enters the living room all cute and fresh with wet hair. He studies the little one, who's finished his meal and tries to move his physical boundaries, defying the chair belt and leaning forward so far that his hands touch the floor.

"He's all determination!" Evan cries. "He'll go places!"

"Yes, he's aching to stand and walk."

"Ha, to go his own way. I can't believe he's my flesh and blood."

Why not? You're full of purpose and strength too!

Anne is astonished by Evan's genuine and profound interest, but she gets a grip again quickly. "Because he's quiet and sweet or bright?"

"Yes, all of that, so he takes after you. But what I meant... I can't believe I left you two behind."

Anne is also reflective, with a finger on her chin. "To tackle the rough part."

"Yeah, getting up at night and stuff – I'm so sorry. There's no way for me to catch up with that, or make amends, is there?"

"Doesn't matter. My mom is almost gagging to stand in – or move in!"

He shakes his head, suppressing a grimace of pleasure. "And you're still not keen?"

"Spare me! Which is harsh on her, because she adores Reg. That's no matter of course for her."

Evan is ready to go, but he's dawdling. "So... will you call her or me when you need someone? Or can I come back once or twice, for a small chat – with you or Reg? If I kindly leave now?"

<>

At the picturesque little marina a boat is lifted in a rope frame, and by the gate is a deserted police car, a real one with its bright striped colors. Dilli is bold and nosy enough to walk around it and peer in, but nothing happens.

"Of course," she says, "they're looking for Art."

"Come on, let's watch the boats and big ropes," her grandfather says.

Roving the narrow and moving pontoon paths across the water, they hold hands tight again, especially when she tries to push and rock a boat.

A few times she can look inside – good hiding places! She likes the word "saloon", to act out at home when Art is back. At the far end, after square bends in the floating path, one-day duck chicks are bobbing around. "Riding the ripples of life," Bernard says to nobody.

One boat comes in, puffing, another sails out to the canal.

"Are boats going far?" Dilli asks.

"Sometimes, yes."

The sun is so hot that you'd like to jump into the water, and she can feel his hand squeezing hers, so she asks, "Has a boat gone far with Art?"

He's not answering yet, but his hand sways with hers in it. She's trying to see and hear everything: his answer, a bow and anchor, the high wall still to climb, toward the ships in the distance... "Oh! The police are there, at the car! Can we go too?"

It's not safe to run here, but they go light-footed, to reach the officers on time, in their very white shirts: a man and a woman.

They're outside the open car door, and Bernard asks, "Have you got one minute, please? This girl would be the happiest in the world if she could take a glance in your car."

"Then we'll do that," the officer says.

It's beyond her expectations and she's terrified, but the man says: "I've got one this age" and he puts her on top of the seat at the wheel. Sitting on her knees, all can be seen and felt, but she's looking straight in front of her, gasping and not pressing a button.

The one minute is almost long enough to get used to it and do some thinking. Luckily the others are talking together, and one good moment she dares to ask it: "Are you finding Art?"

3

LET GO AND HOLD

<>

The officer knew who Art was, and he told Bernard, "Do you want the raw truth? After forty-eight hours chances are slim."

After weeks there was no trace of Art. The scarce tips and leads had long stopped coming in, even when Mark and Nomi had been on television, needing to control their emotions firmly, following a formal part by Hattum and the presenter –

"Whoever you are, and where, are you treating Art well? That's what matters most. If you know how much we miss him, or if you love him yourself... Maybe you couldn't help it. If it was an accident and Art is dead, do let us know. "Otherwise ... Can we please have him back? We promise that it will be anonymous. We don't seek revenge or prosecution, it's about Art himself, and Dilli, who doesn't understand either."

Dilli was not crouching on their laps, it was dramatic enough. They were filmed at home, without a script, only a few notes for Nomi and Mark, with directions from Hattum. Dilli was filmed in her and Art's room, and all shots were edited, but they looked spontaneous, without anything corny.

Nomi conquered a lot of shame and was actually helped by the fact that it went overwhelmingly fast. Afterwards, off-camera, came her outlet of emotions with fear and fatigue. "The abductor is meant to see this, but what if it's on a large screen when Art is having his evening bottle, and he's watching too with wide open eyes? Will he recognize us?"

Or, she thought to herself, could this make the abductor mad and aggressive? And what would be a consequence if the man panicked?

Surely no woman? But never a man either, please!

· · ·

The longest days of the year have gone by and on television it's also summertime. People get ready for their vacation and forget the Art episode of *Searching*.

The News brings so much misery each day – how many dead babies here and there? – that our skin thickens or the soul's callus hardens.

The way the days are shortening again subdues Nomi. At first it's not really noticeable, the trees have gradually turned a denser and darker green, until the changes make her aware of a deeper difference. Everything continues, diminishes, withdraws and begins anew: nature, life with or without Art. He grows and builds up without her – in heaven or on earth? Every memory of her will be gone completely, also if he's alive. When he lives. Wishing and longing can be stronger than common sense.

Dilli still talks about him and impersonates him, she drinks from his bottle and keeps her 'balance-fly-bike' for him, all ready for age one. But the moments in between become too long.

The fact that there's nothing left to do for Art, stretches Nomi's feelings of guilt and shame, which even increase when their modest business is almost booming, in defiance of recession and summertime, including the general tendency of buying and selling without an agent. This could be something to do with the pity of clients, who all know about Art, or plainly their curiosity and sensation.

Sincere support and compassion can also trouble her, by rubbing it in during small spells of not thinking of it, the allowed relief.

In order to specialize, the agency is even more selective taking new assignments, and it may be this very reticence that leads to considerable success. The creative side of the job keeps Nomi healthy; it feeds and heals her where possible.

Thanks to a series of large transactions they can do something concrete if indirect for Art after all: they offer a reward of twenty thousand, although a sum like that should flow back into the business as a buffer or an investment.

They don't go on vacation. No plans come up, and other people are quiet about their travels.

Dilli's pre-school is closed for the summer, but a new day-care center nearby will have her three mornings a week. That's exceptionally obliging – because the center needs the money?

Other days Dilli plays by herself and with friends, also on the lake's beach in water pools where babies can sit and splatter for fun.

Mark and Dilli work in the garden, fix a gate upfront, climb a stepladder to prune the wild and climbing sorts. Nomi and Dilli wash the car, they go swimming, they run or skate on wide sidewalks, where tussocks are dangerous only for Nomi's blades.

The weekends bring visitors again, who come hesitantly without presents but sometimes with flowers or home-made pastry. They don't ask to see Art's room, that stays exactly the same.

There's no police at the marina anymore, and somebody else calls out, "Kids have to wear life jackets here!"

Not until then does Bernard see a sign that says: "No trespassing", and they're even more watchful. Has Art fallen and drowned here or anywhere because he didn't wear a life jacket?

They need to go and buy groceries, where Dil can be snug in the cart, munching a fresh slice of bread, and another one, passing by the jars of ready-made baby food. A long time ago Granddad bought some, saying, "Comes in handy."

<>

What would someone lie about or make up to get a reward of twenty thousand? Anne has read about it in a local paper and she's unsettled by the thought of the police coming by after a tip-off, just in case, only to exclude Reg and her from their inquiries.

When a boiler man comes for the annual check-up, Anne would like him to take his shoes off, because Reg is asleep, but she says, "Please wipe your feet, because I've just cleaned."

He says, "Don't worry!" and takes the stairs to the attic in his heavy boots.

During intensive work in the narrow boiler corner that could make the kindest man claustrophobic, he might invent anything loony for cash, to buy a new car or take a dream vacation.

She shows him the way and apologizes for the confinement. "This is also my storage nook, but I have removed some."

Sufficiently?

The wash-drying racks on the railing were not expecting a sturdy man. Brushing and bumping, he worms his way past them, and she says as lightly as possible, "Give a shout if you need me?"

Anne does the dishes in order to 'drown out' the noises from upstairs. Please, don't wake Reg up. The hall door down here needs to be open, in case he'll call her.

She doesn't want to make a fuss and already she's pleased that a day's dishes are being done, but her musings are crudely interrupted by a sequence of sharp clatters. Is it something she did not clear there?

Out of politeness and apprehension she stays downstairs and the man doesn't call her. His footsteps come thumping down a few steps, there's more loud stumbling, then he walks out – leaves the front door open – and returns without a word, to thunder up the stairs again.

Is Reg flabbergasted and goggling?

Moderately calm, she finishes the dishes.

Finally the boiler man mumbles something of which she can hear only the last word, "Fixed," and he's off. Good thing that she neatly wraps up in the kitchen, because he's back once more, for her signature on a device, approving the payment or automatic withdrawal of $20.50.

She won't ask him to clarify. Surely a man like that can be trusted and her bank account won't be plundered?

Upstairs the drying racks are flat and undone on her bedroom floor, like the skeletons of aliens. What a blessing that he didn't barge into Reg's room. The gods are with them! She can more or less put the parts together again and back in place on the railing, proud to have done it straightaway, without moaning and moping. Better tidy her room before Reg is up.

She's taking an optimistic peek into his room, but what a funny and fitful day of fate is this? Not very gently a ladder is flumped against his window. Are reward hunters fanatic enough to check all the houses with babies?

It must be simply the window cleaner, for another regular and necessary breach of peace and privacy. Yet, further real thoughts are sneaking into her head: creeps and peeping toms, dressed as work people, can get far, for example if they know when she's out, with or without Reg. Will she ask them for identification from now on, or would that cause problems? Nosy and desperate thieves or junkies do reckless things and succeed with impulsive speed or calculated slyness.

She didn't draw the curtains in his room. He should get used to some light in bed, so that he'll sleep well in daytime too. He's probably thinking: what crazy racket are we having now?

Yes, darling, welcome to life!

She leaves the door ajar and stops here.

Routinely the cleaner is banging his wiper on the window – and looking inside? She could run and ask him to skip this room,

"Sorry, my son is asleep now and he needs it badly," but she's embarrassed. Last time she had to tell him to come every other month only, and in winter she'll need him for the high gutters.

Evan keeps offering to do odd jobs for her and Reg. That's a lovely form of contact and it's good to celebrate the results with a drink or meal and Reg.

After a few weeks of getting acquainted steadily, the boys make trips together as well. Evan has put a cushion-filled kid seat on the handlebars of her bike, where Reg is firm and happy as a prince.

Proud yet anxious, Anne explains, "Remember, his hat or cap is imperative, both in the sun and wind. Never mind if he disapproves and pulls at it!"

"Yep," says Evan.

She reckons he respects that, despite his stubbornness and his opinion about a kid's toughness or resistance, aiming for immunity. "He needs to grow without too much protection."

She tries, "His teeth make him look big, but that doesn't mean he's not vulnerable."

"Sure, of course."

"And remember: grant him time to get used to people, so don't let them come close if they don't understand."

"I know," Evan says. "He needs a couple of minutes."

"Also, keep your distance from traffic, please, and he can't sit up long, yet."

It strikes her, though, how caring Evan is, as if Reg is a newborn. The man has no nephews or nieces, and he accepts her advice, if with a grain of salt. The boy can be as headstrong as charming. "Taking after who?" is the latest jocular question, not always out loud.

. . .

Evan talks and sings to him with bravura and a touch of subtlety. They practice the word "Daddy" as well, and near the marina – with Bernard and Dilli in the unclear distance – he teaches him the sound of an engine.

When Bernard vaguely gazes their way, Evan and the hat-wearing son are chatting with a bunch of senior citizens, a dog, their grandkid, about the weather and pets, health and safety.

Bernard's eyes linger on the baby whose age he estimates to be the same as Art's, and who knows, if Dil weren't here... But from this distance and in his state of mind, *any* kid resembles Art. There's nothing to see, really, and he can't go on tormenting himself like this, with a heartache rather than suspicion.

The dad and son over there are moving in such free and open ways, close, confident – making for the boat hanging in a frame on a crane – that Bernard heaves a sigh. He'd like to show Dilli the hauled boat from close by, but she's brimful of impressions as it is. That baby – a boy? – would tear up her attention. He'd get too emotional himself, for that matter, which ought to be avoided if it serves no purpose.

<>

"So, tour riders, where did you go?" Anne asks after two hours of probing thoughts, put on paper and in an email to publisher Simon. "You haven't been biking all this time, I hope?"

"No, we stopped at leisure around the boats that Reg loves. He copies the horns and engines! God, the zest is a feast. If I let him, he'd jump into the water, and on the shore he picks daisies, making original arrangements."

"Then he fell asleep on the handlebars?" Anne wants to know.

"Yes, leaning on my arms!"

"Oh, tricky for braking?"

"Nah," Evan laughs. "We've taken the little country lanes, nice and slow, avoiding each bump and hole."

"Next time..." Anne presses her lips.

"Ah, yes, please! When?"

"...take a towel and fold it over the handlebars. Or give him a slice of bread in his hand. That keeps him awake and he can sleep in his crib."

Evan is quick to agree. "I'll be happy to. He's a cool sparring mate, with a great interest in people, and he likes action."

The bike is parked in the front yard, where Evan has all the time, but Anne is impatient. Afraid it's been too much for the baby? And she asks, "There were no annoying people?"

"Why?" His voice is wary.

"Oh, the pushy types who think that babies are toys!"

"No, mostly people with kids of their own, who were natural and casual with him, and Reg wasn't shy at all. He's keen on children, sticks his hands out, wants to talk with them, tell them something, if he could at seven months. Or eight?"

"Yes," Anne says, "he's a truly social child."

"Ha, you can tell already. Has he got many friends around here?"

"Well, he doesn't play out yet."

Evan perseveres. "He does meet the neighbors?"

"Of course, but the past months have been odd."

"Yeah, sorry."

"And this is no street of many family homes."

"Right." Evan falters. "Anyhow, all in due course, and next thing you'll be in a crowd of other parents, on the benches of a playground, or standing and lifting him onto the slide a dozen times."

Or he'll say: *can I sleep over at Dad's?* And: *I want to play with such and so.*

<>

At full speed on her way to the climbing ground, Dilli is steering her bike past the creek and across the steep bridge with geese poops. It's a game to aim for these, which is not allowed but often works.

After looking for frogs among the lilies and king-cups, she races by edges and fences with flower pots. Nomi follows in a run on foot, seeing that Dilli slows down and adapts on time for all perils, or she corrects a sway in a reflex.

The happiness to see her in action is forever clashing with the moments in and outside the bike shop, which are not so much memories but a dormant presence whenever Dilli gets on her bike.

She's learned to stop at crossroads, and her feet in solid shoes are good at braking, also in the nick of time. Nevertheless Nomi holds her breath, calling out from a distance that can grow far in the twinkling of an eye.

She'd like to dispose of this bike, since it's tarnished, and buy a very different one, but she loves Dilli so much that a large part of herself is put aside and can share Dil's fun. What power in those lithe legs of hers; her torse is floating above the saddle, her hands and the bars are one, they swerve and adjust when she looks over her shoulder to see what's keeping Nomi, who's panting – not only from exertion.

She can't keep running, and here's the crossing coming up with cars going faster than allowed in this residential area, where she's always looking around with the eyes of a photographer and estate agent and mother of two.

These outings with one child and no piled or split attention, used to be a luxury.

Dilli rides and flies so confidently that other people should have faith in everything too, still it can be unclear if she brakes for danger on time. She can lose concentration for a tick! Nomi shouts and spurts, hindered by dislocated angst.

Out of breath she clasps Dilli half a meter away from the curb.

Crying and vexed, the daughter calls out, "I *was* braking, I *did* stop, I don't go missing!"

Nomi sinks on the sidewalk and buries herself in Dilli's neck.

The confusion is solved before they've reached the great playground, that offers time to recover from this understandable incident. So a particle of the other, perennial trauma can mellow, to be faceable one day.

After Liza Jacobs's visit, Nomi has hoped to bump into her, regretting that she failed to ask for a number. But surely Liza would get in touch with good or bad news.

She doesn't ask Hattum to what extent the search or investigation can go on without finding a body. CID budget cuts are as bad as elsewhere, and how many children go missing each month?

Now and then Hattum calls her to ask how she's holding up, but she's not very talkative. "We've all done everything we can."

With difficulty she undergoes the politeness and hesitant frankness of friends and strangers in the streets, especially the helplessness of women who'd like to hide their babies in sight. She wants to reassure them, no matter how strongly a kid resembles Art. "Every boy is the image of Art now."

His image will fade as much as his presence. Or it's the other way around: most hurt comes from sensing that he won't know her anymore. For how long did he remember her scent and eyes or smile? Even when he's alive and possibly alright, what will he feel or miss unconsciously as a six-year-old? Would the teenager Art wonder about things? If he lives.

It's been over six weeks now. 'Age-progressed pictures' can be made of long-missing children. The older ones only, or can baby photos work too? For how many months or years to come would the high costs be paid? And if 'outcomes' – guesses or estimates – won't prove to match reality, they'd preserve an illusion that could induce the wrong conclusions one day. What are reliable impressions?

Nomi can picture Art at several future ages. He's running a fever and his breathing is impeded by caked nasal fluids. He plays with raisins in a bowl, chewing endlessly, panting and groaning quietly, and one of them slips out of his hand, down the cover out of sight. He's remaining still, but his finger goes and gropes where it can.

His cuddly cloth lies on his cheek below the hazy eyes. When the letterbox clatters, he says "Dad home." He wants to suck his thumb keenly, but then he can't breathe at all. He lays the cloth in front of him, tries to spread it and lean his head on it.

Nomi would not take a photo. It's all too fragile and precious.

She wonders who will look after him in such times, but anything cheaply sentimental needs to be nipped in the bud.

<>

Off and on Anne can be so absorbed by pleasant work that her mind is absent in everyday matters. Now she's flooded with ideas for the project called *Time-In*: themes, questions, people, confrontations...

Publisher Simon will phone her first two candidates, Josh Gelder and Bernard Bloomsdale, without telling Gelder how critical Anne is of his famous TV show *Little Big Mouths.*

With a pedagogue friend, Bloomsdale wrote the Network a letter about these popular series:

"On television our children appear before an audience unsheltered, with their open-hearted, disarmed stories, rewarded with an applause, also from their ambitious parents, but nobody wonders how that public performance affects the children's developing self-image."

Taking sharp notes to start a column or chapter, Anne watches a number of episodes until they drive her mad, then she calls the pedagogue and Simon.

The book will combine the columns and interviews, interacting, that will contain as much humor as emotion, leading to literary and psychological tension.

Tonight at nine, walking down the stairs to get herself a tall glass of wine, she hears voices in the living-room. It does occur sporadically that a neighbor comes in for something trivial, but before going up, she locked both house doors, didn't she?

Her heart jumps and her legs are faint. She stops on a step. A lot of rubbish as well as common sense enter her head at the same time, until it comes back to her that the television is on: after a session of *Little Big Mouths* she left the World Cup Athletics on to follow the heptathlon during her deserved work breaks.

Her mind is stretched by one test after the other. Even more emphatic than last time, Mom Wil calls again, while Anne keeps doing little chores and making a Reg-fact-list for Evan.

"Annie, I know we're far apart, but please, if you become a recluse like your father, you shouldn't have had a kid! I'm still your mom, whereas Reg won't know me anymore! They change so much at this age, I won't even recognize him! Do you take him out enough? Bring him here for a few days or a week, have some time off, you badly need a breather. I'll bring him back and you won't need to put up with me all the time."

"Mom, don't be shocked if I tell you something bizarre; Evan is kind of back."

"Oh God, why am I not surprised? One man bolts when there's a baby, another returns to claim his share, and Evan does both! Has he come for the good bits?"

"No, I've got to say, he's changed – for the better."

"Has he," Wil sneers. "For how long: an hour or a day?"

Anne pretends to ignore the sarcasm. "It's been a few weeks now, so..."

Wil interrupts. "No wonder you don't want me around. I can't even remember how long it's been, two months? Must be Alzheimer's!"

"Mom, this is not about you. It's complicated here."

"Yes, you can say that again, I guess. Is Evan changing diapers or just planting Reg in his car and by the TV?"

"Well, it's all very nice, actually. More so than I could ever have thought."

"He's not moving in, is he?"

"No, no," Anne says, "I am taking care."

Wil simply continues. "Good, or next thing you'd have another kid!"

"Nah..."

And why the hell am I even answering at all! I've long fled the woman's sticky, egotistic stuffiness. Or her loneliness with sweet, good intentions? No, the witch is not even asking much about her grandson; whether he's quiet or cheerful, if his hair is growing fast and giving him these very different looks! It serves her right if she doesn't know the first thing about him.

"Listen, Anne, please understand, I'd love grandkids that I get to see! I have only one daughter, and you seem happy to be without me!"

"Sorry, Mom, it's just been too hectic. I'm compiling a book with many different aspects."

"That's why I'm telling you: catch a train and bring Reg here. I'll pay for first class."

"How, with all the luggage?"

"Never mind, honey, I've got everything ready here. Come on, what's holding you back? Make everyone happy! Or what are *you* holding back?"

A pause is tangible. "Annie, are you there?"

"Sorry, time is running away with me and I have to catch up. Can't believe it, we're barely past breast feeds."

"Nah, don't exaggerate."

"But I'll call back, OK? This does need some getting used to. A train or car trip would be too much now."

"Alright," Wil says with resignation or indignation. "I'll handle another day or week."

So long as you won't follow your father's footsteps. You do take your medication?

Sometimes Wil bites her tongue, but she dares ask this, "Is Evan still in that busy job of his?"

"No, he works four average weekdays now."

"Oh, at least that's something, I suppose."

"Yes," Anne says. "We're doing well."

"You and Evan?"

"And Reg."

Which is harsh on the grandmother, who ends the call, unlike her usual self.

They're doing so well that Anne makes an easy-going Monday appointment with Josh Gelder, whose 'real life' could be just as funny and cool or sly as his shows, all the more now that *Little Big Mouths* will be cancelled after ten years. Gelder must be eager to promote his new theater show too.

For Evan she makes a know-how list of Reg's food, play routines, and bed times. Evan has grown adept after a "solid internship", as he calls it, "for the main adventure of responsibility," thankful that Anne trusts him and gives him the opportunity to prove himself as a friend and a dad.

"Careful," she concludes her nervous instructions in the doorway, wearing a business outfit on her way to meet Gelder, "Reg is so fast and strong, he'll jump out of your arms or dive off the changer before you know it."

"OK, I'm a warned man and worth two."

Anne watches him. "Don't forget to close your own stair gate."

Evan grins. "I'll trip over it!"

"But not with Reg!"

"No, and his bottle won't be cold or hot, full diapers are changed immediately..."

Anne breathes. "Don't be economical with the wet wipes."

"Right. No TV or music for him, and for the garden or parks, I know all the safety rules too."

She stares at him. The backyard is a tad wild, with a narrow path of crooked old stones and a thorny rose bush. She loves 'old-fashioned', the scents and spontaneous greens. But there should be no poisonous plants like foxglove.

Evan continues with only a hint of irony.

"So, go get 'em and enjoy. You can take your time, have a day out, stay kind and give Josh some credit as well. Do not stumble over the curb here, or over a charged cable there, think of Reg and drive safe, turn the microphone on and keep the recorder on! We'll paint the town red, I mean, we'll spray the lawn."

Anne leaves with fresh inspiration.

On the road she'll need to concentrate, because her thoughts tend to be all over places, and a collision or fine are off limits more than ever. This day away from a teething baby is a frightful gift, she can't even recall the last time.

What a shame that she's in a hurry.

Too soon, the dynamic vibes of the studio are compelling. The set lights are tested, an assistant director is trying out camera positions, and a runner takes Anne to the canteen, introducing her to Josh Gelder.

Who cries casually, "Thank God, here's a serious person to fill my long breaks. I love this job, but the deadly waiting hours can't be abolished, it seems; believe me, I've tried! Will you write about that?"

"Or," Anne starts just as lightly, "use your spare time here to write for the theater? Or write history?"

He laughs and points around. "All is worked out and planned and ready."

"May I?" Anne says, going along, and when he nods, she puts her recorder amid the coffee things. "What do you prefer: the stage or television?"

Amid the abundance of lights, props, busy people, he gives her a wondering glance. "Is that a philosophical trick question?"

"No, it's down to earth."

"At any rate," Josh says, "I like both equally, the way we love our kids."

"But one child may be closer to you than the other."

Again he scrutinizes her face. "I'd say it can vary per moment. We've all got our moods."

"Yes," Anne admits cordially – with a flush? "And your kids don't mind being on your website?"

"Oh... Do they look unhappy?"

"No. It's a beautiful site."

"So what are you saying?"

Thus he can suddenly take charge and put her off balance. She smiles and looks around, takes a sip of coffee and asks as neutrally as possible, "Why are your children perked on your site?"

"Pooh, pardon me," he sighs, "why not?"

"You first."

"OK... I've never given it much thought. And what's *perked*?"

Anne controls the urge to look at the recorder, which is unobtrusive beside a lunch plate. "But your brothers and sisters are on it too, so you did make decisions, for the private part of it."

"Well, it just seemed complete that way, showing a personal background."

For whose sake?

Anne gestures to the set. "And these children have great fun."

"Yes," he says, "but do you think that my family on the site is... exposed or displayed or something?"

"What I think doesn't matter, it's what you are saying."

And he looks a trifle startled by what he asked.

"They're proud of you!" Anne says with a cheerful arm wave toward the studio, quick to add, "The audience has a laugh too!"

"Yeah, they double up, especially the parents."

"But the children realize they're being laughed about."

"Yes," Josh says, "it gives everybody a good time."

"And they?" she persists.

Which makes him exclaim, "They're so into it, roguish and jovial."

"Or insecure, over-conscious of themselves."

"No," he says, "it makes them grow up."

The spot where children are interviewed, is elevated, central, exposed, with the tall stands all around, which must be intimidating in the spotlights, amid crew and cameras creeping up.

"But you often talk over their heads, addressing the spectators and cameras."

"Yeah, with a smile, I hope?"

"Of what?" Anne asks in stern earnest.

"Well, of sheer fun!"

"Yes, with the entertainment they produce."

"Absolutely!" Josh says.

"And you never think that the kids lose their innocence with that public attention and loud massive laughter?"

"Sure, good thing too, they'd better, in this society of ours."

"Ah." For one second her eye is averted. "The vicious circle."

There's a hush, and Josh rubs his head, but Anne turns a screw. "When you address the adults, the children can see that you're amused or triumphant, watching the crowd."

Josh takes a deep breath and gets the plate of rolls. Standing up to reach out and offer her some, he spots the modern, small yet sensitive recorder. What sort of 'evidence' will it store forever? On diplomatic guard he adds reluctantly, "A difficult word here and there does no harm, it's educational, and they understand me very well."

"No, sorry, in truth, they often don't, just pretending and acting away their awkwardness, and then we have these 'comical' misunderstandings. They react wildly, gambling and guessing, which evokes even more laughter, thrilled and satisfied, also from you. That's degrading, isn't it?"

He moves away. "And you seek revenge by doing the same thing to me?"

"No," Anne says, "we are equal, but apparently you recognize the feeling? And there's not even an audience now, no cameras are running."

"Only your sneaky machine."

"Well, that was put here openly." And she asks, "Do you ever see these children again after ten years?"

His gaze drifts: would that be a grand new show? But what would it uncover?

<>

Bernard has faced a spectacular choice that he could not make. His trail-blazing novel *Ventures* was rejected by his publisher, "I love its titillating tension and powerful experiment, but it seems uncommercial."

As modest as daring, Bernard asked if a more commercial title like *Ventures Naked* could help, but his emergency measures are seldom successful.

He wrote a stage script based on the book and had this reply from Soho Theatre, "Original voice, the characters are all huge and interesting, the dialogue is great, stylized and effervescent, brilliant comments and wonderfully witty insights. But its medium is almost certainly TV."

Bernard got even more curious or determined and wrote a screen version, loving the craft of discovering the story's visual dimensions, but after this try-out for television, the BBC said, "It's more like a work of literature than of drama."

As the circle brings him back to the novel manuscript, this resembles a Kafka farce with a grim theme, 'the purchase of a child,' but Bernard grows recalcitrant and sends it to the quirky Proper Press in London, that specializes in eccentric books that fuse art forms and defy anything mainstream.

Idealistic, personal and without commercial pretence, they're enchanted by *Ventures*. The editor is flexible, strict, skilful, direct and clear, which are all Bernard's favorite virtues.

For weeks he's relished the collaboration. They exchange passionate thoughts on satiric word play, a switch of perspective, and the cover possibilities: a colorful abstract painting or a journalistic photo?

Then blue-sky lightning strikes with an enthusiastic message from Aragon House, New York, one of the world's most artistic and literary publishers with a list full of awards with a worldwide reputation and influence. In his previous obstinate mood Bernard submitted 'the 3D version of the novel' combining book, screen and stage elements. It was an off-hand, unsolicited action by email, and here is Aragon offering an advance of $200,000 for world rights, whereas The Proper Press pays no advance at all. There's not even a contract yet, that's how human or naive their mutual trust is.

As to PR contacts or business expectations, The Press has no leg to stand on, where Aragon opens a world of awe and years of security ahead. Going with Aragon is morally impossible in the stage of editorial work with the Press, but choosing The Press would be financially absurd, although steps like that have been known to bring terrific surprises of success.

He's running out of time: each day gone by is one too many.

Bernard reports to The Press that only British rights are available, letting Aragon know that those are excluded.

Both publishers are "disappointed" and ask for a substantial compromise: The Press wants all of Europe and Aragon wants world premiere.

Bernard is honored and ashamed and dazzled. This reminds him of the ambitious well-known actor who was handed a 'choice' in a live show on television: "Your partner or a major lead in Hollywood."

Of course, the young man could have babbled his way out in any direction, but the entire nation watched him choose Hollywood without hesitation. Similarly, Bernard feels like a twisted traitor who is exposed, above all to the publishers and Nomi and perhaps Dilli one day, with her beautiful pureness and candor. Also – or most of all – to Art, possibly *in memoriam.*

Nomi has more on her mind than a sickening, redundant ethical dilemma. How many world books in the pipeline would he give up for Art's return, for a year or a day of life? The happiness of four people would feed him.

After emails and phone calls in his cold sweats, The Press

accepts a minimum of rights, hoping that global publicity will bring them something superb too.

Bernard keeps both the exhilaration and the crap feeling to himself, but there seems to be something independent in the air that's reaching far to touch and connect. He's invited to contribute to a fascinating book, titled *Time-In.*

<>

Friends of Mark's and Nomi's are the victims of a builder's fraud. There are endless delays after hopeless mistakes, inferior supplies and shameless lies with rising costs, but Mark does not say: Where's the grief, compared to a child gone missing! Or gone. He knows too well: a house is our soul, the shell or shield in life storms.

Their own plan to have an extension is not mentioned anymore. The last time, when Mark got cold feet, Nomi said, "Do you want to wait until Art is ten or so? Art and Dilli will be in each other's space by next year!"

The reward of $20,000 is never claimed or earned by anyone, but the money is not spent on an extension either.

As estate agents they have a hard time with properties where children live, carefree, effervescent, omni-present. For viewings Mark has always asked the residents to put toys and clothing away as much as possible.

Nomi's work photo sessions are preferably planned during school hours, but she's forever on guard for the presence of baby things. Usually she avoids the nurseries where fierce colors or cold materials form a matter-of-course atmosphere, but now and then she does hurry through them for a glance out the window or a petrifying sense of 'you never know'. After all, there could be such a thing as 'extreme coincidence,' a strange whim of fate, if something is meant to be and insisting, because it will be good and crucial in an ultimate, concealed way?

The other day somebody said, "Coincidence means that God wants to remain anonymous."

But hey, so can the devil wish and act.

Does destiny leave no margins or give no second chance?

There are people who state that bad luck and happiness are created by ourselves. We're a part of Nature's laws in the broadest respect, which does make more sense than a series of clueless coincidences, doesn't it? If it helps.

Nomi is watchful everywhere, keen on a sign of recognition. The abductors probably don't know that she's the mother, and surely they can't be known to her? That sort of madness happens only in nasty family conflicts.

Once or twice a house has such an indescribable mood, that Nomi expects to find a baby who doesn't belong there. It's close to an obsession, she admits, an illusion or fantasy, yet it could be real just like that.

Without Art, Mark and Nomi can easily explore and view properties together, but they rarely do so. It's not even discussed; it would emphasize what's wrong: in their own house Dilli has plenty of space now without Art snatching her toys or breaking what she's built. Would Dilli accept that easily now if Art returned? Learning that he did such things by accident?

"Do you think Liza can tell if he's still in town or the area or in the country?" Mark asks during a magnificent sunset with a spectrum of low light stretching from the horizon to the front garden: a golden yellow beam is reaching through the house to the back.

"That's been on my mind too," Nomi says. "Liza doesn't see specific places, but she did say *close by*. What does that mean?"

At the most beautiful moments, with singing birds in the dusk and the scent of honeysuckle, the gleam on the grass, a late coffee or early wine, it's just as well that there's bound to be something prosaic or annoying to keep a heap of melancholy at bay: a neighbor dragging his feet toward the trash can outside, the on-going barking of a dog or a motorbike tearing by on the cyclers track.

"If we thought he might be in town," Nomi ponders, "would you knock on every door?"

"Yes, every hour available."

"Me too, a couple of streets a day."

"Friends and others would join in."

"We'd never watch TV or read a paper and book anymore."

"You know what," Mark says, "with volunteers, a whole network can be organized."

"For how many thousands of houses?"

"Let's say a hundred a day."

Nomi counts and estimates. "That's about six months."

"Would we recognize him then?"

"Of course," Nomi says.

The lightest breeze finds their arms in short sleeves, warm and cool at the same time. The shrubs yield the last daylight, while tree tops turn pinkish.

Mark goes on musing. "For all we know, Art can be in the Orkneys or Caribbean. Still, the thought of canvassing door-to-door is a sort of madness that could work. I'd care to sound people out, who may join in."

"And the news would spread."

"Yes," he cries. "The snowball effect! Basically it only takes everybody to go next door, have a good look and ask sharp questions."

In the near-dark something flaps by that looks like a bat, or is it a late sparrow? Between day and night, one's notion of size and distance or reality is easily lost, although their premises are neat and straight, pruned and maintained thoroughly, if not rigid? Wildlife such as hedgehogs or even snails don't thrive here. They might say 'the placed is trimmed with nailscissors.' But plants are never treated with chemicals. Art would have a safe and clean space to play his legs off, if given the chance.

"But," Nomi says, "an action like that could make the abductor feel cornered, and who knows what a panic brings about."

When Art is still alive. If he lives.

"As if other actions don't."

"But this would come close literally, physically."

"That's why it's a good thing!" Mark says. "Even if the freak hears about it and runs, it would be noticed, either here or in the new area. If they move in a hurry, they're likely to make mistakes!"

"Well, if you consider it seriously, please talk with Hattum, about risks that we don't know."

They continue in silence and out loud – in such unison that it makes no difference who thinks or says what.

Why is there never an appeal of this kind in the local or social media?

"Does it seem too simple or are we going nuts?"

"Yeah, it sounds a bit ridiculous."

"At least we'd do something."

"Powerful."

"Or desperate and reckless."

"You mean damn effective!"

Come to think of it more, it might be a genius plan.

This could be called an Art Alert, because it should end well!

"Or we're having a heavy burn-out, mentally."

Next, we'll burst into laughter or tears.

<>

Mark opens the curtains and Dilli cries, "The moon!"

"Ah, girly, it's the sun."

"It's not!"

"Just look, Dil: the sun is shining through the clouds."

"No, it's the moon."

And his lack of view makes her feel rather sad, so Mark agrees without lying. "Yes, it's a radiant sort of moon."

With a searching look at him, as if his face means a thunderstorm, Dil says, "Will it rain?"

A chunk of his heart was in his boots already, because after a restless night of search ideas, he still doesn't know if Hattum would refer him to a psychiatrist. He calls a few friends first. They're surprised alright but would love to take part.

"Why not?" is the general mood. And, "Should it be insane, it means we're beating the creep with his own weapon!"

"But watch out for violations of privacy," Hattum says.

"Yes," Mark explains. "It's just social control, taken a step further, since Art's photos in letterboxes have no effect."

"Alright but tell your friends expressly that it has to be civilized and call us with any suspicion or trouble. Remember, we have no inkling who's behind this."

Hattum is still very involved, without the side-thought that this option is hypothetical anyway, because so much has been done within the media and police means.

A specialist 'ages' Art's best picture by six to eight weeks.

Mark gets the streets map, his personal and work contact files. He borrows Dilli's large noteboard with a brief comment. "We'll do a good search for Art again." And he tries to work mathematically, while Nomi and Bernard write the texts for emails and other media. The police provide a coordinator.

...when you've finished a street, please report it here on this website.

If you're planning to do a street, check there too...

It's a peculiar day when a woman in their own square dies. Barbara was only sixty-four and loved by everyone. She and her husband, Bert, didn't show much of their situation, but they weren't secretive either. Dilli didn't call Barbara "Gran," like other kids in the neighborhood, yet Dilli saw and heard a lot.

Nomi wonders: how many homes with grief or misery are there in town? If only their door-to-door search for Art goes down gently there or goes around them.

Dear Bert,

It's evident and inspiring: the way Barbara says goodbye or moves on, is full of love, given and received. There was a physical struggle, but the love between you has been touching and impressive up to the last moment – will be beyond. You'll keep connected with her invisible part.

You'll miss her terribly and we wish you consolation and strength, to be felt when thinking of Barbara and her good heart.

All warmth, from the four of us, Nomi

"What's death?" Dilli asks in the process of building the highest Lego Duplo tower.

Her mom and dad are also busy with tall orders, so she wants to be more specific, "Does everybody die?"

Even then it's a while before Nomi ventures an answer. "The most beautiful and important part of everybody... never dies. But you can't see that, I mean not with the eyes. It's what you feel when you're very happy. And what *can* be seen with regular eyes, the body, will die someday."

"Oh. Everybody?"

"Yes. Don't worry, it's not as bad as it seems."

"Oh." Dilli goes on efficiently. "Why?"

"Well... All things grow old and wear off, and then you need something new."

"Shoes?"

"Yes." Nomi tries her very best after a brave breath. "For example, because they're worn, or you've grown and they're too small."

"But Art is little himself!"

There's a lull again, when emotions are neither too open nor hidden.

Patiently the Duplo tower is fortified at the base. It appears to be a castle where people have lived with food and water for a hundred years.

"Yes," Nomi can carry on. "We hope with all our hearts that Art is alive, with someone looking after him, but things can go wrong, if that person is mean or ill or crazy."

"Crazy?" Dilli cries. "Why?"

"Hm, that's hard to say. Some things get broken, by accident or on purpose, and that can also happen to people, their bodies or minds. For difficult reasons."

"Not Art, right?"

"No, I think not."

"But Barbara."

"Yes."

"Doesn't matter?" Dilli checks.

"Well, for Bert it's hard and sad now."

"Yes. I'll get the train, with the rails and more stuff. And if something breaks, we can repair it."

As life is trying not to be clunky, while Nomi and Mark are busy with the computer, phone and papers, Bernard takes Dilli for an extra bike ride, if less long than she'd like. Are his legs tired again?

They also read a book and lug water to the sandbox, to make mud, but not around the flowers.

"Is your gran dead?" She might as well ask him straightaway.

And he doesn't need to think as long as Nomi. "You mean your gran, who lived with me. Yes, she died."

"Sad. How come?"

"She had a bleeding in the brain," Bernard can say without breaking.

"Ooh. I won't have that?"

"No, Dil, it's rare."

"Oh. Good."

And safely he says, "Later, we can go and look for the swan chicks."

"Yes. In bed I sing about the swans. And we can have pancakes."

As life doesn't know whether to be fast or slow, publisher Simon is on the phone with an update, "*Time-In* will be a striking and organic whole with parallels and contrasts filled with surprises."

"Compiled and edited by whom?" Bernard asks.

"Anne Hoaver. She's quirky and inventive, always finding more than meets the eye. I'll send samples of her work."

Intrigued: "What are the themes?"

"Above all," Simon is prompt. "Children and public life, public frankness, linked or separate, with room to improvize."

As Bernard is not in the mood to mention Art's life, bitterly or vulnerably, there's no reason for Simon to say that Anne has a boy exactly the same age. It's not for Simon to create a bond between the collaborators.

<>

On the day of their trip to her mother’s, planned by Anne as late as possible, she wakes up at five a.m., after one roar coming from the other room. She needs to make up her mind: feed Reg a bottle now, put him back right away and hope that both of them will sleep again, or let him drowse and murmur with a pacifier. They should try and stretch the nights, otherwise he’ll get used to ‘Five a.m. is bottle time’..’ He loves patterns and systems.

In qualms and all, Anne does doze off, but she hears him again at five-thirty and stumbles to his room, gives him the pacifier and flees the scene, begging for some peace.

Today that’s extra welcome. After weighing all the pros and cons of a trip by car or train – for two days? – or have Wil here after all, staying over? – Anne seemed to know what was best. The grandmother happily settled for two days at hers, presuming secretly that an extension will be feasible with patience and tact and lots of pampering hominess – too good for Anne to refuse.

She sleeps a bit more and wakes up at six, fairly grateful. He can have his next rest in the car, and she’ll take a nap at her mom’s – if the woman won’t do any stupid things with Reg, in plain sight of anyone.

After a full bottle they share a nice hour of playing and chatting, while packing for the major adventure; it’s been due too long, she admits. They have a shower together and get into the car. She’s freshened up and he is favorably languid.

With the first sign of a traffic jam, the rumbling of unrest begins on the backseat, and Anne pulls over at a gas station with a green and secluded parking space, to feed him fruit and half a bottle.

They take a stroll around the fragrant warm foliage and pines of the woods fringe, so unlike her landscape of shoals, turbines and pastures without end. Satisfied, they breathe in deeply. He motions to birds and trees, turns over on her arm, grabs a wisp of hair and nibbles her cheek.

Back in his seat, he watches the strings of cars, lost in wonder.

After three hours in total, they arrive in the arms of Gran Wil. She sheds a few thick tears, but Art is wearing a protective 'coverall' hat.

"At last, at last! Welcome, sweethearts, had a good trip? Ah, Reggie, you're big and heavy and so different, as far as my poor eyes can see. I can't believe this, I'm a weird creature, true, but it's been too long: two months? Your mom ought to be ashamed of herself. And me, sorry! Let me tell you, I'm getting new glasses anyhow. Or is it a strike of Alzheimer's? Oh, sorry if I babble from nerves! What have I heard: you've got these handsome teeth? Show your gran! Hm, he's changed too much..."

Overwhelmed, he turns away and clutches Anne, who says, "I apologize, it's been long. It was beyond me. Wait, I'll hold him for a bit. It's like a new start here, isn't it? But give him ten minutes and he'll know you again."

Meet your Gran: the loony lady, or the sly actor with normal eyes? Hawk-eyed? Hiding things to herself on purpose, as she's done all her life?

"And I'll know him again!" Wil says.

"Obviously. Let me just put his hat right. Was I that shy as a kid?"

"Are you joking? You could be hopelessly rude, embarrassing!"

"Still am, I suppose," Anne says.

"No, I taught you different! Come and sit, or stretch your legs after the trip? We'll walk around the back. Look, Reg, remember Gran's lovely garden? Smell these roses, mm... Oh, I'm so thrilled you're here! Anne, would you like fresh tea or cold juice? Go through, I've got the bags."

. . .

Presently, her glowing hospitality is appreciated by the grandson, although Anne politely declines the sugary treats on his behalf, which Wil can't grasp at all, while the ladies relish the festive strawberry cake in the fancy garden seats under the parasol, with tiny wonder bites for the smiling child.

"Like it, Annie? You do look knackered and skinny."

"Well, it was late last night, five o'clock this morning, and it's been a stiff drive, to which I'm not accustomed anymore, clearly."

"Yes," Wil says. "What an eternal pity! But you know, as a free-lancer you can move house into this region. There are such good opportunities here. At last we could be close again."

Anne doesn't react. She dives into her bag and gives the curious boy on her lap a piece of dry bread.

There is enough space around the detached house for privacy, which doesn't have to be intimacy. The chairs on the back lawn are not close at all, as if Wil shows off, or she likes keeping her distance among the shielding charms of many greens.

"Why was it a late night?" Wil asks.

"Hm, I had some good ideas, and then there was too much adrenaline, I think."

"Beware, Anne, don't get a burn-out, will you? Especially with a baby; you wouldn't be the first. Do you know how many millions of people take anti-depressants?"

"Are you saying I need a cocktail?"

"Well, better not sink into a crisis or something. It happens enough to writers and young mothers. Take Helen Van Roy and Vasalis."

Anne keeps frighteningly calm, although she shrinks to hide behind the upright back between her hands. "I thought it was Vasalis's husband?"

"Oh, I believe both, or maybe not officially. At any rate, I know what I'm talking about."

And Anne's mind rushes off as far away as possible. Would Van Roy be an interesting asset for *Time-In*? Yes, with a nice girls fight, but Van Roy gets too much attention as it is. The Vasalis offspring are put on her *Time-In* wishlist.

Still pre-occupied, Anne says, "Anyway, Evan is awfully helpful."

"Is he? Or does he want his portion of Reg?"

"Well, today, so without a portion of Reg, he's doing handiwork around our house, making me very happy."

Wil frowns. "Like what?"

"Repairing a lamp, cutting a tree, fitting an insect screen in Reg's window."

"And then he'll watch TV for days again," Wil says. "Only to meddle and mess up and run off again. For example with Reg!"

"No, don't be a cynic. Evan has changed so much, it's a revelation. The other day Reg got hold of a sharp knife from my plate..."

"Dear God. So typical."

"No, listen, Mom, I was in the kitchen just one second, he was buckled up in his chair and I still don't understand how he did it, reaching for my plate and knife, so quick, smart, strong, that's how he is, but Evan saw it on time and kept very cool, subtle, so that Reg didn't do anything scary."

"Oh." Wil almost faints. "I don't know what to say first!"

"Never mind."

When Anne is fidgeting with him too much, he pushes her hand away. His hat slips off and Wil looks on without her reading specs or sunglasses. She gestures toward Reg's head and says, "Is the cradle cap gone?"

"Actually," Anne hastens to say, "I was just going to inspect it, but he doesn't like that."

"No. Boy, is he clear and direct for a shy child. How come the cradle cap is gone now?"

"Ha," Anne plays assertive. "He loves water, the baths and showers, and it's summer, so we got lucky, just soaking it off."

"Well, he's remarkable. Or I'm deteriorating. But then I've had only one child."

Wil glances at the missing-boy's picture, somewhat lost in the newspaper between other things on the garden table, left there just in case for a suitable moment, if ever possible, as a warning or a careful thought with a sticky suspicion. But she shakes her head as if a silly secret is kept unwillingly. As if she'd turn her own daughter in – what monster would do that? IF the most preposterous of her thoughts had a grain of truth in them! She couldn't take the boy in full-time now at her age, could she? Even if Anne were arrested, God forbid, if that were the best thing to do, who knows, to be acquitted later! And who'd be there for herself to confide in? Besides, one's imagination or anxiety can also run wild and gnaw at the mind. That's best defied by going out and mingling!

What if she accuses her daughter of madness and proves to be mad herself? 'Again,' someone might say. That would be fatal for Anne and everybody in any circumstance.

Wil moves the paper out of sight. "So, Annie, will you come and choose new glasses for me? I have been to the opticians for measurements, but I'd love your help for the frame. You have an eye for taste."

"Sure, if we can fit it in between his naps."

"Of course, plenty of time, and he comes first. Shall we make him a nice and easy meal? I've bought vegetables and fruit in excellent jars."

<>

In Anne's house, Evan does the promised work at leisure, and he answers the door. It's a friendly, elderly woman, who gives Evan searching looks and also peeks inside. Impolitely? "Hello, do you know anything about the abducted boy, called Art?"

Annoyed, he says, "Sorry. My son is called Reg and he's just away a couple of days, to visit his grandmother."

"Oh, is Reg alright? And there's no little brother or friend for him?"

With a laugh of surprise Evan says, "No, why?"

"I'm in the local watch group for Art."

"Sure, I'm the handyman now, and I need to get back to work."

"Oh," the woman says, "I have a list of odd jobs! What's your rate?"

"Sorry, no time. They'll be back and there's lots to be cleaned."

She smiles and looks inside closer.

But still kind and resolute, Evan closes the door.

When Anne tells him nearly all about her days of strangeness, it's tragi-comic and oddly vivid, as if she's narrowly escaped from a catastrophe. "The entire suburbs had been informed. Wil considered herself entitled to a great deal of catching up."

"With what, the Reg-time she missed? You can't blame her for that."

"Don't know. She had us roam the parks and sit on benches, where ducks and crowds came. We entered the best shops, had drinks in restaurants, she insisted on treating us, and most of the time it was no disaster. Wil kept trying to feed Art anything and show him off to friends and neighbors, making me edgy and rebellious like a teenager. Good thing I shirked successfully, otherwise the place would have embraced us!"

"To suffocate!"

While Anne is chatting and unpacking, Evan is happy to take care of "his boy," and all are having a ball, hearing their reports.

Anne seems relieved indeed after a timely escape. "Reg took the goodies when he could, he underwent the spotlights, then he slept like a log."

"And you were not overstressed?" he asks.

"Occasionally, yes, but on the other hand I had some time off, willingly or not, so whenever I managed to relax and ignore Wil, I had a real break, and that worked for Reg too."

"How to ignore Wil? Even I never managed that."

Anne affirms, "Maybe her thrills and diligence pulled me along. Somehow it was infectious. You know, despite all, she can be caring, neat, responsible, and Reg does have a Gran like that. So I'll accept the fact and set limits again, to shield Reg and keep our distance for now. But hey..."

"I see," Evan agrees. "Once you've tasted a break, the vacation mood..."

"Yeah, something like that. There are strong and contrary feelings."

"As you've deserved it, we could take a week off or so."

A trifle coy between irony and earnest curiosity, Anne says, "Oh, could we? As *you* have deserved it."

"Sure, if you like, the three of us?"

"You mean, in a tent in pouring rain?"

Evan shrugs. "Or just Reg and me, if you want a quiet week of working."

She looks out, where the sun is all flames around storm clouds. Forecast showers often blow over, or they unload in one spot when the wind drops dead. Behind the lake, a black sky can threaten and stall while the swallows are still clear and wild in the light on this side.

She wonders, where are those fluttering birds on other days: too high for the eye or hidden in trees? And at night?

"I've never seen a swallow in a tree," she mumbles out loud.

Intrigued, Evan looks out the window too. "Now that you mention it, we don't know the most regular things."

"As if we like the abnormal, do we? No, the unusual. I mean, we humans in general. Sensation on the News..."

"Yeah, this morning there was a funny kind of vigilante lady at the door, about the taken baby."

"No, that was ages ago!" Anne says.

"Yes, but now there seems to be a sort of patrol going on, and as far as I could tell from that picture, that missing kid looks a hell of a lot like Reg."

"She showed you a photo?"

"Yeah," Evan cries. "Uncanny, after all this time."

"What did you say?"

"Nothing. I must have looked pretty sheepish, because dumb stuff went through my head. I don't live here, but Reg is my son, while another dad is searching desperately. I never saw him the first six months, and for a minute it got so bizarre, with my sense of guilt, and hope, longing – for your coming back safe today, the two of you."

"What happened?" Anne asks.

"Well, I stammered something like 'handyman', as a joke, and 'Anne is away with Reg'."

"Who was it?"

"I think the lady down the street, two or three doors away."

"Didn't she remember you?" Anne checks.

"I hope not! Maybe it helped, as a red herring for my dumbness."

"So she won't come back?"

"Nah, I've chased her for good."

Anne looks at him, pleased but unsettled, which has been

called a tricky mix or trigger of risk. With goosebumps, she grows hot and shivery, craving for a thoughtful and tenderly sensual caress, prickling and mutual, building a bridge from the past to a future of some certainty.

As if it's inevitable, she grabs every scrap of him. He is wholly and happily taken by surprise, turning weak and hard. He succumbs, until their lust and emotion are one.

She feels the wind and clouds inside the house, on his skin. Their nipples and muscles are touching. Held by him and the sun, she pulls him into her hollow and clutches acres of buttocks, back and legs.

How strong and soft he is, robust and supple. It's been a long time, but she's catching up, he makes her young and limber, tireless. Their first years are back, just as physical and impetuous, but sweeter and complete, and upstairs a young boy is asleep, weary after the car trip with flashes of light through the chinks of trees and fleecy clouds.

Formerly Evan would return to work immediately, or he'd flump down and sleep; now there's after-joy in a daze, groping for the new phase, of which the first step is offered by a voice upstairs. For another minute they stay naked and intimate, scarcely lost between love and doubts.

After the vehemence, Evan stays inspired, energetic, eating and playing with the boy.

He asks, "Do all the neighbors know about Reg?"

"What do you mean?"

"That um..."

He gets up and a finger rubs the wings of his nose. For a moment he stands with his back toward Anne, but the broad shoulders turn around again and he says, "I mean, do they know why you've been on your own?"

"Oh, as far as we meet and talk... They haven't seen you for a year. On this side of the street, they've had the birthcard. Of course, there's a distance between the houses, literal and figurative, and still I don't understand who it was, at the door. What did she look like?"

"Slender, in her sixties, old-fashioned. What's the fuss?"

"Ah, that must be Mrs Hoyst. She loves a chat, and I've held her off too long. Did she invite you for tea?"

"No, God forbid."

"I'll go and drop by," Anne promises. "To be on the safe side."

"Why's that?"

"You know, apologize, explain how busy I am, and about you."

"What will you say?" he fishes.

"No idea. It's nobody's business, but I don't want any wrong conclusions; better be on good terms."

"Yeah, just in case, although you're not all alone anymore – looking after Reg. If you want."

"One day at a time," says Anne. "You don't mind? I won't keep you dangling, but you'll understand that we can't afford any confusion. I've just survived Wil, who said: 'Watch it, girl, quid pro quo.'"

"Hm, tit for tat? Referring to me?"

"I didn't ask her what exactly she meant and regarding who. She can't have thought of sex, can she?"

After the tension with honesty, both laugh hard and Evan says, "Do you want me to get fish and chips or cook a healthy meal or go home before the rain?"

Now she can't keep her eyes off him again, can't believe how real he's become, but her face drops. "It's too good to be true, is it? A year ago we said goodbye definitively."

"I know, what a shame. Shall I make it less good? You do deserve it, though."

"Oh, you're growing more handsome by the day. Will you choose between cooking and getting chips?"

"OK, and no vacation by the sea just yet."

<>

The early hour is fresh, still overcast but windless, and nature seems to be drenched, satiated. There's no car to be heard, a pigeon coos and even the magpies are endearing, all granting one another a part of the acacia. Their wings go at ease, making Bernard wonder: what's the word for this beat sound on a peaceful Sunday morning?

Separate from any memory.

Untouched by anything else.

Without a weight on the conscience.

He gets a chair and absorbs the idyll with heart and soul.

The climbing roses are almost top heavy, the balsam is reaching the sky. The monkshood is also exceptionally tall and upright this year, joining the drifting wisteria strings, called 'blue rain' in another country. The hues of lilac and purple deepen one another. Hollyhocks used to thrive here too, and he can't understand why they've all gone in one winter – due to the frost? Or does that happen just like that after a number of years?

He knows little about gardening. The unruly grape bush has entwined with the hawthorn, creating these accidental combinations that are praised greatly by birds. Less by the neighbors, while a major part of the splendor clambers their way.

He doesn't know much about birds either, but a choir wish him good morning because he needs it. The mildest raindrops are taken in his stride, and the light through a chink in the sky is hurting his eyes. He thinks of The Proper Press and hates his ego with the business side. Except, how to survive otherwise?

He misses his wife, Hannah, who did hear the birds here but doesn't know that Dilli calls herself a grasshopper after doing athletics on the lawn. He misses Art in the same pore-pervading way that can't be shared. Perhaps with Nomi in a dozen or thirty years time.

He's afraid of self-pity and anything selfish.

Even the balsam leaves are dead still now, until it's raining. How can drops from those heights land lightly?

He's writing a poem about "the seven-arm balsam, embracing forever," wondering if it's for children or adults, and it hits him that Art was often here in springtime. There are two highchairs on stand-by, one bought recently, the other stored by Hannah.

Art would copy the birds and probably call them 'sirbs'.

Simon phones and asks Bernard's permission to give Anne Hoaver his number and email address.

"Alright, if you trust her, of course."

The past years Bernard has been less generous with personal details, but his contribution to *Time-In* is a private story of two years ago, which he'll send to Anne in these words:

My mother has toy cars from the past. Toddler Dilli can feel how solid they are, with supple wheels. The driving part is even more important than their beauty. She pays less attention to the woman of eighty-four, who is by no means offended. She'll live for weeks longer but gives the cars to Dilli now, to take home.

When Dil stays with me three days, our favorite vintage car goes missing, the royal-blue Austin Mini with a white roof. I look for it twice in every spot where Dil has played, and once more on my knees in the very best daylight, because it simply has to be here!

She stops asking for it.

In the course of months, I'll still grope around spider spots with bare fingers, moving boxes and bags that have been there for years. Then I'll give up.

My house has corners that have not seen a human being since Hannah died, because I don't know them or I'm not shifting a closet and oven without probable cause or visible reason. However,

I must have remembered that the heavy and clumsy *drawer* of our old oven can be moved. It contains the baking gear that Hannah was the last to touch. But from where this impulse or offhand decision?

After some tinny and noisy friction, the drawer is out on the kitchen-floor tiles, leaving a gaping hole with dust in flakes and trails, where slim creatures take to their tall heels before the hoover is placed in position.

On all fours and with a red head of shame and effort, I behold some dried food remnants, old matches, a bill, a draughts piece, pen, and a jar lid, and in the dark back corner there seems to be something under spider stuff and more. Some shine has been preserved: you'd say it was a beautiful blue and white.

I get the Austin Mini without a glove, to wash it gently, apologize for the ten-month delay and hand it to Dilli.

Although I haven't mentioned the car since she was one year old, she says "Mini" with a smile of "all is meant to be" and places it in the row of vehicles as if it was yesterday.

Bernard has been writing and musing in the garden, but behind the dense hedge that hides no sound of these linked houses, a new neighbor's door opens, whose kids are about ten, and her smoky cough is preceding her out, over-loud in the calm fresh air.

She must be holding a cigarette, while her cough is a raw and dry, endless hawk. When she goes back in, the door is left open, it appears, because even then Bernard hears every stage of her coughing. Often enough he's retreated inside the house for this kind of reason, but now he'd like to be out for hours.

He can see why the Ipomoea is called Morning Glory. He sucks his lungs chockful and clean, looking forward to teamwork on *Time-In*. After a long time, these contacts may be relished, if tempered by Art's absence. But he can't manage to ignore the coughing next door; the woman is not at all trying to muffle the noise.

Before his courage or recklessness is gone, he tears a piece of paper off, writes a website address on it, gets a photo of Dilli and Art, walks over around the hedge, and knocks on the neighbor's yard gate. He opens it and goes through toward the baffled woman in the house, to say less confidently, "Excuse me, sorry, this door is wide open, and I heard you. May I?"

In her robe and slippers, she's gaping at him – angry or nervous? He stops in the doorway and holds up the photo. "Sorry, you know Dilli and Art? They've been playing here, staying over."

She nods from her distance and Bernard has gathered the guts to continue. "I hope you'll have grandchildren some day. But that will be a while, of course."

She's pinned to the floor; only her cigarette moves.

"I do hope too that you will be in good health, because it's a unique privilege, which can happen before you know it. In Nomi's case it all went fast. With the state of your lungs, by the sound of them, it would take a mountain of willpower to break the habit, stop the poisoning, but there are good methods and it's worth it. When a child goes missing, we're mostly powerless, but a grandmom should be valuable, important, so if you wish..."

He leaves the website note in the windowsill by the door and concludes, "These people offer terrific help. Good luck!"

He goes home, with the sweat on his back.

<>

Mark's box of TicTacs has run empty. He washes it and keeps it for Art: a little piece of wood in it can make an attractive sound. Wish-dreaming in private realism: Art will move it deliberately and later he'll be able to open it with his hoping fingers and smart eyes.

Mark is musing and losing himself in what may happen too: Art will discover the telephone buttons and suddenly a voice says, "Animal Ambulance, how can I help? ... Hello? Who is this?"

Art keeps quiet and the voice grows impatient. "Abuse of this number is a felony."

Dilli joins the guilt or adventure and together they crouch in the landline cabinet, waiting for what will come to pass.

Nomi takes the train to a convention on the future of estate agents, and she can permanently feel how Art would enjoy himself here in a year's time: he walks down the station platform, going almost out of sight, and he rides the elevator as well as the escalator twice. Pigeons – not people? – are allowed to walk on the rails – everywhere! – and at Granddad's he'll see those birds in the acacia and say, "Here they are again."

The sewage is renewed in the street. For weeks a monster digging machine has been busy with pipes, water and heaps of sand. When it's done for the day, all big children like Dilli build bridges across the daring deepness behind barriers pushed aside, and the little ones bring their tip-dig-shovel-tractors to a patch of "clean sand".

Meanwhile there's a re-run of *Little Big Mouths*, marked as "'Entertainment' in the national TV Guide: "Children are lured to say cute things about issues of grown-ups."

Another channel shows a scientific documentary about cruel experiments with babies who are taught to fear random objects.

What scientist is normal or mentally ill?

"At the cost of Health Care," the makers declare, "*Science* receives billions from the government to collect knowledge that can also be found in the streets of life, in bits of natural wisdom."

Could some of those funds be transferred to the search of children in actual peril?

Mark and Nomi can't grasp why the last action for Art has no results. They can imagine and visualize him so tangibly, they experience a 'soon or later and next year with him' so realistically –

"He likes mixed fruits," Nomi tells Mark out of the blue in bed, lying beside him on her back, not seeing him. "Banana and mango."

"Or strawberry and apple," he says, looking at the ceiling.

"Such things will be noticed, won't they."

Mark and Nomi keep agreeing about Art in turns.

"At bedtime, when he needs to sleep, he's so sensitive to sound."

"A loud car, household machines..."

"A screeching bird, the squeaking faucet and creaking stairs."

"If only they're aware of that on time and give him some slack."

"He's got so many particulars. I hope they're open to that too."

In the course of another week, it's the present that becomes unreal. To Nomi a memory and her hope for the future can feel equally real at special moments, for instance a scene like this –

By dinnertime, Dilli would like to stay and play longer in the square across their street. Art is having a good time there in the buggy, viewing the colorful social motion, and the outdoor air will enhance their appetite.

"OK, Dil," Nomi says, "I'm just going to put the rice on and get the vegetables, to peel them here with you. I'll be right back. Through the open door, we can see each other, yes?"

Dilli nods. "Will you watch?"

"Yes, absolutely, the whole time."

Putting the rice on a simmer, Nomi peers through the hallway and front door, past a car. In the quiet moment Dilli looks like a gnome with a toy buggy and real baby. She must not run onto the street, where cars come unexpectedly. Does Art's buggy have the brake on?

While Nomi finds the vegetables, a pan and knife, she sees Dilli standing totally still, a hand on the buggy, her eyes tight from responsibility.

The fridge is still open. For seconds Nomi wonders how long Dilli would be waiting like this.

4
THE UNLIKELY EVENT

<>

"The chapter on Josh Gelder is flirting with sarcasm," Simon says in an email. "Please, avoid satire!"

"Thanks," Anne replies, "and don't worry, the part on Bernard Bloomsdale will be a different story."

She leaves home and drives off in a state of irritation, that doesn't seem to have a clear cause. Yesterday she arrived at the chemist's after opening hours and lost her temper, but that fiasco was shaken off, wasn't it?

She panicked about the wall cabinets in the kitchen: too heavy with the many special offers from the shops? But Evan swears that she's only haunting herself; no cabinet will be coming down! He also promises that the mass of ants outside the kitchen window will not march in. She never leaves anything sweet lying around, but ants are shrewd, with special antennae, and once they're in these columns... Hey, is that what it's called?

One of Reg's precious, handmade gnomes is vacuumed by accident, but it should be found when she'll empty the bag. He bawled in bed because Bear slipped out of reach, and she put it back through the bars.

These days he's waking up at the strangest hours, because his head is stuck in a stubborn spot. Bear's minute of toy music works miracles then.

With Bernard, she has a ten a.m. appointment at The Kew, a rural restaurant between their towns, and Anne left late.

Rushing the car, she needs to slow down for kids playing ball in the street and not exactly moving aside. While she's pushing on close, the ball keeps rolling, so-called controlled. With each meter she's expecting a bang and scream from anger or worse. By the time Reg will play outside, she'll instruct him properly.

Further down the road there's a narrowing with the red and white arrow sign. An oncoming van seems to reduce pace for her, making her hesitate. Oddly slow, the van does drive on, and Anne waits, frustrated. The next car stops for her definitely and now she sees that the arrow on her side is white. She laughs at herself – your eyes and brain are growing as bad as your mom's! – and she pledges never to get upset again before it proves to be necessary.

The road bumps and pits don't bother her terribly anymore, although she needs to slow down and watches the clock.

"What's a source of annoyance to you?" is Anne's first question at 10.15 a.m., after a short introduction in a corner of the lovely country restaurant. "Apart from people being late?"

Quasi-rattled, Bernard says, "By all means, do begin with a delicate point, make me talk about that and we'll be here all day."

"OK, the publisher pays."

"Ha, for my candor?"

"Is it that bad?" Anne asks. "Can I tape it?"

"If we stay polite."

"And if we don't overdo that."

"But what a shame," says Bernard, "to start on a negative note, such as kids in the yard next door, shouting to someone inside, who can't hear them because the TV and computer are on for shows and games with loud foreground music. So, the kids keep on yelling without moving. Nah, let's not go there, shall we?"

Beaming from anticipation, Anne checks her recorder, reluctant to take notes on paper. "No, we'll start with a lot of brunch treats. And I'll ask the most positive question: what's your biggest blunder, as a man or writer?"

Bernard covers his mouth and before speaking he chews the nut cake, a specialty of the house that was ready on the table. "I was a guest at the Boston Book Fair. After a good interview with the major daily paper, they wanted my picture. We went out on the street, where a woman asked for my autograph, and too late I realized that it could have been the photo moment, spontaneous and active, because I can't pose, let alone beside a conifer, when the photographer has no better idea. In such predicaments I tend to have muscle and brain failure."

"Excuse me," Anne chuckles. "I asked respectfully for your worst moment in life, and you come up with a cute small tale – as a smoke screen or red herring?"

"No," Bernard sighs earnestly, "I just didn't know where to start."

"With something you want to get off your chest," Anne says half-seriously too. "Something you need to get rid of. Be glad with a chance to set it right at last."

"OK... After an interview with Woman's Weekly they granted me a look at the article proof. That request of mine had nothing to do with the quality of the reporter or editor, only with my mental defects during press moments."

She waits and says, "Hm, tell me all."

He clears his throat and smiles. "In the proof I saw the word *very* nineteen times. Unnecessary! Obviously, that was the spoken word, surmountable, but the lady had faithfully saved all nineteen, and that became disturbing on paper. I mentioned it without much emphasis, and she was vexed in a sweet way: 'I detected a pet phrase too: *Profound*. I've deleted three out of six.' For which I was genuinely grateful. Not until months later it dawned on me (don't ask how that works): she thought that I thought this *very* had been used nineteen times by her! As if I would have been so plain about it then. Dead awkward."

"Well," Anne says, "very many thanks for this very thoughtful hint or very concealed warning. What did she say when you explained?"

"Oh, you see, I forget the main part again: I never did repair the damage. By that time it had been too long and the strength failed me."

"Boy," Anne says. "What a confession!"

"Yes, your recorder has red-hot ears. What exactly will *Time-In* be: a gossip rag in posh book form? Or is there a camera behind a plant here, for this TV show called *I'm sorry*? Let's blurt things off our chests in turns. You're up next. And mind: we want a rising scale of disaster."

Pensive, both take a sip and bite of this and that, which have been brought on a charming antique trolley.

"So," Anne says, "all your private and career calamities appear to involve interviews."

"Ha, like this one! Spooky, isn't it?"

"Don't you have an excellent experience with the media?"

"Alright," he says, "you want a highlight or the all-time low?"

Looking at him, not sure if he's amusing himself or her, Anne is modest and sympathetic. "I think my choice would make no difference."

His smile shows recognition with admiration, and he says a bit gravely, "My book titled *We Need To Tell You* came out in Europe, non-fiction on the gruesome death in a family, a week after a massacre at a school. For a page-size feature, The Inter Daily flew a reporter and photographer in. Remember, in those days the newspapers had a great deal of influence. The Inter Daily had millions of readers back then, partly after sensation, but I thought: they can't get any sensation out of this book, so bring them on for the good cause, let's have some beauty and consolation in this Daily for a change. Arrogant, eh?"

Anne doesn't blink and he continues. "At the airport they rented a car and drove to me. The reporter was a famous, posh woman, the photographer a skilful and jovial good man, very kind. I offered food and drinks, but was mighty shy if talkative, about the book and its background. In hindsight I caught a funny glance from her when I happened to call it a children's book. The publisher had renowned successes for adults. But I turned off that alarm bell."

Anne takes a note after all, inconspicuously, and Bernard goes on. "The lunch and photo shoot went well too, for my timidity, and before I knew it, they were off again. When I felt guilty about their long and heavy workday, they said this was a field day compared to other assignments. Afterwards the publisher's marketeer called, curious as well as anxious, 'Certain press people can be ruthless.' And I had nothing but good news."

Anne laughs, waiting for the climax.

"The Inter Daily used to be in all the shops and stands, and every day I went to check, but the article was never published. The marketeer stopped calling too."

"What happened?"

"Officially I've never been told. The first months I didn't stir either, I was just stupefied, but I had the woman's name, and later I sent a letter, only because they borrowed private photos of my family, with my hearty consent. That's how truly good the mood was. I'm still positive about that."

Anne is on the edge of her chair, but he drinks his fresh juice and has a nibble of quiche before going on. "When there was no reply, I wrote a letter to the editor with a sort of threat – imagine."

"What kind of threat?"

"That I'd publish the story the way I've told it to you now."

"Ha," Anne says, "for me to publish it! And then?"

"Promptly there came an apologetic and elegant letter from the reporter, 'No idea why the editor had a change of heart,' with the family photos, and a series of large, fabulous new prints from the photographer."

"Have you ever traced the truth?"

"Well," Bernard thinks out loud. "It may be that the story didn't offer enough sensation, and I suppose they would not give much space to a children's book. They were probably cross with the publisher for not telling them."

"Why didn't they?"

"I assume the PR people just kept their mouths shut and hoped for the best."

"The best being a calculated misunderstanding. So, The Inter Daily sent a team overseas without having read the book?"

"I reckon," says Bernard, "a chapter from the manuscript, wrapped in strategy. Who knows what Promotion told them. If only they'd let *me* know what they kept quiet about – something as minor as a child's book. My lips would have been sealed for the greater good."

"Would you've lied as well?"

"Yes, I think so."

Anne asks, "The book is highly praised by adults too, isn't it? Parents, teachers, therapists..."

"Yes, you're well-prepared."

"Which makes the Daily's decision a disgrace all the more."

Bernard is fierce. "Makes them distressingly wrong, but not for my sake. Children are the future leaders! Their minds and souls need fuel."

Anne shakes her head, nods and scribbles, and asks, "You excel at writing from anyone's perspective: man and woman, especially children. Why are they protagonists in your work for adults?"

"Don't know, it's never a specific purpose or plan. A story or a theme comes up that involves children. It's logical, in a sense, as they are a large part of life. And we *stay* children a bit, I hope. Maybe because I only have one."

"Who is not on your website."

"No," Bernard says. "Why would she? The site is about work."

"Or about you and the extended background."

"As little as possible."

"But," Anne tries harder, "your readers would like to know you and the loved ones around you, as an inspiration. I haven't found many personal details – after looking extensively!"

Bernard hides a touch of exasperation. "Sorry, my whole heart is amply present in the books. Exposed, I'd say."

"Yes," Anne agrees heartily. "That makes them beautiful and valuable, but we're only human. Readers love to be touched by the person and his life: contents and sources, virtues and weakness. That could help us."

Bernard wipes his hands and mouth on the napkin beside his plate. He gets the fork to break a piece of pie with care. "Mm. Do you have children?"

Her eyes drop. "A boy, and we're not going to dwell on him at all."

She seems to be blushing.

"Sorry." Bernard waits and says with a diffident smile, "I'm no scandal rag, I just like dialogue, exchange, two-sidedness."

Anne's reaction is slightly delayed. "Watch it, I'll have to delete your countless times of *sorry*."

She is used to vigorous conversations, she often starts them, but the mood of this one is unusual, and a part of it is beyond her control. On the other hand, it's more as if she's his biographer, with a bond of years, a peculiar fusion of the professional and private. He's right: this encounter feels natural or autonomous because they're speaking as equal humans and colleagues. Nonetheless she wants to keep her distance.

<>

"How did it go?" Evan asks with keen interest – before she does.

"Oh, Bloomsdale is amiable, witty, moving, wise..."

"Well well!"

"As vulnerable as engrossing. But so reticent on a certain level. It's almost disconcerting."

"God, I've never seen you this charmed or lost, as if he's cast a spell."

"And we haven't finished. This man is a treasure, perfect for *Time-In.* But instead of a chapter there's material for a separate book."

"Wow," says Evan. "You can do something about that!"

"Yes, I'll put it to Simon: *Life, The Search.* What a true cliché. And how did it go here today?"

"Super. This kiddo is melting my heart. He answers to his name now as well."

Anne is beaming. "Then you have his heart too."

"Yeah, it's a joint venture."

"So, it was no plight?"

"On the contrary," Evan says. "When will you go again?"

"Possibly Saturday."

"Good. Remember: Wednesdays and the weekends I'm available all day. The rest by appointment, plus a pile of spare days. But I'm not imposing, I won't mention a cabin in the dunes again – for now. No more reserves?"

"Evan, it's still hard for me to accept all this."

"Yet it's all acceptable. I have to say, I'm dazzled myself, but one year can make an insane difference, with my new job for a start, with normal hours, and what Reg brings about..."

His voice fades and he wipes an eye. "Sorry, fear not, I won't go mental and sentimental."

"But Reg does touch a tender string, I know. He brings tears to my eyes too."

"From fun and emotion," Evan says. "Plus three filthy diapers. How long will the teething be this messy?"

"Wait for the molars! More than a year, I believe, altogether. I'll check. At first I didn't want to know what I was up against."

Surprised, he asks, "You don't visit a health center?"

"We do, but not every week. Would you like to go, for vaccinations and everything?"

"Ah, no need!" Evan says on second thoughts. "His brain is good, for one thing. On his way to bed, Milord cries and protests on purpose. His tummy is fine too; when he's had enough to eat in his opinion, his mouth and eyes shut tight. He won't be diverted one second. And his muscle system is top, he can sit up and correct his balance."

"Next," Anne says, "he'll get out of bed by himself."

"To go where he wants!"

"Yeah, it's killing my back to lift him."

"There's one problem," Evan says, "he calls me Momom."

"Ah, he sees your tender side. Wonderful."

"Or he sees no difference. You're not jealous then?"

"No, Evan. Did you get the groceries?"

"We did. He finds the supermarket fascinating, and a store girl fancied us."

"Oh?" Anne says.

"At the bread section I asked for an Allinson loaf. That was fetched from the back, so fresh that the bag needed to be open, still warm, and so good that we ate some right away, all snug and sauntering. At an aisle turn I looked back and saw that the bread girl followed us with her eyes."

"Oh..." Anne frowns. "In what sort of way?"

"Amused or endeared, I guess, with Reg, of course, not with me. At least I'm glad she didn't start about the missing kid. She must've seen how close and true we are. Nobody thinks we met only weeks or a month ago."

"And then what happened?"

Evan is pleased to report. "I put a thumb up and pointed to the slices of bread in our hands. I could see her broad smile from our distance, and she waved a hand, so enthusiastic!"

Anne seeks a minimum of humor. "Or she worried and thought: wait for the boy's bowels to act up. Because the delicious Allinson bread is full of grains and seeds, too prickly for babies."

"Ouch." Evan shrinks. "Forgive me. I need more internship, after all. As punishment I'll put new batteries in the thermostat, or else you won't have hot water."

"Thank you," Anne says. "I need it badly."

And Evan asks, "Will you go to Bloomsdale's place?"

"Why?"

"Well, obviously, for a personal impression of the man behind the author!"

"Nah, he doesn't like that, although it would be fascinating."

"Or," Evan presses, "invite him to come here; you'll get special insights."

But she doesn't answer.

"Anne? Is that original and smart or stupid?"

"Yes and no," she says. "Are you sure the heater works now? I can do with a good shower."

"Absolutely. I can join you for back-up?"

"Yes, please. Reg won't wake up yet."

<>

Life can pause.

Between high dunes, Dilli is going down the slope where sand lies and glides on stones. Below, shells prick her bare feet, until she's reached the wet beach by the big sea, all clean and smooth and equal because nobody has been here yet. She can run as light as the wind, almost out of the world or into the sea with a spray of splashes.

In the distant blueness a sailing-boat is white and still. A baby sits here in the ripples on the edge, wearing his diaper and a top. Art's tops are in the drawer at home, so what is he wearing now?

More and more people arrive, and the sun grows hot. Then it's not so bad anymore when you crash into the water with your head and all. But another girl keels over in her plastic "life belt" and she can't get up again, it's the belt that keeps her down now, her head under – with a lot of salty water in her mouth when she cries out. The legs are floundering hard, till her mom sees what happens. On time?

Nomi is peeling an apple and cutting it into the best slices, but watch it: they can slip from your hand and get sticky in the sand.

The fancy lounge beds are for other people, they cost money, but Dilli turns one of them into a trampoline and lies on it 'by accident', while a baby boy wants to join her and cries because he can't climb.

Parents rub sun lotion on the kids with caps and hats. The little boy says hi now as if she's known him all his life. He roams around with a big slice of bread, and after a bite in the middle, he wears it on his elbow like a bracelet.

. . .

After hours of digging (sand canals to fill up at high tide), track-making and wave-jumping, there are more lotion rubs, a proper swim and lying-drying on the large and warm towel, before they go home, onto the glowing-hot slope again, where some babies are carried.

<>

Life seems to be narrowing: there's no sun or rain and wind, and Anne is inclined to drive more slowly than usual. Today she's not frustrated by those who drive forty-five where fifty is allowed, or by a roadblock and detour with wrongly placed signs.

It does bother her that it's busier than average in The Kew.

"If you badly needed the money," is one of her first questions to Bernard this time. "Could you be a ghostwriter?"

"Well, these days that's no bad or mad question. But not for a murderer, I think. Fortunately, I've just had a windfall."

Anne turns her device off and says, "Can you tell me off the record?"

As briefly as possible he talks about Aragon House and The Proper Press. "Can I trust you? If you write this down afterwards... Oh well, I won't keep it a secret anyway, but for *Time-In* you have enough tall stories now."

"Alright," Anne says, before switching the recorder on again. "Perhaps I'll come back to this, because it's a wonderful theme: loyalty vs livelihood and self-preservation."

For two seconds, Bernard looks in her eyes, murmuring. "And I will count on your integrity."

"That goes without saying. Whose ghostwriter or biographer could you be?"

"Oh, interesting, and difficult. I'd like to think about it, but not now and here. Can it be homework?"

Anne nods with a smile and disappointment. "How far would you go, as a writer or a human being?"

"Ah, too far. Been there, done that, but it's over."

"Never mind," says Anne. "I'm not the Gossip Rag."

"Hm..." He's on a fence. "In the early days I thought I needed a trick to get an agent's attention, so I used an eye-catching pseudonym. One can't brag about oneself. And believe me, some bragging is required, sadly, when good things are snowed under by... *Oh dear*, hear me sounding like an elitist."

But Anne shakes her head. "You can brag your heart out here. Please do!"

"No, thank you."

And she asks, "What are you sincerely proud of?"

"Ah, the honesty I have maintained."

"What are you happy with most, regarding yourself or a book?"

"Um..." He's taking his time. "That somebody has come to life, who wouldn't be heard otherwise."

Instead of asking for an example, she says, "What was the pseudonym you had?"

"Ha, long gone."

"What happened?"

"I saw this film: *Shattered Glass*. Do you know it?"

"No."

"A true and staggering story, that should appeal to you particularly. A journalist of The New Republic publishes fake articles, fabricating all the 'facts and sources' with so much conviction, the scam can go on for years. He gathers fame, until the whole caboodle collapses the hard way. It's so unsettling and real that I got nightmares from guilt and shame about *my* trick. Don't tell anyone!"

Anne's laughter is too loud, out of proportion, getting looks from other guests at The Kew. The restaurant has the mood of a 'village inn': a friendly and attentive openness, where people tend to share – perhaps more than they care to admit. Bernard and Anne are not in the middle, nor in a little corner that both would prefer.

Now she turns terribly solemn and says, "Your own work is real too. The way you enter a character's mind and soul is beautiful and outstanding, intense and true, you *are* all these people. How come?"

He fumbles with his napkin. "Beats me. I never give it a

thought. It's a freaky cliché, how often my fiction and reality overlap as one truth."

"How do you mean?"

"Well... This unconscious of mine seems to have crazy and creepy links. When a plot or name or theme comes up, I run into all kinds of parallels and similarities, like extreme coincidences. Carl Jung wrote about the collective mind of mankind, and sometimes I'm scared: can fate be tempted? Or does that sound wooly?"

"No," says Anne. "So long as you don't proclaim it's 'coming from God.'"

"Oh no, like this pop star did?" Bernard checks. "Cheap music received from above?"

"Don't tell me."

"Or criminals hearing voices," he adds.

Anne's laughs are so exaggerated again that Bernard feels embarrassed and looks at his watch in a reflex. She pretends not to see that, but she calms down and makes a note, neatly breaks off a piece of croissant and asks once more, absently, "Whose biographer would you like to be?"

He stares at her until she looks away, and his own eyes drop, seeing more than he cares for: is she having a sad blackout or is this a stunning, bashful lapse? She's not being rude and defiant, is she?

He gets light in the head himself, as if a virus actually makes him 'wooly', and he wants to eat something savory, but he gazes into nowhere and says, "My grandson's."

While an aspect of her face dies, she can't but ask, "Who is he?"

"Arthur, eight months now, but he's been missing for two. I'd write him back into life: happy, active, loving, generous, full of purpose. Until *he* can add what's lacking."

"As a matter of fact," Anne says, but the tone and volume of her voice are nearly gone. "This is more than sufficient; you fill two chapters already."

Abruptly she stands up, takes the car keys from her purse and leaves, bumping into a table and chair, creating a stir around the restaurant. Guests are gawking at her and at her seat, the purse is dangling on her shoulder, but Bernard's eyes return to the soup bowl and plate, glass and cutlery in her spot at the table, with her pen and notebook next to the recorder.

The jacket hanging on the back of her seat, looks as if it's handed over, surrendered, as if one can change persons, body and soul.

<>

Life shrinks and time will catch up.

On a warm and glowing October day, months or ages later, Art is walking barefoot, in and out the garden door of his new old house. At first, he stumbles on the threshold, then he takes his time to feel and shuffle his way to the three-wheel bike, not to ride it yet but touch and sense the greatness lying ahead.

In a yard corner stands the full water can, where his hand goes to get some and lick it, if given a chance.

"It's a funny, lucky miracle," Nomi tells Mark and Dilli or the world, "that he doesn't drink from the sea."

"But from the bath," Dilli says. "And he can't, right?"

When he doesn't understand and cries, it's still hard to be stern and forbid him the dangerous things.

Because of Art, Dilli can play with her marbles only at the table that's too high for him, but sometimes an extra smooth one slips away, and Art is so quick to spy and pick it up, it seems he's always ready for this. She knows that a marble can stick in your throat.

The word danger is used many times.

It's still weird to be angry at him, even when he escapes their attention again at dinner and drops his plate with a hundred crumbs on the floor once more.

"Clear enough," Mark tells him. "But there are limits to statements."

Or in a flash Art makes a far-reaching painting of his mashed peaches, that would awe Jackson Pollock or wow an art student.

"Is this age-related?" Nomi asks.

"I can't remember if Dilli used to do that."

"In any case, we should give him some respite."

After what's happened, is leniency normal?

<>

Before time caught up and made amends, Evan reported one last day: "Reg is growing smarter by the hour! Now he's offended by the pacifier! In the highchair he drops his plate – intentionally – and studies the way it falls on the floor. Yeah, how else to explore? He tiger-crawls all over the place. Why didn't you tell me? We'll take him swimming, I'm sure he will love that. Next step, he'll stride around and discover the wide world. But the latest trend is less nice: he's found the reach of his voice, with long and siren-like screams, they won't stop, he's just mesmerized! Look at him, he knows we're talking about him. But Anne, what's wrong? Have you eaten something bad there?"

She didn't answer.

He could not ignore it, should have realized earlier: she was lethargic and alarming even before the doorbell rang. She seemed to lose weight in an hour. How much blood can be drained from the face? She didn't respond to anything, and Evan went on talking as if to keep her conscious, also keeping an eye on the boy on the floor, known to him as Reg. His shoulders were athletically energetic, and the rest of his body followed the rhythm.

"A tiger or soldier could learn from that," Evan said. "And no, I don't *teach* him, I'm just putting the things he wants at some distance. Look, he likes your shoes. Careful, he's right at your feet."

When the bell rang again, longer, something had to be done, but Anne was stock-still, nowhere between coming and going, giving no sign of life.

Resolutely heading for the door, Evan picked up the lively and investigative son (afraid to leave him behind?), telling Anne, "Do you know what he does too? He waves to a specific person, all deliberate..."

And with increasing concern or an attempt at comedic urgency,

Evan added over his shoulder, "You'd better sit or lie down. Call the doctor!"

Carrying the curious boy on his arm and shoulder in a fine, safe routine, he opened the door and saw a man of about sixty, holding some things of Anne's, it appeared. In the second instance this man grew pale and gaped square past him. He squinted and dropped the things, peering closer, then gasping. Both his arms reached out, but he reeled, laughed and cried, and waited – from caution or politeness, hope for a sign of recognition, all mixed with disbelief.

5
NO THICKER THAN WATER?

"It's a kind of madness to be wise among fools."
Jean-Jacques Rousseau

"The space between wrong and right is occupied
by common sense and humanity."
Martha Costello in *Silk*, BBC

<>

Art's coming home went well, it was nothing festive or exuberant but moderate, humble. At first there was too much fear: the happy ending seemed just as unreal as the abduction itself. Those two months were a life by itself. Nomi felt much older, and she hardly recognized Art, with his teeth and hair. He didn't remember anyone from home, which never bothered Dilli. He was not disoriented or anything, but they needed to restrain their kissing and cuddling. They could smother him with a hundred variations of love and guilt.

It was Dilli's fervent joy that he accepted first, her stroking his whole face, the dancing and singing, a piece of her cookie and the gifts from her toy box.

In its turn all that attention required some habitbreaking as well, and a week later the two of them were fighting fiercely over cars and Legos, when Dilli was less keen to share what caught his eye. It had been all hers for too long.

When Arthur turns two, he enters a toddler's wayward phase, as if nothing has been out of the ordinary.

"Or have we spoiled him?" Nomi wondered.

After his gap months, that danger is lurking. Mark realizes it too and they protect each other against it. "First and foremost, Art needs to feel safe now. He was almost gone for good."

"We do know it when he's trying to impose his will as any other kid."

"Sometimes he gets the benefit of our doubt, but we're no pushovers."

Nomi confirms. "There's no need for us to be soft, is there."

He didn't suffer deprivation.

Plenty of people still warn them, "Babies can be spoiled in

early stages. They've got antennae for a parent's weakness and inconsistency. The first years can do the damage."

Upright in his highchair at the dinner table, Art is refusing to try and eat one bite. Tactfully Nomi aims to be bold and mild at the same time. "It's cauliflower with cheese, it will melt on your tongue! Look, here's a spoonful with extra cheese. You can smell it."

They're watching each other, and the way he does not flinch could be mollifying or comical, but it's been a long day, the meal has been cooked with care and he needs it, because February has been a bleak month with coldness and storms, consuming vitamin reserves.

The hell was twenty months ago. How long before the harm has worn off with or without guilt? Avoiding anything too corny, Nomi wants to look after him and give her warmest all, grounded enough to enjoy it.

<>

In Evan's modern part of town, in the middle of a calm street with terraced houses, there's a car stopping with the engine running and two doors wide open. A man gets out and walks to a house door.

On her bike Anne has pedalled slowly, then she brakes just in case. Without looking left or right, a girl darts out of the car, just missing Anne's front wheel. The child screams, the father sprints back and gives Anne a prodding push, making her reel and let go of the handlebars.

The bike falls down with a clatter that rebounds in her head, enhanced. She keeps her footing but staggers. She'd like to walk over to the girl and check if she's unharmed, and she wants to explain to everyone what happened, because apparently the man did not see that. There's no question in his mind at all – about blame or cause and effect.

Another kid sits in the car, and in the front door a woman has folded her arms.

A role-model family? Anne thinks with delayed anger.

"Sorry," she says on the safe side.

"Got no eyes in your head?" the father calls out.

She could strike back or stamp her feet and whine harder than the girl, but after a questioning gesture she takes a step and lifts the bike from the ground, to move on carefully.

Anne has been in this neighborhood for six months now, in Evan's apartment, and she's never been conspicuous before, good or wrong.

The choice between train and car was not difficult this time, since the weather is fine and some exercise like cycling to the station is good for her body and mind. Almost composed again, she rides on, and it's easy and free to park the bike. See: often enough life is no problem! There's even a whiff of spring in the air, although she's wearing her winter coat.

It's still February, but on the platform there's a teenage boy in a t-shirt. Now who is being abnormal here? He looks a bit lost, as a matter of fact, or is that an eerie sort of projection from herself? During a year in the clinic, she learned about limits and mirroring, but some things remain deceptive and may come unexpectedly.

Anne parks her bike in the station lot, and proceeds to the far end of the train, hoping it will be quiet. By the door, this boy in t-shirt waits next to her and lets her get on first. She hurries to the upper deck and nestles in a good seat, in the direction of the train and out of the horizontal sunlight that would shine smack into her eyes elsewhere and expose each part of her face.

This carriage is fairly empty, but the boy sits right across the aisle, now restless, then staring into nowhere.

A few booths further down, a woman is on the phone and Anne can follow patches, about a new love affair. "I miss you already but isn't that bizarre?"

She'd be mortified if people could hear all kinds of personal or intimate things about her.

One man is reading a book, and that gives Anne such a warm feeling that she could send him a smile or go and give him a hug, if it wouldn't create a confusing scene. With a book you always have a friend around, a kindred spirit.

Hardly has she plugged her ears and closed her eyes, than a guard arrives and says, "Good morning!"

It's a while before she's found her railcard. "Sorry, so clumsy, I should have it at hand!"

With my criminal record and all. If no jail time.

Next there's commotion around the boy across, and she can hear fragments with a heavy accent, "In my jacket... Gone..."

He turns a shoulder as if his coat was on a peg behind him only a moment ago. He has nothing else on him, not even a plastic bag, which could be strange on an intercity train. Is he telling the guard that his coat was stolen here? Has this fib never been used before?

The kind man throws a searching glance around. He mumbles something slightly wary, but he stays friendly – to prevent aggression? The boy has no ID-card, he needs to give all details and spell his name. "Yasar."

Anne won't "betray" him, not even when the guard asks her if she knows anything about the coat.

"Dark gray, CoolCat, with a furry line," Yasar says.

Not until later does Anne realize how quickly one gets a wrong impression, but not because he's foreign. Eventually she thinks he's looking sad, and that's not about guilt or vexation being caught, is it?

The guard's manner toward Yasar is encouraging and sympathetic. What a pity that she'll never know the whole truth of this and how it will end. That blank touches a part of her own life and keeps it smoldering, or aglow.

On a train, Anne feels more part of society than in a car, where she can be overcome by a sense of isolation, both in traffic jams and on distant roads, with the rhythm of windshield wipers.

A train offers agreeable distractions, but they can also be risky. Last time she took her glasses off to rest her head on her coat, and she got off without them. She had to run back without the camouflage, terrified that the train would leave again with her still on it, as if one station too far would be the end of the world. In fact, having to go through something as trivial as that, compared to the past years, should make her feel stronger, if anything.

As a mental shield the glasses might not be necessary anymore, but she's grown fond of them. She knows the Stockholm syndrome, that strikes when you have so-called empathy for the person who's abducted you or taken you hostage for a long period. What's this condition called when you miss the one you kidnapped?

That sort of questions come up during the sessions with Doctor Grant, who supervises her reintegration thoroughly and with relative toughness, after conferring with GP Mullan, who retires –

because he's old or failed? They suggested an 'adapted identity' and for the time being that seemed to be a simple solution, the least she could do for the sake of herself and everyone. The word 'amends' has never been used.

When she's ready to get off the train, the door jams, which causes a spell of claustrophobia. She finds herself stupid and insufferable sometimes, but in the end, once her feet are firm on the platform, she tells herself that life is full of bumps and obstacles. "So what?"

People are watching her. Because she's talked out loud?

Her coat is no part of the 'disguise' but a valuable shelter.

Walking down the sidewalk along a busy road with large buildings, she looks immersed in life again, amid various workers in the streets. A couple of old trees are replaced and there are pits in the ground for repairs on tubes and cables. Thank God there are experts for such things. Now watch the crossing, because people in fast cars don't heed patients taking shaky new steps, big or little, back into the world as if it were the first time.

"It's a useless cliché," she tells Doctor Grant. "But one or two years can be like two days and an entire life at the same time."

Somewhere eight weeks are lacking, mislaid or erased, and she can't check the waste or recycle can yet, from which many things can be recovered.

"However," she adds when Grant smiles in silence, "normal people often feel that way too, don't they?"

He nods. "What's normal?"

"Ah, for example, when I don't steal children."

"True. But who knows what kind of hardship others go through, with deep grief or big mistakes..."

Anne almost hastens to say, "A third of the people have burnouts or depressions, a third have ADD or dyslexia, and the rest are therapists or mental coaches or life trainers and whatever they're called."

"Like me?"

"Yeah," she teases back. "Where does a shrink seek help and safety? At the hair salon?"

Grant moves his legs and rubs his knee, saying, "Sudden infant death is random and not rare, as you know by now, and a mood disorder is next to regular."

"Yes, like asthma, diabetes, a heart condition, epilepsy."

"But those are not disturbed in most people's eyes."

"Quite," she mocks. "Not so deranged."

Grant has a short laugh. "Still there are medications for them too, for a part."

"Also with side-effects?"

"Correct. And in many cases there's a form of accepting, fighting, suffering, clinging on. Your combination of circumstances was harsh and abrupt, like a stroke or a heart attack."

Anne is crying, but she keeps it low.

After a moment Grant asks, "What's happening now?"

She's glad it's no insipid routine question like: are you OK?

Softly she blows her nose. "It moves me, your interest without judgment. And I realize that some people have three strokes or attacks."

"Yes, that's regarded as medical bad luck, while you are considered lunatic, dangerous and guilty?"

She gives a shout. "Because I've made victims!"

"Yes, that's a big and tricky difference, a double tragedy. Was it deliberate?"

They've had this conversation before. How to know if we feel something for real at last? Would you be safe then, to yourself and others, or could it go wrong again after more bad luck?

It won't happen again is a daring expression of regret.

"No," she says, "of course not."

"What?"

He makes her say it: "I didn't do it on purpose."

"How then?"

"Unconsciously, by accident, in a mental fit or spasm or seizure. Which lasted!"

Grant stays calm. "Like a melt-down of the mind. Why?"

Right, she got the point ages ago: he wants *her* to state it all, out loud and convincingly, like an oath or an "I do" – but no guarantees – to show that it's genuinely sunk in, and not out of duty or obedience.

After breaking an oath, one can be sent to prison. At least she's been spared jail-time, leaving her eternally grateful to him and everybody. Now she mainly needs to keep away from danger. If only Grant won't push her with his questions, not yet, please, because certain words are too hazy or heavy in her head. In what ways is a patient better than a criminal if the result is the same? There was a lot of talk about mitigating circumstances. Apparently, professionals were totally convincing. About her!

<>

When Bernard's novel *Sudden Depth* is out, he sends rather personal promo-emails to a selection of bookshops and libraries, literary festivals and clubs, magazines, acquainted filmmakers... What amount of networking and platforming is average nowadays? He enjoys the journalistic browsing, with fine discoveries, such as the English editors of major European papers.

Most replies are polite or downright enthusiastic. One or two are less amused: "I object to your littering my inbox with your silly self-promotion."

That vehemence – is the man right? – makes Bernard tremble in his seat, but he won't send a guilty apology, he tells himself: this ethics professor could be depressed or hot-headed, he may have a bad day, or he's fallen out with his wife and a child.

After reading the book, the famous film director Paul Baldwin writes, "This story is exciting, moving, real. But in principle I only film my own ideas, and ever since the Oscar nomination I'm short of time as it is. No doubt there are colleagues and producers who'd love to take this on. Good luck!"

"Can you refer me to anyone?" Bernard asks.

Straightaway he receives the names of four producers. He googles and explores and finds the email addresses of their companies. To all four he writes a note, quoting Baldwin's beautiful first sentence, who sends a furious email, "How can you do this without my permission? Now they're all checking it with me!"

Bernard is nauseous from shame. His ardor, naivety, guts, impatience, and hesitation are all ravelled and topsy-turvy. His venture spirit defends itself, arguing that by toady elbowing and shoe-licking or worse, well-known people have had success with flying and shiny colors. Why can't I?

But his modesty also persists and tells himself: you were out of your mind! Where's the line between zest and misconduct? Mr.

Bloomsdale, you are no better than those who sell their souls to the devil!

"Dear Paul, I'm horribly sorry! It's just that I didn't want to bother you again; you're very busy and it's extraordinary as it is that you've read *Sudden Depth*. Therefore, my false step is all the more wrong. So often did I wait for comments and opinions month after month, I thought it was finally time to be forward or even rude. Forgive me!"

Oh well, the rebel in him reasons that countless job applications are submitted full of self-praise. One has to display oneself, how else will they know what you're worth?

In the course of days there's one more email from a filmmaker. "Thank you, Bernard, could you please send the synopsis and treatment? With thanks, Debbie Atkins."

She's an independent executive producer, and her note comes from a private email account, which makes him feel even more positive. Other information found on the internet sounds awfully good as well. She's involved in all stages of filmmaking, from development to financing.

After sending a sixty-page Word file, he badly needs fresh air and exercise, for his back and mind.

During a solid walk, his thoughts are pleasantly engrossed by plans and chances, but passing by a garden that looks lost between winter and spring, his eye is caught by a few blades of bulbs trying to find some space around a flowerpot with an old chrysanthemum plant. Are they late crocuses or daffodils, with more stems blocked by the bottom of the pot?

The door opens and a woman of about thirty asks, "Can I help you?"

Bernard doesn't know what annoys him most: the phrase *help you* or the fact that her suspicious tone is understandable.

"Excuse me." He clears his throat and gives an amicable smile, pointing to the garden spot. "Could this pot be put on the tiles? Then the bulbs under it can come up too."

But her eyes are saying: should I call the police or a shrink?

And Bernard tries to prevent a grotesque scene; he moves the withered-flower pot and continues on his way before the woman could be alarmed and have him certified.

<>

The minute they ride, Art in his seat on the back carrier, and Dilli behind or beside them on her own bike, they start singing hard. In the clear morning air, their uninhibited voices make people turn and look, with or without humor, and Nomi decides, "Loud is alright only if the two of you sing the same song."

Sometimes she still finds it difficult to leave Art behind at preschool. There are moments when anything can remind her of *back then*: a smell or sound, a look in Dilli's eyes, a newspaper headline, the posture of an unknown woman in the street, a bike with a baby, a police officer, or nothing specific as far as she can tell. Her muscles and skin have their own memories.

Art was gone for fifty-eight days. For how long can something remain in the subconscious?

The kindergarten front door is locked and has a code-key box on the wall outside. But with a smile and some inventiveness every bad man or woman can pretend to be a parent or grandparent who has a blackout and can't remember the code, saying, "Alzheimer's has come early for me!" Or "My mother is dying, and my mind is blurred."

Or holding a child's bag with a total matter-of-fact air, they can wait for someone to enter, put out a cigarette casually and follow them in, muttering, "I'm an idiot, I'll quit, this was my last one."

Each of the children would be there for the grabbing.

Nomi is ashamed to think of these tricks, as if she's just as evil and crafty as kidnappers. This Anne Hoaver may be a free person again, declared sane or cured, coached by social work, unrecognizable and welcomed in a community that doesn't have a clue. The headlines and questions or outrage are over. No punishment, but psychiatric treatment. No danger to the community. Prison would have been an aggravation.

Whose consensus was that? Unanimous or doubtful?

Nomi has heard that 'such people' are not allowed to go anywhere near victims, but who is checking that all day? They must have a kind of repeat urge, an instinct, like these women who marry a man resembling their violent father. An inclination can be genetic, in the blood, always prone to relapse.

She hates her fits of bitterness, also when she thinks: are there any support groups called Abductors Anonymous? She'd recognize that Hoaver woman from a photo, wouldn't she? Not from the instant when Art was discovered in her house, and she sat on the floor in a sick, vacant daze. In retrospect Nomi can see that extreme pain being in violent contrast to her own joy.

By now she has stopped looking around on the alert and discussing the risks with a teacher. Despite herself she does read about riots after the whereabouts of a released pedophile have leaked. She understands one side of the matter, "Nowhere near my child!", as well as the other, "It's a good thing to have them in sight."

"Give these people a break!"

"Who deserves a second or third chance?"

How she'd wish and fear to set eyes on Hoaver!

To her surprise it's Mark who says, "They do need to live somewhere."

"With house arrest or an ankle monitor?"

"Not like lepers in a camp outside town."

Nomi hisses, "This woman buried her kid in the yard and acted as if nothing had happened."

"Nome, she was in shock from grief, among other things."

"Yes, I'm sorry."

Who knows what she says about me, and rightly so?

"Be glad," Mark says, "that you're not in her shoes. I mean, would you swap as victims?"

"Oh, I know, forgive me. She's lost her child and her life, *and*

Art! You are my saint or guardian angel. But imagine, she lived on, she spoke with Bernard at length on two occasions!"

"Good thing for us that she did, instead of taking Art to a place like South America. I'm still as stunned as you, but anger doesn't help anymore, does it?"

"No," says Nomi, "that is a sore beside our happiness of now."

"And the very thought that she can be watching us somewhere..."

"Exactly, observing Art wistfully!"

"So," Mark asks, "what would you do if her care team were there for you?"

"It may sound childish, but I don't want that kind of help, I want the two months of Art back."

Or rather the hour before them, to live that differently and change the mistakes completely. But wishes like that are futile and stupid. I need to pull myself together, to look ahead and live forward.

"Would it help," Mark says reflectively, "if you could go and see where Art was?"

What does 'you' mean here: that Mark doesn't need this himself?

"Yes," Nomi says absently, "that has occurred to me."

"But?"

"Everybody would declare me mental."

"Who is everybody?"

She smiles with a grimace. "That woman to start with. Or you?"

Suddenly she realizes that few people would need to know, which is a tremendous relief.

"Never mind," Mark says. "I'm not keen myself; it's about you."

He has told her what people think of her, all the sympathy he's heard, but that's no good unless she can feel it herself. And she knows for sure that many don't speak their minds. No blaming out loud. Words like 'neglect' and 'abandoned' churn in her head of their own accord. This second year, Art has begun talking, babbling as if catching up. Too bad he can't report anything retroactively. He can't accuse or forgive in language, although he seems expressive enough.

Off and on Nomi instructs the kids needlessly or in vain, "When you're playing outside, do not forget what?"

"Button our coats," Dilli says.

"I have!" Art says.

"And you must never do what?"

"Go with somebody," says Art.

"Only if you know them," says Dilli.

"Know them well!" Nomi urges.

"Granddad."

What's the line between warning them for 'strangers' and scaring them, so they lose their natural faith? She's never said things like this: if someone takes you, scream hard, even if they're very kind.

Instead, they have had this chat –

Nomi, "What's the best food in the world?"

Art, "French fries and ice cream."

Dilli, "Cake, chocolate, cookies, liquorice, pancakes."

"Now listen and focus. If anyone gives you all that, you tell them 'No, I can't.'"

"Says the police?" Dilli checks.

"Yes, and you rush off to a teacher or parent or anyone you know. Then you'll get the treats here at home."

"Now?" Art asks.

Nomi swallows her "no" on time and says, "Alright, by way of example, if you understand and never take one thing from strangers. OK?"

They nod ardently and for some reason she won't ask: promised?

A little devil in Dil's head might whisper: So, in order to get what you like at home, you can just claim that somebody wanted to give you goodies. But she would not be so cunning as to make up a description of her assailant, although children are frightfully bright when it comes to obtainingsweets. Unintentionally, with funny fibs, they can cause massive havoc.

<>

In general, a good friend needn't be told 'have a seat,' but it would make sense if Cindy were tense.

Her laugh seems out of place, before Anne has asked, "Coffee or a stiff drink?"

Then Cindy sounds as direct and familiar as in the old days. "Coffee, please. How are you?"

Or that question is a trifle investigative, Anne frets, but this paranoid crap of herself has to stop. She won't answer with a cheap or conjuring 'fine' anymore, she clicks the coffee machine on and gets the treats. "I'm alright in a small way, considering. Or is it uncanny acquiescence?"

"Neither excludes the other, does it?" Cindy says.

"Sure, of course." Anne looks at her thankfully. "How are *you*?"

"Well... I have some weird news. There's a baby on the way."

After a second or two, Anne checks, "Why weird? Is it unexpected?"

Why didn't she say: I'm pregnant, or: we're having a baby...?

Cindy hits herself. "Sorry, sorry! I've been worried that it's tough on you, but now I've *made* it difficult. It's not unexpected, no, and yet it's a miracle, isn't it?"

Anne gives her a hug, but she's caught unawares by snotty sobs, that she stops to get some tissues.

At the clinic she cried after months of numbness, and never when other people were there, apart from Doctor Grant. It's still easier to be derogative about it and call it 'blubbering'.

For a moment she sits on the couch with her back toward Cindy, and both keep timidly silent, until Anne turns and murmurs, "Don't say sorry again."

"OK, Annie."

"It will be hard, of course. Just always tell me – for my own good – what you are afraid of. When are you due?"

"By the end of August."

Good, that's very different from winter, when Reg was born, and from early summer, when he died. She's uttered that word and his name only in front of Grant and Evan. More things needed to be discussed, though, and she managed with Evan as a go-between.

When Reg's body had to be exhumed, Evan wanted to be there. She couldn't even bear to hear him talking about it, let alone be present herself. "Step by step," Grant said a dozen times. The police asked her to point out the spot, but she couldn't, and Grant intervened. He let her draw and paint, scratch and make smudges, until her hand was autonomous and created a vague shape, deep red among crooked pastel strokes. Eventually there were a few black details, that Evan was able to interpret as a spot in the garden.

She wouldn't grasp that he stayed in that house, or stayed with her – for whose sake? – but he came around at the clinic until she understood that he had not abandoned her. "Not a second time."

Cindy and doctor Mullan came too, finally Simon and Wil, in that order and with all variations of hesitation, guilt, caution or courage, with flowers and books, painting gear and music, few questions outside regular life.

For a long time, she'd prefer to be alone, but she wouldn't say so and sound ungrateful or disaffected, and who knew what was the good thing to do? Grant kept matters open, or he left them with her.

In the beginning there were episodes with misgivings of a conspiracy, a pitfall, an illusion. She'd weigh her words or remain silent, and weeks lasted only hours or the other way around. Grant proved to mean well by her, and he was working on the medication. That sent her back two years in time, or they were millimeters, now with the gait of a snail or a hedgehog, then with a bird's eye.

She was at reasonable liberty to roam the clean, spacy, and neutral building, to go for a meal and drink, to do a game or sport and something artistic, talk with Grant or with... What were they called: addressable fellow patients?

She was terribly lucky with this "punishment". Wil made that clear enough, but Wil reminded her of a woman who was no visitor here. Once or twice, Anne screamed when she entered, her room or somewhere with other people, who were surprised or unperturbed.

"Sshh," Wil called out. "It's only me, your mother!" Which helped insufficiently. Her "don't make a fool of yourself!" had more effect. "Come, Anna, let's walk to the garden and get some color in your face, if possible."

It was a fenced yard without any breeze, too hot in summer but snug in the fall.

Toward Anne's discharge from the clinic, Evan suggested confidently that he'd stay in her house, and she'd move into his apartment – without knowing for how long – and here she asks Cindy, "Are you hoping for a boy or a girl?"

Makes no difference, as long as it's healthy is a frequent answer to that question, honest or evasive.

"I don't know yet," Cindy says. "I thought a girl."

And head-on Anne asks, "Because that would be easier for me?"

After a hitch, Cindy says, "And for us. But it's ridiculous to have a preference anyway, to leer at this technical screen and look for a willy, as if a baby is a product."

"Will you have the ultrasound?"

"Yes, on second thoughts. Rob gives me no choice, really."

"Do you want to know the gender then?"

"Or we'll decorate the room lilac! Or yellow and spring-grass green."

Anne gives her a hug again, happy with plain time, almost sisterly or like fellow mothers. Anne lets go and says, "If you do know the gender, will you tell?"

Cindy doesn't ask: did you, when you were pregnant with Reg? She answers, "No idea. At any rate, I won't tell the name."

"You have names already?"

"Yes, I need to be careful, I tend to give them away. We use the boy's name all the time, instead of 'the baby'. Anyhow, it's no disaster if it does get out, nothing fate-defying."

Now they're on sensitive ground again, and Cindy sighs. There seems to be more that she's not saying, but Anne asks, "Would you have an amnio, if there was a reason?"

"Oh, I don't want to think about that."

"Sorry, made no sense at all."

Since we can't be prepared for everything.

"It does, in fact," Cindy says. "If we start ultrasounds, we have to be ready for bad news and be brave enough. That's why I shrink from it all, because where to draw an abortion line? If the baby has spina bifida or a severe cleftlip?"

What goes without saying: the baby's interest always comes first.

What horrible disease or disability would you let Reg have in exchange for his return?

Cindy stands up angrily. "I'm a no-go hero. I might choose the coward's way out."

She bends down again and takes a sip of coffee.

"Is it lukewarm now?" Anne asks.

"Yes, but no problem."

Cindy takes the cup of coffee to the kitchen, pours it into a pan and heats it.

Anne hasn't budged. For the first time since... She's considering a new column for NUNA, about the space between murder and mercy, that many people may have to tackle, but her brain is working too fast for her feelings.

When the news of Reg broke, editor Brigit sent a condolence card, leaving NUNA matters open. Has Evan saved all the mail or only the friendly cards and letters? And his photos of the exhumation? For over six months she didn't dare read the mail that Evan brought, but Grant said it would be important one day – for the rest of her life. "Anything is better than no reaction, from people you know, even something hostile. At least it could grow into a dialogue. It helps you being there again, in the present or future."

But some envelopes have not been opened yet, from people in the street.

And the reburial?

Or cremation.

It was needed.

After the body was released.

Reg was released.

Evan saw to it and talked to her.

And someday she will be there yet.

Life can be retrospective and feel ahead.

<>

The prominent film producer would like a shorter version of the story. That's a shame, but the request implies true attention, one could say. "Do you write your own scripts? Do all the press quotes refer to this title? Best, Debbie."

This kind of interest is good news, isn't it? Or is her query an omen?

He won't dwell on it.

When a neighbor is drilling into a stone wall, Bernard leaves the premises. With brunch and a thermos of coffee, a tiny chair and a sizeable towel, he installs himself in the lee between woods and lake, to work on his novel called *And Walk.*

After the postponement of *Time-In,* publisher Simon asked him to elaborate on exhilarating plans.

This day in the first week of March, the sky is perfectly blue. By noon it's wondrously warm in the sheltered sunshine in Bernard's low chair. When the light prickles his eyes, he closes them for a while and breathes from the feet up. Each of his senses is highly receptive, with the scents and birdsongs, the budding shrubs, lesser celandine and flowers called "honesty" in the vernacular.

Hardly has he written a sentence and boldly taken some clothes off, than a big black Labrador comes blustering up to him, all tongue and spring-bliss leaps, panting and drooling. Far behind it, the woman master calls out half-heartedly, in vain. The dog with its mud paws and instinct is jerking at Bernard's towel and sticking its snout into his coffee, that was ready for the next paragraph.

The woman is still shouting impotently.

Bernard knows how a dog reacts to fear. And to fury? As there's no trouser leg to be ripped now, will it grab some hide and hair? As forceful yet neutral as possible, Bernard tries to push the animal away. He has a variant of territorial behavior himself, which is probably not the reason for the Labrador to withdraw. There's blood on the towel, but not caused by a fight.

The woman is keeping her distance and Bernard screams, "Discipline, please, or keep the beast on a leash!"

While she walks by timorously, he stands up and shows her the smeared towel, asking. "Has it got a bloody foot?"

"Oh," she says at a loss, "So sorry, I'm only babysitting, and I thought that wound had healed."

Bernard stays grumpy – taking other things out on the woman or dog? "If bloodstains are not rinsed at once, they'll never go away, but I won't leave, I've just arrived."

Do I always meet weirdos or saddos, or is it me: are other people the normal ones?

Nervously she fumbles at her cardigan, gets a wallet out and asks, "Will you buy a new towel?"

She gives him a tenner and inadvertently he takes it. She and the dog move on. Regretting his bluntness, Bernard wants to give the money back, but stepping out of his wood-edge lee, he sees that the Labrador is thundering to the next unwary man, and the useless yelling starts anew.

Bernard recants his regrets and lays the towel to soak by some reeds in the water – where no coot or pike will have a bite at it? He drapes his clothes over his chair, and the coffee is delicious, not from the cup where the wet snout went, but in the thermos top.

"You need to socialize more," Nomi has been telling him lately. "Take up sports and dating!"

Because fifty-plus youthfulness will fade away if you don't maintain it.

By nature, he's a spirited and credulous person – formerly gullible – with a dose of shyness, so that mistakes get to him hard and make him insecure. He found Anne Hoaver interesting and attractive, she was frank, witty, skilful and above all original. Boy, what a sharp judge of character he is! Could she still be that? Deep inside?

Alright, self-mockery is unfair, now that he can look back. The shock and disgust of the final scene outside her house were so mixed with the sublime joy of seeing Art again, that he felt schizophrenic, a stranger in his own mind.

Later he would know the cause of her insanity, but that still divided him: how to have sympathy for someone who was destroying the lives of his loved ones?

He can be repulsively nostalgic about their unknowing encounters, with the agreeable exploring, discovering, creative collaboration, the love for words, harmony of contents and form. And in particular – what an irony from hell – their thoughts on the power that media, commerce and politics have over children. They agreed and got along immediately, and the affinity grew, with humor as well as feeling.

As to her age, she could be his daughter, but that didn't seem relevant. Or did she have a father complex? At the time that question never entered his mind. After their lengthy and intense interviews and a number of emails in between, he thought some signs of falling in a sort of love were mutual. But for her there proved to be a special, pretty stable relationship with Evan.

Bernard knew that it was no flirtation from either, and this Evan was the father of her child, who looked after her despite his own shock. It was heartrending, the frantic way he wanted to take care of Art and her at the same time while dealing with the intruder. Both men stayed calm or frozen, sensible and tactful, in the first place for Art's sake, who he went on calling Reg. They didn't pull at the boy, nor scream or call each other names. Bernard didn't even need to control himself; after the perplexity there came a primal stillness over him, as if to force everyone to take their time, a few minutes or hours if need be – after the eternity of uncertainty.

For an instant they were staring at each other and at Art, but Evan must have seen the sincerity of the senior's emotions, who dropped Anne's personal belongings helplessly.

Bernard began murmuring, "Art... sweetheart... Arthur?"

Although Evan did know the kidnapped boy's name, the truth remained unreal to him too: how could this have anything to do with Anne and via her with himself? But a minute ago her icy return home said enough, with slow and retroactive effects.

In a reflex Bernard's arms reached for Art again, and Evan handed him over instinctively – "not the way one is happy to give a child to his granddad," a passer-by might think. And Art was fine with it, always curious.

Although only a part of Evan got the picture then, he stopped mumbling "Reggie". It would be days before Anne was able to speak at all, and much longer before she could say what had happened to Reg. She had no idea that she lost two babies.

<>

"Does Art have this talent for falling and bumping," Nomi says, "or is it me and my stress?"

Is his presence that prominent?

"It's driving me nuts too," Mark admits. "I'm holding my breath all day, waiting for a bang or clatter."

"He's so different from Dilli, isn't he?"

"Has always been," Mark says. "I mean... Except the first six months."

"Yes, when he wasn't crawling around yet."

And after that... They can't remember if it was like this when he came back. Those first weeks after, they got lost in time, they were in a holiday mood but seemed worn out. Dilli could skip school for a day here and there – on very special leave – and at first she didn't want to go back.

Art stood and took his first steps along the pen railing. Then he fell ill.

"Is that a reaction to this fast development?" Nomi asked Mark.

"Or it's all the big changes. And some children's diseases are inevitable. Some doctors will say 'necessary'. But not the first year?"

Art stood up anyway and his legs literally gave way. After three days he was better, but Nomi and Mark were woken a few times each night, confused between fatigue and relief: what would they have given the other week to be woken by Art numerous times a night?

They went to check on him and couldn't sleep anymore.

For weeks they cancelled as many appointments as possible, but sometimes they were aimless when he slept long hours – in his own cot – and they couldn't sing to him or take him cycling or swimming.

Initially they were unable to be strict or angry when the children 'teased' each other, or one woke the other up at six a.m.

They were on the News again but gave no interviews, in spite of powerful and persuasive requests, "Your story can be an example. You will inspire lots of people!"

Substantial 'fees' were offered, also by magazine and network editors with integrity, which were declined without much thought and ado.

"But you could donate the money to great children's charities," a friend or two would suggest. And "Use it to create something wonderful for Art, for later." Or they told Nomi, "You can show your side of the matter, to get rid of people's doubts and blame."

After a month or so, life seemed to grow tolerably regular again, as if the two months before had been caught up with.

"The poor darling," Nomi says, "he's covered in bruises and never whines."

"Not about that."

But Nomi worries. "If we see a doctor, he or she will be suspicious."

Instead of "How do you mean?" Mark asks, "Don't you think that something is wrong with him?"

"Because he fell on his head once?"

In the rare careless failing presence of Mark or Nomi – a risk for any parent, fit or tired.

"Or who knows what went on *there*."

Phrases like 'that house' or 'the gap' are still avoided when possible.

"For all we know, he may have fallen down the stairs or something. That happens in every family, but we wouldn't know about it."

"Nor," says Mark, "what she would've done."

"The smallest brain damage in a child can cause a muscle disorder, a lack of control, showing when they grow and seem wild or clumsy."

Mark swallows. "Did anyone ask the woman about such things? The police, a doctor, her psychiatrist?"

"As if asking would help."

Nomi remembers – wouldn't part with Art another minute, during a medical check-up, but there were standard police procedures and she understood that, she wouldn't make a scene. He looked healthy and happy, well-fed, developed in all aspects, but nobody knew what Anne's mind had been like. Nomi obliged silently; she didn't want them to find her possessive or hysteric.

Outside the house where Art was discovered with a streak of fate, Mark asked, "Do you want me to join you in the hospital, or collect Dilli first?"

Why did he leave it up to her? At that moment the whole world consisted solely of Art, and she couldn't think properly, but she said, "Collect Dilli, please."

Of course?

"It's creepy, though, to leave you alone. Well, you're with Art. Holy Mo, Art is with us again!"

It's too crazy to scream or cheer and jump or stamp, like winning a sports final.

Nomi shook herself awake. "Will you and Dilli come over directly?"

"Yes, she'll be part of it all. That's good for everyone."

When Art was carried off, Nomi stayed close, but in the hospital they took her to a waiting-room. She made no fuss and didn't go mad from derision. A psychologist came to have a chat with her. He was personal and observant – to see if Nomi could cope? Whether Art would be back in safe hands, with people of sound minds? One of them left him behind in the street.

While Art was elsewhere in the vast building, soon after he was found, she wanted to kick and yell, but she put on an armor and kept so cool that the psychologist studied her even more. He gave her a compliment but asked new questions.

He gave her his card and said, "Feel free to drop by no matter for what reason or when. It's a considerable plight, what you've been through, and still are."

Free of charge? From the goodness of his heart, or as a case study for his PhD?

Would he have this kind of conversation with Mark too?

Who knows what he'd tell Hattum or anyone: Keep a sharp eye on her.

But why not accept his kindness at face value. When will she be able to trust herself and others again?

When Dilli came in running and glowing, Nomi burst into tears and hurried to explain that grown-ups cry from happiness. It was a minute before Dilli agreed.

The psychologist smiled at Dilli's uncomplicated and unmitigated excitement. As far as he could see, this girl had no symptoms of any problems whatsoever.

"There's no need to go and talk with that woman yet, Anne Hoaver?" Nomi asks between hope and fear. "Are the tumbling and scrambling a part of Art's character?"

"You mean," Mark says with a grin, "he trips over his own legs from eagerness, interest, liveliness, willpower... Taking after Bernard and you?"

"It seems," she says in earnest, "that he's got absolutely everything of you and me together. He counts for two! And he will find his balance alright. Or should we make inquiries with someone else? Because in those two months, anything may have happened, at his age."

"You know what, Nome, if you truly wish... That man of hers

looked like a decent guy. He had no clue either! And the way he yielded Art or gave him back... Bernard said it was heroic."

"Yes, to prevent appalling scenes. With a gut feeling."

Mark thinks. "We might get in touch with that partner, if he wants. Maybe for ten minutes and see how it goes?"

"Via Hattum?" Nomi asks.

"Or we should leave it with Bernard, who was there!"

"But he's got enough on his mind, I believe. I don't think he's been very fit. And would that personal role be wise?"

<>

It bothers Anne sometimes, that Evan has done so much for her, including finances. The contrast with 'previously' stays eerie. Is he too good to be true, the kind of person who thrives when his help is needed, for a sense of purpose and feeling useful? Action and tension can fill empty days. That goes for most people, but in some it's more obvious or sinister than in others, and she's awfully dependent. When will that be over?

Never mind, you fool, and be fair: Evan has an interesting job in Marketing, he's fine without the crap.

Doctor Grant thinks it's time for big, new steps. Fortunately he's not saying: You're making nice progress. Has she always hated that phrase or just now?

Grant would like to see Evan several times as well, and Anne has praised him vigorously, but Evan is no fan of "therapists and such", and there's no obligation at all. About the TV shows of traumas and tears and vulnerable love, he says, "The networks make fortunes out of this national peeping!"

"Evan, I'm not going on television, am I?"

"Sorry."

She jests wryly, "The ratings would hit the sky and cause a powercut."

It's the first time that Anne makes a self-mocking joke on the subject, and Evan dares adding to that, "Just hypothetical, if you had the opportunity to clear your name with your part of the story, for example sided by Grant or Cindy and doctor Mullan, in comfortable surroundings, not live, and you'd have a say in the editing, would you consider that?"

Anne gazes at him and he continues hastily, "Not to bare your soul but give the facts. Not as emo-TV, but as journalism in a quality program, in your own way, like your best article!"

The tragedy has not messed with your writing.

What's there to lose?

Sure, let's do a confrontation with the other mother.

Anne's sarcasm is fierce. "For how much cash would you do it?"

"No no, Anne, I didn't mean anything about money, and sorry, what's got into me?"

"You see," says her own devil's advocate, "it could be a true possibility, for my own sake, to show that I'm no monster or loser. The dough would be a good-cause bonus. So, for what figures would you go on camera if you were me?"

"Ah... A million?"

And he laughs his words away, but she says, "Mind you, before you know it, your bluff is picked up and you've signed a contract."

"Well, with a load of money, you could start all over, build a new life."

"Without a job?" Anne asks with a torn mind.

"That would be your call. For a thousand grand you can change identities."

"Right, in a far-away country, I suppose."

"Of your choice," he says.

"Ah, you know a lot about it."

"Hm, you have no idea!"

And Evan's charm is enchanting again. He can be so himself, open, and honest with humor and toughness and feeling all in one. What more could she wish for? It also means that he's taking her seriously, including the playfulness, if that's what it is.

Grateful, she flies around his neck, and they kiss and caress, for the first time since the other life, into which she's hurled back now, under an avalanche of warm snow with chunks of ice, touching her intimate spots. In a mount of mixed feelings.

She's not letting go yet. The incongruous contrast of hardness and softness keeps her hot and cold. It's quite different from times ago. And she thinks: how has he managed? His urges must be bursting, a man of flesh and blood would crush boundaries, or has he found satisfaction with others? That would be only natural. Don't ask!

His erection tarries and makes her melt. They sigh and pant. Their lips and fingertips are looking for tender bits of skin. Shirts and jeans are slipping off. Each body fiber is susceptible between the muscles and pores of tensing buttocks and spreading legs. He licks her hollows, and she clasps his heart and soul.

Next they fold like spoons, nearly motionless, feeling each other from head to feet without a thought, not even that lovemaking can be a deep consolation.

Her legs pull up, so that her tailbone presses on his stomach and crotch. His arm can feel how supple and smooth her breasts and front neck are. Eventually the power of his penis moves between her thighs and bottom cleft, down to the front side. They're heaving and sharing a climax.

After prosaic fidgeting with tissues, they're lying on their backs, as close as can be.

"This way, we haven't made a baby, have we?" Anne says as if it's another era.

She looks dreamy, and Evan can't actually tell if it was a remark or question, jocular or melancholic.

"No," he says. And after a lull, "I take it you don't want to?"

"Do you?"

He clears his throat. "Maybe some day."

For the ultimate second chance.

Her "surprised and anxious *with me?*" remains unsaid.

"Have you thought about it then?" she asks.

"Well, about the possibility."

Or the risks. Wish and responsibility.

"You?" he asks.

In God's name, what sort of egotism are we talking about?

Her hand is on the nearest skin: his upper leg. He wipes his eyes, puts the arms behind his head and stretches his body. She turns and lies on him at full length, her head on his neck, suppressing a memory: it's the way Reg lay on her between life and death.

"No," she says. "But Cindy is pregnant."

"Oh. That's brave too."

"Why?"

He blows a wisp of her hair from his cheek. "Same for everybody: the future is going to be a rough time."

Anne slides off him again, but a hand is left on his chest. "Ev, you're not saying that parts of the world will be flooded, are you, due to climate crisis?" It's everywhere, on the daily News, not sparing people who scare easily: the damage is done.

"Even the Vatican is anxious. I guess they expect a second Flood and want good seats in the Ark. Reserved and deserved? Anyhow, it seems a big deal to be raising kids with confidence."

Especially with me.

She does ask, "Why has that been on your mind?"

"Because I'm no pessimist. I like challenges, torch bearers, the continuance of life with or without Noah."

It might be good or disastrous for us, as a bitter cure, but not for the child?

Two years ago, with the first pregnancy, didn't he have doubts – in the second instance or second life?

The switching from Reg to Art and back, dead and alive, their boy and somebody else's, began with the smallest steps and shocks of awareness at Grant's. Later on, her own at home and in the outer world, not in words yet, not in emails to anyone. That might be possible with a stranger. But a new stage is drawing nearer, as she's noticed in spite of herself.

The baby of Cindy and Rob could induce a breakthrough, but

the very thought of a baby in her arms again someday... A child can't serve her purpose this way and take the rap!

Television displays adorable babies alive and kicking, in spotless commercials with perfect mothers, in celebrity shows and reality soaps about adoption, with tandem parents and sperm donors, reporting: "I put my profile on this website, there were sixty replies, I picked a couple, and we went out for dinner and one of them clicked so good. We had a few shots at it and the second time was a hit."

They celebrate the New Normal.

She can switch channels quickly, but babies or abortion and death also feature in good films, whether thrillers or romance and comedies. Then she turns the screen off but will see the same things in books or the papers. And if life is turned off...

I'll ask Grant about the pill again.

Evan's hand is traveling her arm and side, dawdling on the hip before it returns.

She may have heard him asking, "When the time comes, will you babysit at Cindy's?"

Or maybe he said, "Can you?" as in "Will they let you?"

Such slips of the tongue or misunderstandings occur easily. It's too late now to raise her head and hear better. Nor does she ask him to repeat the question, and without an amendment he's waiting for her answer.

"Oh," she says, "that's six months from now."

Anything can happen before then.

"Yeah, sorry, first things first."

Similarly it's no use thinking of the baby clothes that must still be in the wardrobe or a box, available to someone else? Or to be preserved for when she'll be able to dispose of them – in a charity bag?

. . .

It's broad daylight on the carpet, where they're lying in the sunshine, but she shivers and gets up to put her clothes on. All of a sudden, it sinks in sharply that this is temporary, her staying among Evan's things here in his apartment, because life was turned inside out. Her house, that belonged to both of them first, is theirs again, if not on paper, and he keeps or guards it for a future of some kind: a restart or closure. This anonymous building is a perfect place for her to lie low.

So far 'one day at a time' has been sufficient and safe. Evan took charge for her sake;, he knew what was necessary for her. Today she stops to think about all sorts of things. She needs to act somehow, can't wait and see anymore what others do or ask from her.

She can see that he wavers with his clothes. Where is his home at the moment? The choice between taking a shower or not can be significant to both of them. They miss those days in the house with the action and sweetness around the little guy, who required care without the least preference, politeness, or sentimentality. There was just his pain during diaper changing when he had a bad rash from teething.

Now she wishes that Evan had known Reg, the right one, and the thought is too fresh: that possibility can't be over yet, can it?

<>

"Thank you, Bernard, I will read *Sudden Depth* and forward it to a director I am working with – we are actively looking for material for her first feature. Best, Debbie."

He gives an ecstatic little yell: he's in direct contact with a producer/financer and a director who are interested in the story for their feature film. He googles Debbie Atkins until he's found the director. He goes on searching, watches trailers of their work and thinks that *Sudden Depth* would be a great match.

To regain his breath after an attempt at tax returns – with delay permission – Bernard casts an impulsive glance of distraction, just for a laugh, at *The number 1 dating site*, that he happened to see in a commercial before the News the other day. Does everyone need an excuse like that?

At once the screen is filled with model-like photos of gorgeous young people – all real and seeking? Coy, eye-caressing, self-assured and sometimes hesitant, they're looking at him, arranged around the flashy invitation: *Enroll for Free*, made extra appealing by the announcement that 49,276 members are now online. Is this hot & cool on a Friday afternoon?

The Safe-Dating Quality logo is reassuring, but before he can learn more about these fellow, curious humans, there's a lot to be filled out.

Promptly after his click on "I'm a man looking for a woman", all the photos are women - still pretty and young! His age selection "between 35 and 55" doesn't change anything here.

With "year of birth" most people will lie a little and so should he on equal terms, but that's not how Bernard wants to begin this nudge of fate, even though it's merely a brief experiment, having heard so many success tales about it. Sincerity should be a good method of selection.

To protect his identity, the date of birth is adapted.

Undaunted, he clicks on CONTINUE.

With the postal code he'd like to cheat slightly too, but in stern red it says, "Your postal code is not valid." And after his correction, the name of his town jumps into sight right away. Hm... What is 'careful or paranoid'?

"Your profile. Tell more about yourself. Members with a full profile have 15 times more visitors."

To what extent are you open to a relationship?
- ☐ I'll keep that to myself
- ☐ We'll leave that to fate
- ☐ Not at all
- ☐ I'd love to

At the section *relation status* will he say "widower", or would that put women off? "I'll keep that to myself" sounds revolting here.

The paragraph "Your personality" has about twenty adjective boxes, of which he'd like to tick four, but no matter what he tries, only one box stays ticked.

Hey, there, a man can be both social and sensitive, can't he?

What about "occupation": will he veil *Writer* as *Editor*?

Ah, "Tell us more about your job" can be skipped!

"Your headline" seems to be a shopwindow or eye-catcher. Will he use keywords like love, humor, adventure, feeling, sharing, authenticity, honesty? He needs to find and describe what he stands for. How to finish this fast and unscathed, with enough meaning?

Help! They want an all-in profile text, forcing him to take an objective look at himself. Will it be something like "Profound, eager to learn, thoughtful, physical, emotional, homey, fond of nature, still waters run deep"? Or is that silly and presumptuous rubbish?

Photos will bring you 7x more attention.

But then every psychopath might recognize me!

So what, who for Pete's sake do you think you are?

Ha, that's what should be in this profile, for instance, "An absent-minded introvert, wary of society with its testing demands and noise and devices, but he's also a cocky extravert who contacts film-hot-shots abroad."

OK, a recent portrait of his is uploadable and won't do any harm; it's no revealing close-up. Anyway, this is research – claim all the authors when they do ridiculous things.

"Congratulations! Your entry has been completed."

And what has this fishing expedition brought forth?

Yuck, "Fun girl seeks fun guy for fun things," or, "I'm looking to share ups and downs". However, there are a few beautiful and engaging photos, also from a woman in his area. *Find out more!* the site shrieks. Before paying, visitors can see just enough to be enraptured and tantalized.

"Kind and quiet woman, 49, would like to meet a sweet and honest man. Cheerful but realistic. Faithful with a certain personal freedom. No-claim loyalty. I can enjoy tiny and ordinary things. According to others I'm warm, caring, respectful."

But that lovely person is on the other side of the country.

One candidate lives close to Nomi. "Pastime: ramble around nature, bird-spotting, play the piano, cycling, read novels, computer, cooking, be snug on the couch by the fireplace with a glass of wine and classical music, musing after a fulfilling day. Favorite places: the mountains and coasts. Latest book: Anna Enquist."

. . .

Presently Bernard is lost, with a tingle in his heart and crotch. He can start *Special Membership* at a reduced price, but he's heard about the risk of being "stuck forever". *Send unlimited messages, discover your true match!* Ah, with all his career plans he has no time for this! Moreover, he's an unsuitable recluse, or a chicken.

Now he's too tired to resume doing his taxes as well. Is his ongoing fatigue natural? It's more like a chronic touch of flu, both cold and sweaty, with a sore throat. Or something even worse?

While there are chores that he keeps postponing – and perhaps that's what makes him sick – he walks into the garden to see what's budding there. Mm, the singing and winging of sprightly birds fill the windcalm with promises.

Alright, this afternoon he'll go for a hike at a firm pace and see friends. But the phone rings and it's Dilli, pleading, "I want to play in your house so much. Not with Art!"

"Oh, Dil, that's fine."

"A long time?"

"Has Mom said that?"

"Yes, because Art knocks everything over."

"Your Lego?"

"Yeah, the plane!"

"And you've just built it?"

"Yes, finished."

"I see. Is Mom there?"

"In the bathroom upstairs. Art has thrown up on the carpet."

"Oh. How come?"

"From nothing, he's OK. You know, when I'm six, can I pick my clothes?"

<>

In the dead of night, Nomi can hear that Art is awake. After drowsing and saying little prayers, she feels him crawling into bed beside her. Admiring him for coming down the stairs in scant light, she's glad that he's made no noise and deeply thankful that he's home – two years after – but the sleep is still dominant.

She sees him constantly with her eyes closed: lean and lithe, the deep expression, his hair growing darker and thicker by the day. If wise for his age, how come?

Even with her back facing him, she's not too worried anymore that he'll be crushed or smothered, as before and after the two-month hiatus. It's faded, not forgotten, and she has been thinking about it frequently these days – due to the news about criminals being released?

She doesn't want to relive any instant from back then, but all things lacking keep her incomplete and divided. To her distress she'd like to probe that woman's life yet. It's insane, as if she'll be a better person when she knows more about the 'culprit' or 'perpetrator'.

The nouns have been kept as neutral as possible. 'Abductor' or 'kidnapper' was too charged. The police and Mark did mention her name, but Nomi kept aloof and shirked from newspapers too.

She still has bad dreams about some raw moments, and by day they tend to linger, undermining, independent.

On television one sees only the initials of murderers and high-profile delinquents – to hide what? Everybody knows who they are! The News will show photos with these bars over the eyes, as if their identities are hidden this way! And what is posted on YouTube... Even the police make use of such videos.

Nomi hates to toss and fret and lose her head.

A small hand is climbing her shoulder, exploring her neck and head, before resting on her face. She seems like a drunk lying in a park or under a parked car, touched and prodded by kids.

If Art knows that she's awake, her keeping still will feel like a rejection. If she lets him stay, he'll come every night, and in one way that would be a joy.

She whispers, "Hi, Artie, it's the middle of the night, I need to go on sleeping."

Still trying to find the right thing to do, she can't feel his hand anymore and dozes off.

Thirty minutes later she sees that he's quietly made a jigsaw puzzle on the floor, in the semi darkness.

"Come, sweetie, we'll change diapers, and you can sleep nice and comfy in your cot again."

He does not protest.

By eight in the morning Dilli has built a complex railroad in a town around half the living-room. At a rectangular junction she tells policeman Mark, who drives a sleepy car, "Here you must not look round but look square."

Mark doesn't answer much, he asks Nomi during her slow breakfast, "Why won't Bernard come and pick her up?"

"I think he's struggling with his health."

"Bernard tells you that?"

"Well," says Nomi, "not in those words."

"Was it your idea to drive Dil over?" he asks.

"Yes, you are taking Art to gym class, and I can do with an outing – to my old home."

"Oh, since when?"

"Ha," Nomi laughs, "as a young adult I needed my distance. Didn't you?"

"Yeah, I came all the way here, and my folks are still jealous of Bernard, being close."

"But they have each other!"

"Yes," Mark says. "It's still a shame about Hannah."

After a minute's pause it's Dilli who says, "When I've been dead and I come back, can I be a boy?"

Mark's police car stops at a rail crossing a long time.

"Yes," Nomi says, "that would make sense."

"And can I choose a Mom and Dad?"

"Um... If you wish..."

"Good, I'll be with you again."

"Oh Dil, I'd be over the moon." Although it's probably not supposed to work like that. "But first you're here now, for so long that you can't count the days."

"A thousand?" Dilli says.

"And much more."

"OK. And Granddad too, with his health. But how old is he?"

"Fifty-six."

"Oh. Let's go."

Before it's too late.

After chewing a pensive bite of breakfast, Nomi says, "Yes, Dil, in about an hour. I'll have a shower first, before Art is up."

The times they got edgy when Art never seemed to wake up, are in the past, particularly now that he's fooling around by night – no one knows how long, and why?

At Bernard's, Dilli expects to go cycling and racing down hills or watching the ships immediately, but Nomi tarries with coffee and a cookie, or something preying on her mind.

"Wait, Dil, do a puzzle or a drawing first?"

"No, I've done them at home."

"Oh. Granddad will be out with you soon. You go and look where the birds can build their nests?"

"Yes, and ride my bike to the other path?"

"Up to the street corner, where you can hear me if I call you. No further!"

Bernard shares her doubts about giving Dilli this freedom, but they don't want to be over-protective, or pass concern on to her.

"Call hard, Mom, cos my bike is a motor!"

"OK. And you brake on time on that fast motorbike!"

They wave arms as if Dilli goes traveling, and she tears out of the garden.

Bernard holds his breath for her, the plants, and pedestrians. As well as for Nomi, asking her, "Special plans today?"

She smiles and surrenders already. "How did you guess?"

"What?"

"That I'm up to something scary, which I'd like to keep a secret for now."

He says, "I prefer scary to nasty, so tell me all about it, and my lips will be sealed."

The other expression, 'be silent as the grave', is not used anymore.

With a twinge in her face she asks, "Are you still in contact with this publisher, regarding *Time-In*?"

"Simon. Yes, it's pleasant and titillating, but not about that book right now."

"What's the partner of that woman called again?"

After an instant, Bernard understands the leaps of her thoughts. "Evan."

"Yes. Do you reckon he still lives there?"

"Hm, I think it was her house, but other than that I don't know."

The moment outside that house comes back to him so close that he shudders, which Nomi can see. She recognizes the twisted mixture of rare joy and horror; the way one can be hot and cold from the flu. It's hard to believe how they're talking about it now, with the name and all of somebody who was in a different world. At the time she did hear how the "contact" came about, but it hasn't sunk in till now that monsters may be human too – with whom Art had a normal time? – with a life ahead of them. Their memories of Art will forever be shared unequally.

6
RETURNING AND FORWARD

<>

Cycling to the station, Anne sees the election posters on tall boards, disfiguring the pretty town. As they can't be 'read' from a bike, let alone from a car, it's a pointless eye- and mind-sore. A striking parallel could make a good column for NUNA: the tobacco industry saves billions a year, owing to the publicity ban.

She'll process her brainstorm, because she can go back to NUNA, can't she? Her pseudonym should be intact. Even *Time-In* could be continued – under any name Simon likes – and she has more time than ever, if she's ready.

But her bike almost hits a wall: how the hell could she forget that Bloomsdale featured in that, or still does. For that very reason she has more time than before.

From self-hatred, the contempt of her stupidity, madness and more, she needs to pull over and wait. But it's also a good sign, since forgetting means leaving behind. Except when the ground sinks from beneath her.

She doesn't want to miss her session with Grant. In a weird way it's a good thing that Bernard Bloomsdale has crept into her head again after the black hole. She takes another look at the crooked, cheap nailing and pasting of the political parties. The elections are over! For how long will these blotted and scratched leaders be hopeless here? As if they are the mental patients!

With new strength and feeling in her legs, she straightens her bike and herself.

There's also a growing and tormenting wish to visit playgrounds and farms for children. The salt in a wound will smart, and that may clean it. But hers is covered in a thick and big plaster cast, where the soreness is followed by itching, which means healing. And if you can't scratch? That resembles an aching need to visit a kids farm or playground.

Her entire body longs for a child on her lap, in her arms, at home and out in the crowds. He would run off to play again and return, to share both fun and pain. She won't be egotistic or possessive or pushy.

On the train she gets her laptop, but the seat opposite is taken by a woman of about eighty, with a wondering and sweet eye that Anne finds hard to avoid.

"I like the top deck," the lady says with a smile, "so in case of a crash there's not very much to fall on top of me."

"I like it up here too," Anne says, glad to be not the only one with thoughts like that.

"The steps are tricky for me these days but getting off it's downhill."

"Yes, which is better than the other way around."

The woman laughs. "Hello, my name is Pat."

"Um... Anne. Are you traveling far?"

"I hope to Limeport, I'm not sure yet."

"Ah, as far as possible?"

"Yes, exactly," says Pat. "But I won't disturb you."

"No, that's not why I asked. I'm a disturbed person anyway."

"Oh, so am I!" And Pat wipes an eye. "My husband is driving me mad, and he doesn't notice or won't act on it. He won't wear hearing aids, for instance. We have bought a pair, don't ask what they cost, but Cas finds them tiresome. It would take some getting used to, but he won't give them a chance."

"Hm," Anne says, "I have a mother like that."

"You have?"

"Exhausting."

"True," says Pat. "I can't speak loud all day and repeat everything, while it's unnecessary!"

"It gives you a sore throat?"

"And more, indeed. Is your mother hard of hearing too?"

"Something like that," Anne says with a grimace.

"Is she in your care?"

"No, God forbid, she wouldn't. We don't meet very often."

"Oh," Pat says, "that's tragic. Does she live far away?"

"Yes, a whole stretch toward Limeport."

"Ha, are you going there now?"

"Nah," says Anne, "not that far."

"Too bad. Sorry, I won't bother you."

"And um, Cas has no idea that he's a burden?"

"Well, I do tell him, but if he won't hear..."

"So, you're on strike now?"

"That sounds good, yes. At first I just stopped talking. But that's sad too, isn't it? And he keeps asking questions, driving me up the wall! Now I leave notes, like the names of visitors. It's silly, isn't it? I mean, we were at the audiologist's half a morning, and his hearing aids are ready for use! I do love him, and if he were genuinely deaf, I'd be happy to help, invent all kinds of smart and comical support."

"But he's just being obstinate?" Anne says. "And you thought..."

"No, I stopped thinking. It seems I called a taxi and packed a bag. Look: wallet, toilet bag and a book."

"To stay the night somewhere?"

Pat is still surprised. "I didn't realize, till the driver said, 'Where to?'"

To one of your children? Anne would like to ask.

Pat goes on, "The station was the first thing that came into my head."

"And now you're here. Very well done."

"So I'm no lunatic? Thank you, thank you. I feel ashamed and guilty, but that's not helpful, and I will go back, I won't leave him in the lurch."

"No." Anne is firm. "You're going to tell him that *he* is letting *you* down."

"Do you think so? Does Cas know what he's doing then?"

On the other side of the aisle a handsome and fancy-clothed young man sits down, who appears to have looked for a quiet spot at great length. Perhaps he was out in the cool air for a long time, since he's sniffing considerably, and he may have a cold, because the annoying sniffing won't stop.

Pat has gazed his way a few times and blown her nose demonstratively, as an example or indication, then she takes a half-full packet of tissues, moves to the man and offers it kindly with the words, "Can these be of use?"

Gaping at her and the tissues, he takes them automatically, but before Pat has sat down trimly again, the man gets to his feet and leaves.

"Oh," Pat whispers to Anne, "I was going to say: I won't need them back."

Anne restrains her laughter until the neat man is gone.

"Too bad," says Pat. "Or do you have a man? Sorry, I'm overwrought or bonkers, but let's hope it's temporary. And I won't be nosy."

"Ha!" Anne wants to embrace her, but she puts a hand on her knee politely, saying, "Your mind is one of the soundest I know. People who've lost it – hear who's talking – may not agree, even if it's plump in front of their noses. This gentleman can have an excellent job, but he doesn't know what kind of noise he makes."

"And," Pat says, "if he has no clue, he can't be blamed. I should've done this differently." And with a nod toward Anne's laptop she asks, "Do you have an agreeable job?"

So many thoughts are flashing through Anne's head that she's like a multiple personality. If a station was coming up now, she could hasten off the train, although she'd miss the appointment with her case worker, the start of new times, that she needs more than ever. Between stations she could sneak away like the fancy man, dodging lies. Or she can tell Pat: Yes, good on you to remind me, this needs finishing today.

With an apologetic gesture she opens the laptop unambiguously, without hurting Pat's feelings.

Pat gets her book and looks for the page where she left off when Cas asked if it was Thursday for the tenth time while the note *Friday* was in front of him, as well as today's paper.

"I've had a wonderful job," Anne says yet when there's no pressure.

She's gazing past Pat, who wasn't reading attentively.

The pause is open and expectant rather than uneasy. They're looking at each other, at their hands and out the window, where fields are gliding by, some with sheep and horses, until a stretch of woods bring unrest to their eyes with the sun flickering through trees.

"And yes, there is a man," Anne says. "We used to live together."

Pat waits placidly to hear if there's more.

What time is it: a quarter to nine? Is that why the train is quiet, or only this carriage?

"Do you have children?" Anne asks in a low and respectful voice, bending over a little.

"Yes," Pat says, "two sons. One in the city and one down the coast."

Her voice and breathing give away that she has a lot to say, but her eyes convey that she'd like to be modest or let Anne speak, who visibly has difficulty with that.

The variation in the landscape and sounds of the train try to help.

"We had a son," Anne says just audibly, more or less for the first time in her life. "He died after six months. Cot death."

Her throat is burning, and her forehead is feverish, but she's so cold, as if her bones are exposed.

When the loudspeaker announces a station, some stumbling begins by the door.

The phrases *I'm sorry to hear that* and *Sorry for your loss* are dreaded by translators. Most languages have no more than *condolences* and *sympathies*.

Pat has been silent, softly wiping her face.

The train stops and new passengers get on. A girl and boy in their late teens flop down by the window on the other side and show each other funny things on a tablet.

Before the train is rolling again, Pat stands up and takes her coat off. She picks up the things from the seat next to Anne, puts them with her coat on the seat where she was, across, and she sits down close beside Anne on the aisle side, so that Anne is concealed from everyone and won't feel Pat's eyes on her either.

The train is making a steady sound again.

"When was it?" Pat asks.

"Almost two years ago."

Then I took someone else's baby, could be said now without much danger. Even if Pat were to blab and tell the tale, which most people already know, there would be no problem, unless she'd shout here: are you this hideous kid snatcher?

There would be long and anxious minutes to the next station.

But Anne says, "Reg. His name is Reg."

As if to taste how that sounds in public.

What a good name, Pat would like to say, after anyone? But she doesn't trust her voice. She'd hate to create a drama for Anne.

"The present tense is strange, isn't it?" Anne says. "But it is right. His name is still Reg, if tough to say out loud. I couldn't bear it if another boy were called Reg now. When a popular TV presenter mentions the name of his newborn, a thousand will be called the same."

Pat must know that babbling about banal things can be a defence against pains of the soul.

Anne takes such a deep breath that Pat's side can feel it through her clothes.

Pat hesitates and says, "I think it hurts extra if the present is separated from other times, especially the future."

Anne sighs and nods. "I'll have to make for the past first. I should hit the emergency brake of time, to take a slow train back and get off at every station."

"No, don't, only at central stations."

Anne trembles. "There are sprinter trains with these sharp tones when doors open and close – like sirens."

"Made for people like Cas!"

Anne's laughter is too loud. "They give me headaches. They make me understand how a dog feels, that hears the high tones ten times as hard as humans. It's about safety, but why no lovely tram bell?"

"Yes, have you told them yet?"

"Ha, they'll see me coming – from the loony bin."

Pat grins, but she casts a glance at Anne and is startled by her seriousness. "Tell me about it. Half the world is a madhouse."

"You mean the White House?"

And they continue as in a polyphonic song, where it doesn't matter who sings which note, as long as it's in harmony.

"Just like Wall Street and The City. Or Brussels and Hollywood."

"Not to mention Beijing and Moscow."

"Japan slaughters a thousand whales for so-called science."

"Toddlers go to schools with laptops."

"And behold the results. How is their English these days?"

"It's called Media Speak."

"And universities... There's a Professor of Pop-Music Marketing now."

"So there, who exactly has lost their minds?"

"Do you have grandchildren?" Anne asks, and never mind the abruptness.

"Across the ocean!" Pat says immediately. "I tell them: don't fuss for my funeral. They run a small hotel in the hills there. Another slope has been felled for skiing, so there will be a mud flood, I suppose. And then I can't go to their funeral. Oh, my girl, forgive me!"

She grabs Anne's hand and squeezes it, rubbing it with her thumbs.

Anne recoils an inch, wringing both hands. She stands up but sits again and looks out. The couple on the other side are busy with digital devices, wearing ear sets.

"Ladies and gentlemen," it sounds clear and businesslike, "our next station..."

Anne gathers her things, but she sits another instant and says over-calmly, "When Reg died, I stole a baby. I'm sorry."

Without looking at Pat, she leans to her sideways and gets up. The train passes point and sways, a danger that children love to feel in their legs. With an effort, bumping left and right, Anne keeps her balance and makes for the narrow aisle to the door. At the top of the steps, she needs to hold a post in order to stay on her feet, although the train has steadied again.

Pat stares after her until the train has stopped. Then she looks for a pen and some paper frantically, she tears a blank piece from her book and writes her phone number on it.

She worms her way past people coming in. From the doorway she can see Anne going down the platform slowly. Calling out, she gets off and hurries up to her, waving the note.

Anne has turned around, but she stays put.

Pat hands her the phone number, panting. "If you want... Be

welcome. I'm not due anywhere, that's to say... I would join you now, but I don't know... And my things!"

She points to the train and stumbles back on time.

"Don't worry," she cries out of breath, "Cas never answers the phone!"

Anne shakes her head and nods, not yet realizing what Pat was trying to say – for possibilities, a future based on fellow humanship?

<>

Nomi can't ask for directions along these lines: do you know the house where the abducted baby lived? Without knowing a street name, she can't but follow a damaged memory or her intuition, which was rattled as well. With her bare hands she needs to grope for sharp fractions of the broken past.

As an estate agent, she's used to observing neighborhoods. It can give an inspiring prickle to look ahead and see through facades. Mark and she detect their professional deformations: the interest in properties even in painful situations.

However, Nomi can't remember where she was when Mark phoned and blurted, "Stay where you are and wait for me, I'll come and fetch you, don't budge."

Certain facts can't be uttered on the phone. He could not keep his voice under control. All the same it was just as well that Bernard had called Mark first, who knew where she was at work.

From the soles of her feet upwards she felt that it was about Art. Unable to ask for details, she obeyed and didn't do anything foolish. A delicate certainty spread slowly. Each minute froze and melted.

The unbelievable didn't reach her completely until Mark arrived and held her. "Art is back. He's alright. Bernard has found him."

She can't recall how and when they were joined by Hattum. Firstly, Mark was driving, and she still can't understand how he could. Even now it's taking all control to steer and watch the signs and find the way. Thirty or twenty miles an hour is nothing, but also hazardously fast.

Right now, she needs to be dragged back into a time that turned her inside out. She's inclined to close her eyes, for the right or wrong concentration: to persevere or to flee and dream away. Her clammy hands can slip off the wheel and her lame feet may skid off the pedals. Watch it, you have two children to look after.

In registered therapy practices with integrity, people are hypnotized and led back to places and moments that were wiped from their consciousness. These are physically provable, and yet one word or finger click from the therapist can hurl people back into the here and now, for explanations or integration.

Not for shows on television, prodding armors.

Nomi has watched sober documentaries, and she does believe in the works of the unconscious, but who'd get her to go that far? She would only if it could help Art.

She's reached the house where he lived those months. Diagonally across the street she parks her car with closed windows. She turns the engine off and puts her sunglasses on. She's on the sidewalk side of the car and assumes to be barely visible from the house, across the garden and street, through the car.

The oddest thoughts pop up: it's a good street for children to grow up in, with broad sidewalks, old trees and hardly any traffic. She could live here; it's a touch rural as well as close to town, neither posh nor cheap.

She takes the binoculars that are always in the dashboard box, usable here when nobody is passing by on foot or wheels. Over the low net curtains of the house, she discerns the main curtains in corners, the top of a closet, a ceiling lamp. The premises are well maintained and newly painted in good taste. The garden is very green and there's a hedge, but no fence that fully hides the house.

After nearly two years of getting used to upheavals, Nomi's mind is quite lucid. She's not breaking the law, there's no restraining order, but any consternation needs to be avoided, in order to keep chances alive for herself.

After ten minutes she gets out and walks along this sidewalk to the corner of the street. On the other side she returns, close by the house in question, where no sign of life can be seen and no name plate, only the number: 17.

At the other far end she turns back again and crosses the street once more. Now she tries to perceive something on the upper floor, where Art must have slept. But the picture of him 'all at home' there clasps her throat.

She's never felt over-nostalgic about his baby time before. Couldn't afford that.

Suddenly she's aware that more people are around: an elderly woman is pulling a grocery wheelbag, a boy kicks a football, a woman and man are working in the garden.

Nomi gets a few folders and leaflets from the car, she walks up to the boy and asks in a business-like manner, "Who lives at 17 now?"

He makes the ball bounce, catches it deftly with a foot and says, "You mean Evan?"

"Yes. And his wife?"

The boy has large eyes. "Don't know."

"OK."

When she stays put, he asks, "Do you want me to tell him that you've been here?"

"Nah... Thanks."

He goes on, for whose sake? "Is it still about the baby? He doesn't want that."

"Oh, no. I thought the house was for sale, but there's no sign up. Maybe it's a mistake."

An ethical mistake to be here at all.

Is 'false pretense' much worse than a white lie? Or the end justifies the means.

She leafs through her papers and says, "Thank you. Oh, um, did you see that baby then?"

"No, nobody did. I mean, we saw nothing special."

The boy lives up to an adult responsibility, and he sounds 'experienced'. Maybe the media have tried to pry here for ages.

"But you and Evan do talk about him?"

"Only once, when Evan said he didn't want to. The little kid wasn't even his, turned out. He'll play ball sometimes, and my sister is nuts about him. He's cool."

Art is not very keen on the toddlers' gymnastics anymore. One class resembles the other too much, while he likes adventures and discoveries.

He finishes the assignments with a grumble and cheat.

Going home by bike, Art buckled up in the carrier seat, he won't wear his woolen hat.

"But you have to," Mark says. "I mean, you've sweated, and that can be bad in the hard wind, without a hat. I'm wearing mine, see? We're tough guys!"

They ride off.

Mark peeps over his shoulder, since Art can stoically take the hat off yet and hold it in his hands or drop it.

Before crossing the busy Borough Street, they have to stop for traffic and wait in the full side-wind. To set an example, Mark looks left and right double sharply. "See, Art? We're just waiting until there's no car nearby." And he's astonished to see their own Ford pass by, in which Nomi is looking straight in front of her.

"Hey, look there, where's Mom come from now?"

Art says, "Not from her gym class?"

<>

Bernard and Dilli are ready for a formidable bike ride to the best farm. "We'll dress warm," he says, "because there's a strong cold wind."

"We *are* dressed," Dilli says without any irony.

And he doesn't add a grown-up joke about Alzheimer's. "Yes, I mean the coat, hat and scarf."

"OK."

With the tailwind it's not bad at all on the way down there, and in lee parts of the farm it's up to 12°C. There are one-day lambs and calves, but they stay inside, and after five minutes Dilli prefers the play area with a sandbox almost as large as the beach.

Too bad that lots of kids and parents are here as well. Despite all the swings, the climbing and spinning and plunging devices, half a dozen come storming for the numerous and beautiful sand toys that Bernard has brought – the only one to think of that – and they take them for a public treasure.

Dilli is willing to share some, but she has plans for special building structures. Watched by passive parents, a toddler and baby come lumbering and rummaging around her site, wiping snotty noses during groping and grabbing. A dad takes photos of his boy and leaves him again, to disturb Dilli's work.

Bernard would like to be a social person too, although he's sitting on a damp rock with a manuscript on his lap, deliberately close to Dilli instead of settling on a dry wooden bench quietly, in delightful sunshine.

A woman there seems to be without children, out of place. Gazing away aimlessly, she reminds Bernard sharply of someone, which shocks him back in time. He's trying to think: will he "saunter" over and see if it's Anne? He might have the courage to stop and sit next to her.

It could be a striking and strong coincidence, or something very different, disconcerting. Or a stupid false alarm that says more about him. He wants to go and find out, but the situation in the sand is getting out of hand when half of Dil's colorful and varied sand toys are gone. Dilli screams and he feels like yelling as well, in the process of searching and hushing. Objects vanish in the sand.

The Anne-like woman glances this way, and even if that may be logical, Bernard pulls his hat down to his brow, since this is no place or moment for complications.

A father comes to report that his kids have taken Dil's magic 'ice-cream cones' to the castle structure. "Give a shout when you want them back."

Damn kind, thank you.

In the spring sunshine the castle scene further down looks so cozy and busy that Bernard would like to leave it intact, but Dilli starts flinging sand around, that ends up in kids' eyes too, and she tramples her damaged towers.

"Let's go, Dil. Fancy a sandwich on the bike? They're in the bag there. Come on."

Bernard collects their gear from far and near. He's not pulling them off kids crudely, yet some of them cry hard, making him feel moderately guilty.

He can't wait for some food himself, and he's aching to pass by that woman's bench closely, but Dilli doesn't calm down until she's in her carrier seat on the bike, and he won't look back. Pedalling into the rough headwind, it would be tricky for him to eat. Wind force this or that is blowing through his coat and mind, so he waits.

Halfway home Dilli has finished the portions of both travellers, and she says, "The peanut-butter was delishable," which does and does not help him for the longest eleven minutes.

. . .

At home she also has a share of Bernard's crunchy cheese toasts. His coffee is heavenly as well and Dilli asks, "Taken your pills? For health!"

"Oh, yes, thanks."

After which he becomes the victim of a sleep attack. "Sorry, Dil, I didn't have a very good night."

"Oh, you can have a longer nap. I'll put music on."

She chooses her favorite acoustic songs, and Bernard retreats gratefully.

Over an hour later she's still playing her very personal version of the farm events, and the music must have begun anew.

"Last song, Dil."

"Just one more: *I'm dancing*. It's now!"

He makes tea and tries not to disrupt her dance. For how long will she remain herself when kids are all over the Internet and countless hectic talent shows?

Content, she gets a magazine and sets out to cut and paste Mont Blanc at sunset in pink. He puts his laptop on the table, facing her. A series of emails from dating-site Amore nearly make him cry "Wow" out loud –

You've been added to someone's favorites.

Find out who is interested in you.

You'll like Emma038!

You've evoked some attention.

Your profile is visibly popular, check this now!

A member has sent you a "Flirt".

Make yourself even more popular on Amore.

Take a look at Samantha from Lowpool.

And above all: A member has sent you a message.

Before gaining access to messages, he'll need to be a Full Member. What a shrewd lot they are, with ingenious enticements.

He won't fall for that, will he? But what if she's a sweet, profound, exciting, adorable woman? She doesn't know that he can't answer now, she'd be deeply disappointed in him and wonder forever what the reason could be!

The options are as large as life: $124 for 6 months, $46 for 1 month.

How much would I pay to retrieve a lost manuscript? And above all, remember: what would I've given to have Art back? Everything up to my last cent – to feed on the joy for the rest of my life. "Money is an archetype for the soul," Professor Jung proved impressively.

The $124 can also be spent on drinking water for children who have to walk or wait in lines for hours for half a bottle and share it with the whole family. But damn, if you stop and think about that, there's no end to it, you have no life yourself! This woman's message on the site might be the start of a glorious new love, ready for him here, and together they could do terrific things for others. An impassioned soul can be much more valuable than a craving and lonely one!

It's true that money, sexuality, and creativity are related to the soul and one another. He's noticed that himself in body and mind: the more intense his writing is, the less interest there is in sex.

He pays the $124 and promises to transfer a large amount presently, to selected charities.

"Help me remember," he mumbles to Dilli. "I'll need to pay something."

"Can't you remember good?" she asks, cutting the lucky animals from the RSPCA magazine, of which he's been a member for thirty years.

He's nervously expectant, but the contact request on Amore is as amiable as unattractive, and he sends a short and kind thank-you note.

There are plenty of 'Matches, Flirts, and Favorites' with keywords he dislikes: "...relaxed, have a click, fun, a laugh, a pint..."

He doesn't want to bump into a trauma woman like Anne Hoaver again, even though their contact had a life-saving function, in the very end, and here is Dilli to distract him with artistic scrapbook issues, "Will I leave a bit of white now, between the mountain and tiger?"

When there's no response from him, she says, "Then I will. There, that's done too."

She gets up and passes by Bernard's chair in a flash, pointing to the laptop with total involvement. "Have you got photos? Who are they?"

He does not swiftly click the site away, he thinks and says, "Phew, what a question. These ladies have no man, and I have no wife or girlfriend, so... We might be friends, maybe, eventually."

"So many?" Dilli says. "But you have me. I can stay?"

He hugs her to bits, and she accidentally hits the laptop keys. The women flash away. He doesn't say "No no girl," only, "You are my best friend for the rest of our lives."

"And Art?"

"He too, of course."

"And Mom and Dad?"

"Definitely," he says readily.

They cast a glimpse at the screen again, where something complicated has appeared, and she puts her scrapbook away, reminding him, "Have you remembered the other thing?"

First he writes to Debbie Atkins. "A quiet PS, musing just in case... Would it be a good thing if the story attracted a co-screenwriter from Europe, for some international exposure? E.g. at the Book & Film Fair. But sorry if this is ludicrously premature! Best wishes, Bernard."

. . .

If the original meaning of being enthusiastic is 'divinely inspired', do some people confuse his enthusiasm with 'arrogance'? Instead of luck or bad luck or coincidence, he likes destiny and providence, a mutuality with interaction between heaven and earth – all in combination with free will. That contains love or inspiration as well, in the broadest and humblest sense.

<>

Cool thirty-year-old Lorna will support the next phase of Anne's reintegration, who is not sure which title she likes the least: 'Social Worker or Case Worker'. Out in the streets, Lorna didn't need to get into much action so far, thanks to Anne's disguise and Evan's help.

He is bursting with energy and wants to make a radical fresh start, if need be in a place that's new to both of them. But in spare and weighed words Anne has explained that for the time being they'll need to stay in touch with the house of both Reg and Art. "Only if it's feasible, mind. I realize perfectly what you have done for me."

He sides with her heartily, though, after such devoted work on the house and garden, that it would be hard to part with them.

Ever since her discharge from the clinic, Anne has made herself as useful as possible for him, keeping house, making home and doing research for his PR work – all calmly and moderately. Evan's role in her life has been essential, and to his own surprise he's fine, but parts of their relationship remain fragile or careful.

Understandably?

Does he wait and see?

For a long time after discovering Anne's wrongdoings, he was numb with disillusion and feelings of co-guilt, but without shame and anger. He didn't fret and passed no judgments. In fact, his mind and heart had little room for that. His pragmatic attitude kept him fit and balanced. She tries to follow suit.

He has not told his colleagues about Anne and Reg. He's less jovial and hospitable than before, but no harsh jokes are made about that. They wouldn't dare anymore after an attempt or two with strange or sad answers. Evan is a much-liked marketing man, good for scoops, with a fast work pace and analytical insight. They still invite him to parties and meetings, where he'll turn up appreciatively, if pre-occupied and for not so long.

Evan and Lorna have met to discuss plans with Anne. It's time for her to go out undisguised, or even to "return home", not in order to live there again – not yet? – but to get used to a turnaround.

With simply a different hairstyle in her own color, she might be Evan's Plus One at a work do, introduced nonchalantly as "a friend" who'd evoke plain curiosity at the most, in a large place where everybody goes their own ways. As far as Evan and Anne can tell, they have no common acquaintances there.

No repeat of the Bernard farce and fate, please!

One extreme coincidence will do.

The question has been in the air: could someone recognize her from "that period in the media"?

Lorna asks and answers. "It's unlikely, but we'll make scenarios for situations like that, so you can kind of practise. Anne?"

She's listened alright, knowing that any panicky behavior would catch bad eyes. "Yes, I understand. And I'd love to do my best, I think."

She'll try and face this sort of test rather than visit 'the house', even with the help of sunglasses, a new coat, and a big hat.

Half-happy here in the anonymity of Evan's apartment, Anne looks around. From the ground outside nobody can see her, except when she's at the window or on the balcony. How caring of Lorna to come and see her instead of meeting in her office. Or is that a bad sign? Indicating her weakness?

"At my firm they're all broad-minded," Evan says. "And you'll be with me. You've got nothing to lose."

Hm, which says enough. If it's true.

"*You* have," Anne retorts.

"OK, but I won't." He laughs. "They don't want to lose me!"

These past years his outspoken humor has been dosed involuntarily. He won't say this yet, for example: would you prefer to go and see Wil?

For months he lost his jocular appetite altogether, but old habits… Well, in times of rain, flowers keep growing beside weeds. Take this lungwort in spring, with its two colors in each flower!

"I could be an embarrassment," Anne says, "and ruin the ambiance at work. So, if you want to keep your job there…"

"Don't be dramatic, Anne! You can leave that to me. I mean, it's no use being scared if there's no need."

"Again," Lorna says, "you'll be prepared."

As far as possible.

"Will you join us?" Anne asks her.

"Ho, ladies," Evan plays. "Now I can hear them already: two women, go on then, dude, don't restrain yourself!"

Anne's face clouds over and Lorna hastens to say, "You know, we'll see. It might work, but we don't want complications."

"No, we're just sisters and your flair will divert their attention. Please, Lorn', it would help enormously to have you there!"

"Well, look, with this kind of charm you won't need me at all. This week you'll grow even more self-confident. We'll take a lovely stroll along some crowded shopping-streets, and I'll discuss it with Grant. OK? Buy yourself a gorgeous dress, in which you can conquer the world, at Evan's party or elsewhere. Remember, your recovery so far calls for celebration. You've worked hard, it's been a fabulous effort, and this is a landmark. But sorry, no pressure or emphasis. Wednesday at eleven downtown?"

Lorna takes an official look at her diary.

Anne nods and says, "Thank you."

"Thank you too. You can borrow an outfit of mine, but you have your own taste."

And who knows if that's a minuscule aspect, compared to things that come first.

. . .

After Lorna has left, the restfulness in the room is frail. It's early for lunch, but Evan wants to be busy. He bakes, cuts and butters, offers and says, "I need to get back to work. By the way, should it ever occur spontaneously, I mean the need to go home, or the wish, whenever you feel good, we can always do that. I'm scared as well..."

'Go home' sounds off now. She's tried to be at home here for some time. If not for the long term, one does need to feel right *some*where.

She asks, "How could you stay there in the first place? Wasn't it disgusting?"

"Actually I can't recall. I didn't think much, it was a thick blur. Maybe I lacked the guts to *leave*. I'd never come back, probably, and I didn't want that risk to exist."

Would it also be an ordeal to endure Anne day and night?

At the beginning – after her collapse – each time he went to fetch clothes and other things from his apartment, it was a plight to return to the house, but he persevered, and it made the truth sink in better. Later he grew fond of the place again, when good memories became independent and prevailed, even if the three of them should never have been together.

Attachment is a powerful and peculiar phenomenon.

He forced himself to think of the two babies with their own names. He never knew his flesh and blood: Reg. But Reg did live there for six months. Art was the one he got to know and loved. There was a scintillating summer of rebuilding life, he thought, as promising as unexpected. He was making amends for his brusque and stupid departure. Then with and for Anne he had to start all over once more.

After about a year he began mentioning both boys in Anne's presence. At first he had physical trouble saying Art's name, like a denial or betrayal of Reg. His tongue seemed leathery, and his stomach turned from the mix-up and wistfulness.

The disinterment of Reg's body was too sinister, and necessary. Identification was impossible without DNA. Hattum allowed him to watch only from the house, and that was a good, protective order. Dazed from respect – or what? – he took pictures from behind the window, no close-ups, just rendering the situation, as might be important for some day.

The pear tree that Anne had planted, needed to be removed and transported with its young roots and all. He never asked where to. For months he would avoid that spot in the garden, until the weeds asked for action. Since then he's hoped that he and Anne will plant a new blossom tree there, in commemoration. The house gives an opportunity and a purpose for which he'll stay.

The past year she's bought no pears, which can also be a good sign: that the other past is not dead.

<>

"Do you ever think back of Liza Jacobs?" Nomi asks one Tuesday in the kitchen, where she's making coffee and Mark is getting vegetables for dinner from the fridge.

"Ah, what did we call her again: clairvoyant or clairfeeling?"

"You're not mocking her, are you?"

"No." Mark adapts his tone. "She had integrity."

"Yes, modest and cautious. It says a lot that we've never heard from her again, doesn't it."

"Why's that?" Mark asks. "Would she've liked a compliment?"

"No, exactly, Liza didn't need to hear that she was right about Art. Apart from the truth, her interest and frankness were a huge help to us for a length of time. What a pity that we can't tell her now."

That evening with Liza formed a sensitive calm in the storm's eye.

"Why now?" Mark asks.

Nomi shrugs. "I'm not sure. There's some space in my head."

"Ah, she must know anyhow," Mark says without irony. And with a sigh, "I've googled my head off and it's terrifying, the number of clairvoyants or mediums, or whatever they're called. How few of them are the real stuff, one in a thousand?"

Through the hallway and open front door Nomi looks out, where Art is blowing soap bubbles and Dilli is drawing letters on the sidewalk tiles with outdoor crayons.

Dilli comes running in and cries, "H, P, I... What does it say?"

"Hip," Mark knows.

"What's that?"

"Hm, like cool. When you look nice and tough and modern."

She dashes out again and tells a passing woman that she's hip.

"Me too," says Art, whose bubbles are admired extensively by the unknown woman.

The front door can't open any further, and Nomi makes herself stay inside, watching from the kitchen and hallway. On many occasions she's thought to herself: 'That woman or anyone could snatch him just like that, even when he'll be three.' Those fears have to be over, but now and then her heart jumps again as if it's blocking her windpipe. That will never be totally over.

What would one in a thousand healers be able to do for her before she has heart failure? She herself is the only person who can fill the gap.

They take their coffee to the window in the living-room with the sidewalk in sight. Although – or because – there will be little time for a proper talk, Nomi says, "I've been to that Hoaver house. Saturday I went over."

Art is so kind as to stay on the sidewalk. Dilli is allowed to turn the corner and come back along the other quiet street, on foot or cycling, but not with Art, even if Nomi presumes that he'd keep loyally close to his sister. Dilli will guard him with eagle eyes and take severe measures in case of straying, willfully or not. Or would he get obstinate then and shoot off anywhere?

"What, the Hoaver place?" Mark says. "Why did you go on your own?"

"I don't even know. It was on my way back from Bernard's."

Mark is mildly sharp. "And chance would have it that he wasn't fit enough to drive and collect Dilli?"

"Yes. It was nothing premeditated, that's to say, I had a vague plan and didn't know what would come of it. I wanted to wait and see, firstly if I'd have the courage, taking it per minute. Then it fitted in, and I seemed ready, I suppose, like spontaneous or inconspicuous – as if the chance created itself."

"Ah," says Mark. "Tthings are meant to be, now sad, then joyful?"

According to one's wishes?

His sarcasm contains the questioning earnest again of the times around the abduction. The matter would be touched upon at capricious intervals, and the same bafflement remains, although it's rarely led to quarrels or rows.

Those who believe in 'powers from above' or 'a superior order', can accept both the help and the blows. Ultimately they would have no such thing as insane coincidence but cause and effect in dazzling dimensions.

Accountability as well as forgiveness.

Nomi looks out silently and Mark says, "Why didn't you mention it when you were back?"

"I'm not sure myself. You didn't ask and it never came up anymore. It felt awkward, silly and weak! The way I was peeping and sniffing around there... But I wouldn't lie about it. Or is that the same thing?"

"Never mind," Mark says with a frown of frustration. "Tell me now! Or is that what you don't want?"

"There's nothing to tell, really, there was nobody, I didn't see anything, and afterwards I grew sullen."

From the anticlimax? Either of them can wonder, and the air seems to be stifled. What did you expect: A confession or an apology with a bucket of tears? For the big reconciliation and redemption and the end of it all?

"Have you processed it now?" somebody asked her a couple of months after her mom died. Five years ago that enraged her: as if love or a person can be put behind you!

Art comes in and calls out, "It's raining, but who cares, I wipe my feet!"

He's off again.

Dilli comes in and mumbles, concentrating, "O, V, M, R, O. What does it say?"

Mark imitates a motorbike. "Vroom, vroom..."

"No, what does it say!"

"That's what I mean, the sound made by an engine."

"Oh," says Dilli. "Are the letters wiped in the rain?"

"Doesn't matter, and dinner is due."

"It matters, I still need to read them!"

"But Dil, have you memorized all these letters?"

She fails to understand the good news and rushes off again.

"Would it be better to make an appointment?" Mark proceeds pensively, used to these intermezzos of various convenience.

"Who with?"

"First of all, Hattum, I figure, as he may be in contact with him or her, or with their therapist. Does anyone live there?"

"Yes, it's no ghost house."

"But it would be tricky to sell," Mark says, "and they couldn't live there themselves, could they?"

Nomi needs to clear her throat. "The man, Evan lives there. After all, he wasn't responsible, was he? And he seems nice."

"Well, was mentally blind, for God's sake. But hey..."

"Yes, that must be a grueling mystery to him too. I'd like to ask him. You know what I mean?"

Mark sighs. "You'd rake up hell, ours and theirs."

"As long as I'll clear up mine. Or is that mean and selfish?"

"No and yes, the right selfishness. We're all victims."

"Of her?" Nomi checks.

"Yeah, or the circumstances, and she herself too, I suspect."

"At any rate," Nomi says resolutely after two years, that require a new stage, "I want to know everything now, and see it with my own eyes."

"As proof that we are normal or decent?"

"Or to catch up. And then it makes no difference anymore, what is considered normal – in them or me." She points to the window. "For example, can we let the kids play out in the rain? People will think they're thrown out or neglected."

"Better cook dinner right now," Mark says. "Extra good and healthy. You peel potatoes?"

. . .

Dilli and Art eat quite well, but just before bedtime, Art remembers, "The bubble blower is still outside."

"I'll fetch it in a minute," Nomi says lightly.

"No, me, myself." And he walks to the door.

"Art, wait, it's very rainy and windy. I'll find it later."

"No, now."

"How long will this rebellion last?" Mark asks.

Their moments of weakness are called "only human". They often feel privileged. Other people are craving for kids with Art-like spirit and character: "I'd kill for a baby!"

Millions of children are exploited or abused.

Dilli is in the bath with the door closed, more or less withdrawn from the world. A five-year old would never drown in a half-filled bath, would she? Her parents do listen continually, and their trained ears can hear bath sounds from afar.

Art's bubble blower won't be stolen, will it?

Father and son are in the kitchen, ready for pre-bed business.

Art is lifted onto the sink, and he says, "When you're mad at me, my jar goes empty."

Mark fails to understand this mysticism. During the thorough brushing of whopping new molars, Art cooperates, and Mark is late to discover that he's used not toothpaste but the baby-bottom cream.

It's oddly typical that Art hasn't flinched, and he goes to sleep.

Any minute, in the course of the evening, Mark expects hellish yelling with a tongue on fire. He goes and checks in Art's room a few times, and he asks Nomi, "Should I wake him up to rinse his mouth?"

To have his stomach pumped?

"Well, he's sound asleep, so what could be wrong?"

"He may have lost consciousness! What's in that stuff?"

Nomi is at work for a window display. Spread on a large cardboard on the table, photos and texts are arranged around a headline: *Between city and country*.

Mark reads the ingredients on the label of the bottom balm, but the long Latin words are riddles to him. "A medicinal ointment always has this warning: *not for internal use*. 'Cos it's dangerous!"

While Nomi looks up and ponders, Mark goes on, "This works miracles on the sore bum, so it's got to be strong stuff. Can't be good for the mouth, can it? He won't even spit it out, it's mixed with saliva, he'll swallow it!"

"In case of any harm," Nomi says with minor doubt, "we would have heard him."

Unless...

Full of hope Mark agrees, "Of course there's nothing nasty in it or anything, on the contrary, it's all soothing and sedative. So, no need to call a doctor? Or take him to some Emergency post?"

"No, that seems exaggerated."

"Yeah," Mark admits. "That sounds overstressed, doesn't it?"

"It's no wonder, my love, since you always need to be a tower of strength here."

"OK, we'll take a break and go away, yes? The two of us for a midweek? Bernard will step in. How long has it been? We just went on and on!"

"It's been years," Nomi says. "Before Art was born. We've never even left him at Dad's for more than half a day."

<>

Yesterday Bernard was glad of the rain for the garden, and there was a list of chores around the house. Now he's taken his writing work to Green Lake again, where the moisture in the sunshine has an extra herbal scent.

After a mild month of March, the trees and shrubs are budding early. There are lady-smocks among the shrinking daffodils. The juicy dandelions are heart-warmingly yellow. Do colors have healing effects?

"Each color has its own energetic frequency," he read in the paper the other day. "When that equals the frequency of a virus, the virus can be neutralized."

Is that bullshit or valuable biochemistry?

Bernard would lie down at naked length in the yellow field before him, but at ten a.m. it's only fourteen degrees in the wind there.

He's afraid that a flu virus is not manifest but lingers and pesters, whereas his GP can't find anything concrete. The blood seems alright, although the B12 levels are on the low side.

A heart murmur is heard by the GP's associate, and she makes an appointment at the cardiologist, for an echo and ECG.

Bernard doesn't mind "being on the safe side", and here between his beloved woods and lake, in his chair on the grass with lilac ale-hoof, he shakes it all off.

He's also read something upsetting about an expected epidemic of blood-sucking ticks that spread the deadly Lyme disease. This warmish winter gave them perfect breeding conditions. But then if he frets about all such things, he has no life.

Look, an athletic young woman settles in the yellow patch. Unabashed or carefree, she takes most of her clothes off straightaway and stretches on a large, sky-blue towel. Even from a distance he can see how soft and warm that is. And so may she be herself!

Her hair is chestnut brown, and her skin is lightly tanned, with gorgeous white parts here and there.

Bernard won't stare vulgarly, although her eyes are closed. Her surrender to the elements touches him so pleasantly, more than he finds appropriate. He doesn't avert his eyes very much or move his chair ninety degrees. That might come across as offensive as well.

Refusing to look foolish and prudish, he undresses too, but keeps his boxer shorts on. He spreads his towel and lies on his stomach, sideways to her, his writings in front of him. The work fights for his attention in the same way as the sun and clouds are claiming each inch of the woman.

A little something is walking down his upper leg along the knee hollow, to tickle his heel: an ant, a tiny spider or beetle?

Ticks move slowly; he's learned to recognize their deceptive gait on the skin. If they like white things, they can also appear on his manuscript, where he kills them, or he's merciful and takes them to a dense part of the woods, depending on his mood and energy.

Should he go and warn the comely lady about these treacherous enemies, or would she consider that a ridiculous trick?

Perhaps she can feel something itching too, because her hand is sliding from a breast to her belly and under the edge of her briefs. Or it's a tickle of the skin itself, in spots that haven't had much sunshine yet, and may never have. What madness is creeping into his head: is she seducing him? Freely or sneakily? While his eyes close for a sec, he imagines her fingers on his own body. If she chooses to look at him, she won't have the counter-light disadvantage that he has.

He peers around. Apparently nobody realizes how glorious it is out of the wind. In comparison, the fourteen forecast degrees are unreal. What a delightful woman, to land here deliberately or by accident. She prickles him so vehemently that it must be visible. Good God, how sensual can a person be in public in secluded nature? This corner has become a private spot between heaven and earth!

Even yesterday he was thinking that writing is a strange occupation: you're never finished until a manuscript is completed, and that's only a would-be status too, because you want to read the print-out word by word, undisturbed. Then you have to wait for the opinion of the publisher and editor, or the marketing team.

The job is addictive in the best and hardest way. There's always his urge to finish a novel before something might happen to him, but the birth-labor stages take months. Is his back-up system sufficient? Sometimes he emails a Word file to Nomi. "Please save, don't read; send to such and such if disaster strikes."

Now and then, Bernard lives in two worlds rather literally: the real one can fade away, and he creates another, with places, times and people coming alive. At night he needs to detach himself from them as much as from this earthly Eve some ten meters away. Next thing he'll be hearing the voice of a Satan snake that promises the Garden of Eden but will bring damnation.

Ah, come on, you're a free man, you've been a widower for five years now!

Better have lunch first. He's lost sense of time, but his stomach has not.

He lies on his back at full length. The sandwich is delicious, and the wind is playing pleasantly on body parts. A ladybird stops on his abdomen and explores the area.

Even in this position, 'work' may continue, when a choice of material enters his mind of its own accord, but now he makes believe that the ladybird legs are the refined fingertips of a gorgeously brazen woman, going their ways exquisitely slowly.

When he opens his eyes and sits up to get his bottle of juice, the real-life woman seems to have come closer – moving out of the wind after all? She waves a hand and smiles, as an apologetic gesture? In the manner of: I don't want to interrupt anything, or: it's okay, I'll be civilized?

Both relieved and disappointed, he sees that she's not pretty or young at all. After a friendly "Good morning", just loud enough, he turns on his stomach again, as flat and low as possible in the not so tall grass.

Other days with other people he would fabricate a wall with his chair, bag, and clothes, but that would look rude now, and in curious honesty he doesn't feel the need. She probably wants to blend with nature too, that's all. She has no music on, doesn't spray any chemical suncream on that can be smelled faraway, and there's no unrest about her.

He reads his notes made earlier and alters a sentence, but the sun overwhelms him, the whiteness of the paper hurts his eyes.

He doesn't dare bring a hand to his loins and adjust the hardness there. He shifts a bit and makes room, but now he's pulled a muscle in his neck. He laughs at himself, drops his head and lowers the cap over his eyes. Man, man, take a nap!

It's just as if the rustling trees have spring leaves early, backing the lyrical birdsongs. The side of his neck is glowing in the cool air and fierce sun, he can't feel the rest of his body, and his mind has turned ageless or spaceless. Floating about in a parallel world, he hears no footsteps, but the earth moves and pulls him back when a hand is laid on his shoulder blade, so gently...

He doesn't budge.

The hand goes up and down softly and warmly, like a caress with a question. The lower part of her sitting body is closer, she must be changing position to relax her arm and extend its reach. The hand is roaming his whole back, down each vertebra, touching every muscle and sinew, feather light here, with inquisitive pressure there.

He's afraid to breathe, but he sucks in air through his teeth.

As her fingers are traveling his shorts and legs, she bends over to reach, which gives him even more goose bumps. He wants to do all sorts, crouch or stretch from crown to toes, turn over and answer her silent motion, but there are tears in his eyes that embarrass him just as much as the stubborn if hidden erection.

From his heels upwards, she goes back along his buttocks and tailbone, all the way to the top of his head. She strokes his hair and the skin underneath, she tarries on his neck and descends again, with little outings to the left and right, over his hips and shoulders.

Suddenly she recoils and whispers, “Pardon me, I saw you and your book in the paper the other day, and the story spoke to me so strongly... I’ve read your novels and seem to know you well. But what’s come over me... I love my family.”

Bernard has shrunk and he sits up. He rubs his eyes and looks at her. “What a shame, I mean, it’s good that you’ve said it. I was going to react, but I needed some time. You don’t think you’re unwelcome, do you?”

“No, thanks. I did think it was accepted fondly, like an interchange. That’s why I’m running off, before it might be too strong, for either of us.”

He doesn’t stop her or go after her, nor does he scribble an address or phone number on a scrap of paper or ask her for anything like that.

Back in her patch, she timidly puts her clothes on and waves goodbye with a sweetly painful touch of joy, that he shares.

<>

For an excuse to postpone, Anne hoped it would keep raining, in vain. She's in front of the mirror now to put heavy make-up on. As if Lorna would heed the rain. She'd rightly say, "Nerdy girl, be glad!"

Yes, under an umbrella she might go all natural, as she always has been: no make-up or accessories and trimmings. But they'll enter shops and stop for a coffee or a drink, and neither umbrella nor large hat would help.

So on second thoughts the beaming sun is a disadvantage. At this early hour it's shining low into the whole apartment, lighting up each particle of dust. She keeps the place very clean, but not all specks of dust will be caught, and every movement of hers will make them float again, although she uses wet wipes a lot.

"It's no phobia!" she explained to Doctor Grant with a wink. "It's just that I've got nothing else to do. Look, let me prove..."

Her finger brushed the edge of his desk. "Ah, for how long has this not been cleaned? But I don't scream or faint, see?"

He believed her with a generous smile, saying, "If you want, you can have plenty to do, can't you?"

And Lorna came up with a step-by-step plan.

Anne is still afraid to breathe in some dust, but often she ignores that successfully. She keeps pretty busy ignoring or accepting and overcoming life, with daily satisfaction.

By now she can safely believe that the kitchen wall closets will not come down when she's cleaning them, and Evan keeps being so sweet as to check the construction, yet she carefully spreads the weight of special-offer groceries from all the stores, and the heaviest packets are on the floor.

Once in a while, she broods: does Evan stay and bear with her out of pity or duty? No, they do have good times, they watch TV snug on the couch, buy flowery plants for her garden and his balcony. She ought to say "their garden" from now on.

She washes his curtains, reorganizes his storeroom and wardrobe and paperwork. She stops brooding about the tree leaves on the grass or in the gutter, about a chipped roof tile or the color-fading of objects in the sun. Nor will she fret about lumps in the washing detergent that may cause the blockage of pipes.

Together they celebrate what goes well: within long, her columns will be published again. For instance –

In famous films such as Schindler's List, the Nazis are played by British and American actors, and to make it 'real', they speak English with a heavy German accent, but that's counter-effective: the very presence of any accent ruins the authenticity. As the Nazis had no clumsy accents, we're constantly made aware that these are actors.

And they make love! Which sounds much better than 'having sex'.

They sleep together regularly, but he seldom stays the night, and she doesn't know why. They can indulge and have it on intensely or be languidly long and tender. He's not having women in their house, is he? Obviously he would be entitled, the attractive and virile man in his thirties, who is stuck with a patient...

But no, for two years he's been so loyal to her that she could even fancy the party at his work, to show him that it's worth it, everything he's doing for her. She'd be so radiant that he'll be elated, and no one would have the least suspicion about her sick past.

She can look straight in the mirror. There, the make-up may still be an auxiliary, but one part – or past – of hers will go into the garbage, and this is not her being manic but determined, after a sensible breakfast.

At the clinic she lost so much weight that no trace of stretch or other pregnancy marks was left. Her face changed too, or that's rubbish wishful thinking – as if nobody would recognize her.

She trained her lungs out for fitness there, which helped on many fronts: to ban mean thoughts, rebuild energy, kill hours and days or demons.

"Watch your boundaries," Grant said.

Anyhow, she's back to normal body proportions.

By day she's never peckish, but at night the food fight begins: discipline is a bitch when you're on your own, and Evan has his reasons to leave in the evenings.

She checks her neat, virginal diary and sees the note with Pat's number, which has been mislaid and found three times in funny ways. Too bad it's no email address; that barrier would be much lower.

But, nitwit, why would it be about you? Count yourself lucky that somebody lets or even invites you into her life. Apply your fine intentions and stop inventing fibs! *What* barrier: Pat *knows* what the hell I've done – without fleeing, would you believe – and I'm letting her down?

Pleased with the make-up, Anne stumbles over her legs heading for the phone before the courage will vanish. Without a plan or a sentence in her head she dials the number, and Pat answers.

"Hello, it's Anne... We met on the train."

I'm the one who snatched a kid. Who buried her own in the yard.

She can't remember how long it's all been: Reg, Art, Pat on the platform with the note, that's in her hand now. We're from different eras and worlds, but we did share life, and Pat brings pieces back.

"Hello..." Pat's voice has a mixture of gladness and fear, that Anne understands too well. Here's a baptism by fire, or only a foretaste of that.

Anne almost fades in a tear-laugh, thinking: can I practise on you?

And she says, "This is most spontaneous – or impulsive. Otherwise I wouldn't dare."

"Fine, then I'll dare be honest too."

"Oh, is this a bad time?"

Or you meant something else.

"No," Pat says, "but I've poured coffee, and I like to drink it hot."

"Oh."

"So you'll hear me taking sips."

"And it's alright for you?" Anne says.

"Yes, I'm at a table, and Cas is OK too."

"I'm not calling for anything in particular. Perhaps to say how special it was that you gave me your number. Did you still have a good day then, or were you in shock too much?"

"Yes," Pat says. "I had lots to think about."

"Were you extra happy with your own children and grandchildren?"

If they are around, silly cow!

"Well, I wasn't going to compare. I didn't know anything about you, but it's true, the world looked different. The things we're fussing about or taking for granted..."

"Considering what I did."

Pat is taking her time to say, "When we met, you were kinder, more interesting, more genuine than most people, so something terrible must have happened – before you did it."

Anne's self-contempt is gone. It often works briefly as a band-aid on the pain, that's now blocking her throat. Although nobody can really see her, she'd like to bury her eyes and mouth in her hands, but Pat wouldn't know why she's silent.

"So I've wondered about many things," Pat says. "At the time of the abduction, I did hear some stories, but well, all is colored by the media and general ignorance. They were disproportionate, really, as usual, and short-lived! People love to cry out against something. It makes them feel better than others and that's why we watch the News all the time."

"Thank you," Anne says. "I'm sorry I didn't give you my number. It should have been your decision, to call me."

"Well, this is for the best. Now I'm sure that *you* want it."

"But you forget your coffee."

"Oh, thanks," Pat admits. "You know, we can go somewhere together, soon or later, for coffee or tea."

"Yes, I'd love to. Today it's the first time that I'm going into town without a disguise."

"Ah, good luck and success!"

"Does your phone have my number now?"

"Let's see, my son saw to that. Yes, I'll write it down too."

"Good," says Anne. "Thank you."

"And you. See you next time."

Anne would have been to the hairdresser's, but in salons they have an eye for faces and an ear for gossip. Even previously, the chatty questions of the assistants annoyed her, amid loud curlers and driers with synthetic smells, as well as the radio with mass music and sensation.

How much does one's hair grow in eighteen months or two years?

When Lorna dyed and styled it, they were nervous like teenagers. "I have some hairdo experience with friends of mine, but of course I'm no pro."

"I don't care," said Anne. "I mean, whatever you do, it's OK, if it's not conspicuous in any regard. Only different, please! And *spiky* is cool, so you can't mess it up."

"Well, your bangs caught the eye, so let's pull them sideways or backwards. Do you want the rest in trendy braids or a smart, casual tail?"

They tried the options and decided on sideways and tail, easy for Anne to do by herself too.

"It looks naked, though," she doubted.

"But mostly it's different! And when the sun shines, you can wear dark glasses out there. Deal?"

Anne used to love the old town center with its cobbled quays and little bridges, the ancient coachhouse and tollhouse, the gates to inner courts. The place has never swarmed with tourists, but now she'd like to be lost in crowds, impervious to stares and frowning glances.

Jumpy in the sunlight but grateful for the large and dark glasses, Anne links arms with Lorna to walk along the spots from a past life. She tends to hurry, but one can't be ahead of time and catastrophe.

She's given respite: on this landmark day it would be too ambitious to try and buy a party dress, with the keen and fathoming looks of assistants outside a fitting booth. Thus they have no real destination, only the purpose of walking around the streets, where people can recognize her no sooner than when she'd quicken her pace.

Lorna pauses and says, "Wait. We're supposed to be sauntering, to explore like tourists and friends. You don't need to be aware of anyone, they're not watching you, and if they were, so what? Are you expecting a punch or a kick? Even that would be no disaster, because I've got a first-aid certificate and a phone, I can yell like a Hollywood star, and I've done a self-defense course. That would be a good idea for you too, I mean, not because there will be assaults, but for self-confidence, like every man and woman, as a defense in general – against weirdos!"

"Yeah, there are so many. Says me."

"Right, Anne, enjoy your freedom, the fresh air, my cozy company. Sigh and breathe. Go on then, press your feet on the ground, OK? Where are we going?"

"Don't know. I thought you had a plan. Don't you do this as a routine? See, I'm an exceptional case!"

"You have been here before," Lorna says, "you show me the best places, so think, where do you want to be?"

Anne concentrates and pretends to play a supporting role in a movie. Each take or scene can be redone, and the crew is naked. This old-school trick is still surprisingly effective in dicey situations.

It's quiet in the botanical garden, but unluckily that also means that a fellow visitor could be prone to address her.

"Who cares?" Lorna says. "You love plants and flowers too, so who knows what kind of bond will grow here."

In Pigeon Park with the aviary, fountain, and cabin, a gang of school kids hang out. The group mood is so blue and blunt that Anne hastens away and takes heart for Orchard Street with the marina and city gate, that lead to the shopping area.

"Have you brought a list of errands?" Lorna asks.

"Sure, in a purse with a wallet. Not unlike a usual person!"

And when a man turns to look at them, Lorna says, "Indeed, you've still got it, babe."

"No, he saw you! I've buttoned up my coat like a frump."

"Well, that's alright then."

When others watch them 'a long time' too, it's getting harder to be frivolous about 'making heads turn'.

Lorna says, "We're not looking abnormal, are we?"

"Or women think we're lesbians?"

"OK, no problem."

"I've dressed all dull and boring," Anne says.

"Oh no, we could run into a camera and microphone of the fashion police! To end up on TV!"

"As long as we won't get hysterical...."

Lorna gives her a nudge. "In the meantime, check out the cute guy with The Times, on your left."

He's coming close with a special spring offer: "A two-month subscription for the price of one."

His student-air bravura is engaging, Lorna listens and looks with interest, but Anne walks on without explaining that 'two months' is a charged phrase to her, as if that period ended yesterday, and the price is yet to be paid.

Lorna stands at ease and Anne is getting flushed, keeping still in the promenade stream. Alright, if Lorna is doing this on purpose, as a test or something, she won't fail, she'll move 'out of the way' by the walls, busy with her phone and not looking at anyone.

How many familiar people could pass by here and now? She didn't have many contacts left as it was. She does remember names and faces very well, but most people don't? Look how fleeting and superficial the social media are: in an hour's time we're hopelessly behind! Moreover, those who have no video on some platform seem to be recluses or outcasts. The mind has become immune to basic human contact!

Anne pulls herself together and grins about the way she's being saved by her phone right now, clinging to the thing as if swamped with deep stuff – from fellow humans.

"Come on, Lorn!" she cries defiantly or recklessly, as rough and ready as anyone, to prove herself and show that she's taken a giant step forward, that she's followed Pat's example, scarcely madder than the general public.

Even the sunglasses irritate her. She pushes them on top of her head and calls out, "Lorna, let's go! Or would you prefer to stay with him?"

Lorna takes a card from the young man, she hops over to Anne and says, "Lunch at C&D?"

<>

Art is listening to children's evergreens. *Come riding and riding my cart, and if you can't, I'll carry you.* He walks to the dolls pram and carries the whole thing.

Nomi won't know for how long he would be standing like that; they have to leave and collect Dilli from school. "Are you coming, Art? Let's go."

"No, I stay here."

"You can't, sweet. Come on, here's your coat and shoes."

"I can," says Art. "You always say *back in a sec.*"

"Yes, together we'll be back in a flash, and then you'll play again a long time."

"I want to play now, please."

"No, Art, Dilli is waiting for us. Would you like a sandwich on the bike?"

"No, I can stay home. Then I'm good. Look..."

He puts the pram down and cradles the doll. "He drinks from me, he cries from hungriness, I look after him, Dil says too."

Nomi is silent and Art says with positive logic. "When you fetch me, Dil is alone too. Door closed, key in the pocket. Is the gas off?"

"Art, Dilli is five."

"But I am almost three, and Dil says: I won't go lost again."

The baby doll is wrapped and lain on the Duplo. During another song his shoulders move along rhythmically. Optimistically, he selects the yellow Duplo bricks.

Nomi is sweating as if running a fever. She may know what's acceptable, but she forgets. On their bikes they can be hit by a good driver who happens to be absent-minded for a fraction of time, who's blinded by the sun or has a stab of pain in the chest. On the sidewalk they can collide with a ten- or five-year old, cycling close to the curb and losing control over the handlebars because he's wildly joyous about the news that Grandmom does not have cancer.

Nomi would hate to be a scare hare or have a posttraumatic disorder. She doesn't want a responsibility that's tainted with a bad memory.

She calls Mark. "Tell me, please, what is wise and safe or what's exaggerated fear. My mind has lost its way."

She's trying to be light, but her voice falters ominously. There's no time for consideration, Dilli will presently be waiting at school, with other parents on time in high spirits, with or without a sibling. Essential or not, the decision has to be made now, and she can't let Art decide. Or might she, if he's truly comfy and knows what he's doing? Do children have a primal trust for these things and a sixth sense or an angel beside them? If so, these ought to be respected, untouched.

It feels very different from "the other time". Of course, that was outdoors! And she forgot how good it is to stop and think. But any point of view can be devilish.

"Nome," says Mark, "you'll have to tackle this one day. I would leave Art at home, and most parents would. I'm sure."

Although it's against the law?

And NO kidnapping happens inside the homes?

They still haven't asked anyone about it.

They'll never say it again: what could possibly happen?

"That's my honest opinion," Mark adds, "and I hope it helps, but *you* are there with him."

In other words, it's your call, your action, or maybe with shared responsibility?

"No, sorry," he says, "you can go without Art, that's what I think, since you're asking. We can't be steered by one big incident or accident. We'd be at a loss altogether."

Or have I lost it completely now?

Don't climb, don't go anywhere near the stove... are some of the things Nomi could urge him, but she won't put ideas into his head. In his radical phase of recalcitrance – comes with the age? – any sort of emphasis could have opposite effects, and similarly when she leaves with an easy-and-free "See you, Art," she expects him to come running after her, like many times before. But in adult peace he's listening to *Dicky Dap* and building his yellow giraffe.

Better than dragging him against his healthy will and ruining his beautiful mood for the rest of the day?

<>

The C&D restaurant is known for its good and affordable lunches. It's crowded, and Anne hesitates at the door, but Lorna says, "Fine, we'll blend in."

Anne appreciates the plural.

There's a free table in the middle, where she can't have a seat with her back toward everyone.

At first she hides behind the menu card and Lorna says in earnest, "Please don't turn this into a tragedy or comedy. You don't need to cringe, there's nothing to conceal."

"Except all of me. I don't understand why I was edgy in the streets, where people just pass by! Here they have time to be peering at me."

"Yeah, because you are ducking and whispering."

Anne laughs wryly. Never before has it been clearer how gallows humor can work. Now it takes pluck to face the waiter.

"The quiche lorraine, please. And fresh orange juice."

Too late she thinks of the last time a quiche was ordered in her presence. On the other hand, it's good: she did forget for ages! It's just her favorite.

"Pumpkin soup and a sausage roll, please," Lorna orders. "With bitter lemon."

Anne puts the menu down. She drops her eyes and rubs her hands, that are on the table beside the sunglasses.

"Did you see that film last night?" Lorna asks.

"Which one?"

"The Best Exotic Marigold Hotel."

"Yes. Magnificent."

"With Evan?"

Why does she ask?

"Yes," Anne says. "Initially he was groaning about 'All these old people,' but then he got swept along. Also because he likes traveling."

"And you?"

"Well, yes, to non-trendy spots."

"That feed your columns?"

"Yes." Anne is revived.

But their drinks are brought.

"Thanks," Lorna says, turning to Anne again, chatting away to distract. "Where would Evan like to go? Any plans?"

"He's in for everything. Sun and beach, action and sports, hip city trips or rough countryside. I might steer him a bit." She won't lift her eyes – by taking a sip of juice – and see others. "He's got a load of free days left, as I couldn't go away yet, or wouldn't. What about you?"

"Oh..." Lorna is once more impressed with Anne's interest, which is more than a diversion. Most of her clients live in mental blanks. She's used to listening and enquiring, often with specific aims, but Anne has been different from the early stages on, and she's happy to answer. "I like some adventure, with a touch of luxury, a shower... Nothing exotic and far away. All this CO_2, it's just not on anymore, is it, but then, if we stop the extravagant travels, the economy or the world will collapse anyway. Some countries wouldn't have anything left, and my line of work would be abolished, unaffordable, non-essential."

"Yes." Anne sits up, and her voice is less low. "Social work will be ended before bureaucracy. You know, if diplomats' immunity were abolished, we'd rake in billions from their unpaid fines, cos they do as they please. The climate and economy could be saved yet!"

Her laughter is so loud that Lorna is not the only one to look around in a reflex, and Anne can see her think: OK, girl, forget where you are, or why we're here, and be your good old witty self again, but within bounds, please!

As sincere as civilized, Lorna laughs too, and she says, "Honestly, that's a new column! You're in terrific form. How does NUNA react?"

But all her natural tact and passion combined with her skills, lose their effects now, as Anne sees frowns and scrutinizing looks here and there, flinging her back to that black day in the other restaurant, still deep in her bunker with only cracks or chinks, which are too narrow to allow a peek inside, where a memory can be a bomb or a monstrous magnet.

She's startled by the waiter, who wants to put their lunches down soundlessly. Usually they do that with jovial aplomb, don't they? His elbow accidentally touches her shoulder, and it almost goes wrong in a ludicrous, unnecessary way, that makes her laugh with a boom again.

"I beg your pardon," he mutters as quietly as can be.

He takes to his heels and Lorna says, "Young, maybe a rookie, nervous like we are. Mm, this quiche of yours is something else! It's handmade. Why didn't I order that?"

"You didn't want the same thing as I had."

"And you were first, fair's fair. No," Lorna says, "all madness put aside..."

Now Anne bursts into childlike peals of laughter, that might have been festively infectious elsewhere, and Lorna tries to limit the damage. "You're right, what a funny phrase! But if I can have a bite, you can taste my sausage before I've put my teeth in it. Yes? Anne? Look at this, would you like a piece from the meaty middle or the crusty edge?"

When she's cutting a generous part, a man of about forty arrives to stop smack behind Anne's back. He drops a folded piece of paper on her plate and makes for the exit.

Knowing better already, she'd like to pretend they're in a romantic comedy with a shy admirer, rising to the occasion after many misunderstandings, and he declares his love in this would-be safe way. She loves films with dry humor daringly balanced between tragic and moving.

Is there an icy or expectant silence now, or is that also her boundless imagination?

Men have been known to propose dramatically in restaurants, and even in the movies she finds that pompous, corny, theatrical, preferring something small or hesitant, which is wittier and more touching. But her fantasy stops here, and her eyes don't follow this man.

The bluntness of his note drop has made cracks in her cocoon, through which she can see Lorna, who picks up the folded paper with one hand, squeezes Anne's arm with the other, more or less controlled, and asks, "Do you wish to read it or ditch it?"

"You read."

"Are you sure?"

"Yes, if it's friendly, I don't want to miss it, and otherwise..." Suddenly Anne turns composed or cold, breathing on time and keeping still. "We're here to practice, remember. I'll have to conquer this at some point. This is better, I hope, than rotten eggs or tomatoes in my face."

"And better with me here than with Evan, I mean, you are equal partners."

"And for you it's work?" Anne asks.

"Yes, mostly, just as well!"

Yet Anne is disappointed. "Are you playing a role then?"

"No, why?"

"Sorry, my fault. Just read the damn note, you've prepared me for shit, and I won't let this get to me. Out loud from the start, please, as if it's a Monopoly Chance card. Can I advance to Go? Or let me pass it!"

"Done your time and paid your dues, have you?" Lorna reads tonelessly. *"When will you relapse and repeat yourself? Not with my kids!"*

They don't know who saw the note being dropped. Now it's not ferociously torn up or crumbled and dumped, it's going under in the numbing noise of voices, forks and knives.

When a knife or gun is shown early in a mystery film, it may be a telling sign, but this table is an oasis of food and drinks, where Anne's dark glasses remain as they are, within reach.

"What a loser," Lorna says after a spoon of not so hot soup.

"Oh?"

"Yeah, if he'd shouted this for everyone to hear, there could have been a scene with more effects than this."

"But," Anne says, "he would have drawn attention to himself too."

"Exactly, he's a sneaky coward, a pathetic failure, adding nothing at all. You are much stronger, Anne, and more honest! Eat your quiche and relish the superb herbs. The juice is freshly squeezed, isn't it?"

<>

Outside Dilli's school, Nomi consults her watch once more. The Wednesday teacher has less grip on the big and boisterous class than her colleague, and when they come out late and loud, Dilli says, "I don't want to hear all these voices anymore. I didn't know how to paint 'spring'. Don't walk so fast! I've got a headache, and my legs hurt. Can I sit on your bike?"

They're trudging and zigzagging across the crowded ground in the sunshine, dodging running young teenagers, a whooshing football, dawdling parents who have ample time to make playdates for their kids. One boy is in tears because he can't go with Dilli.

"Sorry, Chris," Nomi tries to explain, "Dilli is very tired after school. She needs to recover."

"Why?"

"I think because she hears and sees a lot."

"Me too!"

His eyes are pleading, and Nomi says, "Will you come on a Sunday?"

Chris's dad nods. "OK, we will."

And he takes Chris with him energetically.

Reaching the bikes, Dilli says, "Can I wear a helmet? Then it goes better."

"Yes, good idea, but we'll need to buy one first."

"Now?"

"No, Art is home alone."

"But we pass by the shop!"

Dilli remembers that Art was gone for a long time. It's mentioned off and on, and she understands a great deal. The bike-shop fright itself is no longer in her young and flexible memory.

Nomi's wish to pick up threads, to find and connect loose ends, is a recent development. It needed to be recognized as a necessity first. Lately it's just been as if circumstances are cooperating.

Fate, including destiny, will rummage and rattle, catch up and repair – when it's right or if you're lucky, since there's also ill-fate. Who is brave or crazy enough to state that life is a matter of cause and effect or accountability? Not ending up in heaven or hell, but acting on earth, the place to learn, as a part of eternity.

Heaven and hell are in this world, for us to choose from every day and fight for the choice.

One or two minutes a day, something of the kind is undergone by Nomi without buckling knees, but not now and here. She doesn't want to know how much time has passed since she left home – left Art. Nothing can be done anymore except stay sane and act to the best of her abilities, one step at a time.

It would be stimulating for Dilli to buy a helmet on the way, a tempting opportunity to get home sooner perhaps than with Dil's whining fatigue or a fall off her bike. Because once she's *too* tired...

"Hey, your hat helps a lot, and I've brought some juice, that'll make you feel better. In spring we're not used to the sunshine yet, but it's full of vitamins."

"I don't see them or feel them!"

"Dil, do you know that famous bike racers wear hats?"

"No, helmets!"

"Anyhow, we're not going to collide or crash. See that cool car there?"

"A Land Rover!" Dilli cries.

"Ooh, do you think we can get past it?"

Nomi's senses are filling up with memories, the hard sun and wind, motion all around, a hundred sounds. She breaks into a sweat and feels nauseous all over again, as if the previous time was yesterday. But all of a sudden, she locks Dilli's bike, hoists it behind the three-foot wall of the school ground and lifts her into the backseat of her own bike, to ride off with the energy of determination and willpower, which seem to give rather than take strength, making amends.

"Mommy! What are you doing?"

"I thought you were tired," Nomi says over her shoulder, riding on.

"Gee, can't believe this..."

Dilli appreciates a surprise, and this one leaves her stupefied, enjoying the relaxed spin that allows her to suck her thumb.

Nomi skirts the parked cars but not the potholes. She's picturing Art at home: on the narrow side of the stairs, and on a windowsill of an upper floor. She has not asked other parents how they do this: leave their children behind, asleep or awake.

And even inside the house, when you're busy cooking dinner or doing the laundry downstairs, your child can get into all sort of scrapes upstairs. But Art has walked up and down many times, on the broad side of the steps and holding the handrail. The windows have safety locks. She's checked them before leaving. He sees the dangers these days and only climbs a stool to look out, through the closed windows.

"Can you hear the gulls?" Dilli says.

"Yes, I love the sounds of gulls."

"You're mad about them. But you're not mad."

"Well, um, no."

And they listen contently.

"But can they be mean?" Dilli asks.

"Absolutely, when they're hungry, or they protect their kids, I mean chicks."

Dilli nods and sucks her thumb, hearing the gull screeches with their striking two sides: endearing and fierce.

Inadvertently they've passed by the bike shop without bringing up a helmet.

At home the Duplo stairs have collapsed, but Art has not flung them around the room. With a chair and closet he has improvised a climbing frame in order to reach the top at about six feet and get a jigsaw, which was there because it's too difficult for him, although a part is finished now.

"A hundred pieces! And I don't eat the sweets, on the shelf there."

More like forty, says neither Mom nor Dil.

<>

Finishing the tax returns at last, Bernard wants to be perfectly truthful and reduce the deductible expenses he entered, but then begins a hassle of the checks and specifications that drive him up the wall. A series of well-meant attempts later he gives up and calls Nomi, who helps out and asks, "Would you be available to mind Art and Dilli for a midweek? Or are you busy dating?"

"Actually, I can't remember what I've typed to who in these clumsy contact boxes. Tax or dates!?"

"Oh, mixing them up? Shall I pick someone for you?"

Bernard's throat hurts, because they're talking about a candidate for her mother's successor. But no, that's nonsense. Life with Hannah is over, and there's room for new love in this universe.

By way of a reward, after sending the definitive tax returns, he casts another glance at the dating site. The place is pretty addictive, buzzing with search-and-find stimuli. The world is close at hand here, his profile draws numerous visitors with photos, plans, hopes, evocative info, with or without kids and interesting jobs. Through one window he can take a look at someone's life, and they're bound to reply. In vivacious emails the site is sure to point at every invitation and reciprocation, direct or by detour.

A woman has added him to her *favorites*. "Quiet yet active, happy gardener (44) would like to share nature, music, film, in the motion of daily life."

There's more worth his while in her profile, but her age frame for a partner is 40-55, which is kind as it is. He could react in various amusing ways – "May I overstep slightly?" – but he's in two lives as it is: the real one and his fiction are mingled as they are. No wonder he's tired or coming down with something. His appointment at the cardiologist's tomorrow is a good reason for postponement and contemplation. Is he actually a social person at all? He shouldn't impose a heart-patient on a 'young woman', should he?

A part of him would prefer to receive a message from Debbie Atkins, the film producer.

Having thought that, between all the horror and action movies, there's not much beautiful and valuable in that business. It's as bogus as the special effects! In many movies it rains out of blue skies. Fighters take positions to receive blows that could easily have been dodged; when you turn off the 'sounds of thumps', the dumbness and emptiness of it all are stunning. Again and again, heavy doors are kicked open by the police in one or two easy go's, and no bad guy copies that. Doing dialogues in fast cars, the drivers look sideways for minutes without causing a crash. Elsewhere there are crashes galore without any plausible cause.

Like a thunderclap the name Anne Hoaver enters his mind: this could be a column of hers! He's ashamed of their 'affinity', with their viewpoints and the desire to convey information as sharply and clearly as glass. They also shared or still share the publisher, and to his dismay he'd like to know how she is.

He writes an email to let Simon know that his novel *And Walk* will be finished in a few weeks, and to ask aside, "Are you still in touch with Anne?"

Which sounds so personal or private that his finger lingers on the mouse a long while before clicking Send.

Then it's high time for groceries and workouts, and odd jobs around the house, kitchen, yard, but on the stairs a sentence for *And Walk* comes of its own accord, and during the brushing of teeth there's a whole paragraph – as if to underline that he's leading a double life. In the meantime, he's downright shivery and weak in the legs. How would that go in a midweek with Art and Dilli?

He'd better take thyme syrup to begin with. It "soothes the

throat and airways", but what on earth has he done: this pharmacy stuff contains sixty percent of sugar. So much for the muscle firmness. Who in this world has gone off their heads?

7

NO FINAL STATION

<>

Every day Anne checks the TV guide for anything outstanding in the evening, also for potential work. Now that the lunch incident doesn't seem to have any consequences (no window is smashed and no door is plastered with nasty words), there comes a degree of self-belief that enables her to make some careful journalistic plans without falling into traps.

Dear Simon,

My apologies in advance if you find this email inappropriate or repulsive. It's still hard for me to know what could be acceptable in my situation, but I can only learn by making a start – or mistake? 😊 Have you planned *Time-In* with another editor? I would understand that, of course. Otherwise, we might someday discuss possibilities because we did love the project.

Modest yet hearty wishes, Anne.

Once confidence has a foot on the ground, it can expand. From a corner of her eye, she sees *Abducted* in the TV guide, a quality docu series, without ripping the page or fleeing into a cleaning spree or making tea.

Mesmerized in spite of herself, she goes on reading, more and more relieved that it's quite different from her 'case': in this program they trace children who are taken abroad by a parent.

She'd never heard of a Center International Child Abduction. It's difficult to take in the details, but she perseveres and reads on. "Most parents whose child is missing don't have the financial means to get him or her back."

Between bewilderment and concentration, the phone makes her jump, but she's happy to adapt when it's Pat, who asks, "How did it go this morning?"

"Oh, thanks, alright, I think."

"Shall I drop by, or would you like to come over? Sorry, you've just been out."

"And how!" Anne says. "But maybe I've got the taste for it now, and you know what they say about barriers: take them a few times right away! I've got some adrenaline left, or unrest, so... Or would you like to go out yourself? Have you told Cas about me?"

"Yes, was that allowed?"

"Why not. I mean, you are the best judge of that."

But keep it under your hat.

"Care to say what you want now?" Pat asks.

"No, I'm bad at making choices."

"OK, I'll come to you. With Cas around I'm never free."

Anne gives her address and says, "Thank you. See you."

"Yes, lovely."

To Anne's ears it sounds like 'I've always wanted to have a daughter,' and the situation would be bizarre, too good for words. Yet it's nothing suspicious, is it? No sign on the wall? There are people who feast on their contact with criminals; they love to visit them in prison. But she's positive that Pat is not like that.

She doesn't really 'hang up' the landline but presses a finger on the button and holds the receiver: today's achievement could give courage – or hubris – to call her mother, with a good possibility to keep it short: I'm expecting company, I just wanted to let you know that I'm fine, much better.

As the phone rings this very instant, with her finger still there, it's extra loud. Perplexed, she lets go in a full and odd silence, until somebody mumbles, probably just in case, "Hello?"

"Anne here," she says out of an old habit, and the astonishment subsides.

"Hey, it's me, Simon. How can this be – so prompt?"

He must be thinking: are you still in the funny farm?

She laughs and explains coherently what happened.

"Fabulous." He sounds more circumspect than formerly, when there was a baby around. "Our paths cross!"

Better than our swords, she holds back on time, because he would not see her illustrating smile.

"So it's a good sign?" she asks without stammering, and her new grin is inaudible too.

"Definitely," Simon says. "Time..."

What's he thinking in his pause: ...can heal wounds and sins?

"...Time can be self-willed."

"Wow," Anne cries, "that's a good title too, or a subtitle."

He whistles between his teeth. "You're right, we're a team again already!"

She swallows and he clears his throat.

They haven't even met since...

"I like your email," he continues. "As far as I'm concerned, you've got the green light for *Time-In*."

And as far as society is concerned...

"And your colleagues?" she asks.

"They'll recognize this as a special opportunity, for both contents and promotion. And after all you have a contract."

That could surely be annulled after her actions, but apparently, he hasn't done so – because he was baffled or counting on a favorable ending?

Anne could scream from joy, but as Grant's best pupil she tells herself that a counter of over-optimism can be lurking behind the corner, turned into overkill.

"Thank you," she says with goose bumps.

In a voice between fatherly and formal he asks, "Do you have plans?"

"Yes, firstly... Brace yourself, it would be audacious..."

"Fear not, we have skins of steel."

"And hear me out, please," Anne says. "Peter Mills is from the Center International Child Abduction. An interview with him would be a meaningful chapter. I'll be in the wings. I'll bring things up and link them. It will be very different from the Van Gelder story."

And Bloomsdale's?

She's carried on to be ahead of criticism, as it were, but Simon says, "Do you know Mills personally?"

"No," Anne says, trembling.

"Good, you go and drop by innocently. Sorry, I mean, request an interview with an open mind. No, excuse me, it's my job to take that first step, evidently."

And hide her real name for now? To prepare them gently. To remove doubts beforehand, of himself and the Center and the rest of the country?

Anne is quiet and keeps her body still as well.

"So, you'll hear from me," Simon concludes. "Thanks for the good initiative. We'll speak soon."

She hangs up and forgets about calling her mother. Simon's sober sympathy – if that's what it is – keeps her fairly balanced, and Pat is on her way – has been how long now?

She is tired, as she realizes late, but it's out of the question to cancel Pat. After a double life of the mind, the body is bound to struggle and trail. It helps to think of Evan and Lorna, to look around the room calmly, tidy up, and put other thoughts in the freezer.

There's no pressure, Pat is lovable and won't expect a neat reception. Anyway, she's always been a social person, now returning after an extensive sort of 'gap year'. This phrase is painfully more accurate here than 'sabbatical'. She needs to get used to the bustle again. In fact, that process or notion is growing mighty real, which lifts her spirits.

Pat has brought a basket of cheerful violet plants, presented bashfully. "For the balcony?"

"Thank you! Have you carried them all the way?"

"In the bike bags. An E-bike!"

"Excuse me," Anne says, "how young are you?"

"Seventy-eight. I take the quiet roads, where possible."

"Do you like grape juice?"

"Thank you." Pat glances around. "Are you alright here?"

"Yes, for the time being. I'm not sure if I can go home again. And this is home too, often with Evan. I don't know what you've read about us..."

"Oh, everything that came my way at the time, without knowing. There wasn't much from your point of view, was there? I read about a court hearing and mitigating circumstances, but I've made no enquiries."

"In any case," Anne says, "it's good to have you here."

"For me too. Do you *want* to go back one day? If I can be of any help then..."

Out of Pat's mouth it sounds so easy that Anne has tears from surprise, dreaming away. She'll have to go back, but now it touches her that she *can* and wants to and will be able to, as soon as it feels good.

She tells Pat, "The house there is often empty. We can't go on like this. I'll need either to let it go or be so drastic as to... No, anything else would be impossible, wouldn't it?"

That's discussed with Grant, but it's been too far away.

Pat almost finishes her drink and asks, "Are you tense about the people in the neighborhood there?"

"Yes."

"About the memory?"

"Terrified."

"And yet you want to go?"

Anne looks away again and says, "Yes."

Across the street there's an office building, where the sunblinds are mostly down, which she's never disliked before. When somebody opens or closes a blind and peers out, they can see her, but they've never said hello to her, as they might with a handwave or a nod and smile. She would greet them. But it dawns on her that she's never paused at a window long.

A gaze from across or any form of greeting shouldn't hurt her anymore, on the contrary.

"Our son, Dan, is gay," Pat says. "He's been happy with a man for twelve years now and they'd love to adopt a child. It's difficult and they miss that part of life. Cas and I don't have grandchildren in this country, but your sorrow is unspeakably deeper."

With her back toward Pat, Anne sags onto the coffee table. There are countless people with pains of the past and aches of longing. We can't compare, we can be touched by the others for reciprocity.

She doesn't want big tears, but her will is melting.

Pat stays put, making herself scarce and musing away too, not disturbing with a word or movement.

After a while of timelessness Pat gives Anne a kiss on the head and leaves without speaking or sneaking.

Shortly after, Evan comes in, not tiptoeing either, and Anne can hear that he's not really 'coming home', even when he gets a beer from the fridge in a routine way.

He says, "At work I couldn't call you. How did it go today?"

"It was good, interesting. But sweetheart, I'm taking a shower, and then I'll tell you."

"Hm, is that a trick to make me cook dinner?"

Anne puts her face in the hollow of his neck. "Back in a minute. You nibble some crisps. Then we'll have fish fingers with fried potatoes and early fresh carrots, yes?"

She turns on the shower hard and hot, and she holds her head in the jet a long time, although her hair was washed and dyed this morning. When the heck was this morning?

Having trouble standing up, she leans against the wall, spreading her fingers, legs and toes. She opens her mouth wide, bows the head between her hands, and the pores absorb the water from her crown down to the foot soles, until the room is full of steam.

She wraps herself into a large towel, pushes the door open and savors the coolness like a cloud on a sticky day. She can smell that Evan has been busy in the kitchen.

After their meal with a number of day reports and his array of awed reactions, he stretches and asks, "What's for dessert: a cup of coffee or a hug?"

Anne is yawning profusely. "Sorry, we can do with both, but I'll have a nap, sadly that's just imperative, and next I need to write or do some research. Sorry, Ev, you are more important, and you know how much I owe you, which I'll show better..."

"You don't need to," he says. "You saved my life first."

"Yes, I want to show you that we can start again with everything. Trust me, I mean, all will be worth our while!"

"Ah, you're building your future but sending me away now."

No, you're free to stay; it's your own place.

She doesn't know how much of his misery is acted, and sleep is overpowering her. As a sign of deep de-tension? She can only surrender and mutter, "Don't you want a night off?"

"Well, once you are working..."

His previous re-start was dazzling and festive, because she let him reveal himself as a dad. He remembers each hour of every bike ride with the baby. All results from the chores and odd jobs he did, the bike seat, stair gate, insect screen, got a gleam from his bond with the boy, until they answered the front door together and saw the expression on that man's face, going as white as a sheet as if his heart collapsed, when he saw his flesh and blood.

Even the smell of a poop diaper lasted and became something melancholic.

What happened to the diaper supply and pile of wet wipes?

Evan can still feel the boy's weight and movements on his arm, the busy fingers on his neck, brimful of newness and curiosity, ease and closeness, with the first speaking sounds of a baby who'd love to be much older. But the man reached out again and took over his grandson, as it was never meant to be different.

<>

After the evening meal Nomi tells Mark, "If you put them to bed, I'll go and fetch Dilli's bike."

"If it's still there," he says grimly.

"Can I come?" Dilli asks.

"Sorry, no, I'll go to the gym as well."

"I can go too!" And she shows them how gym is done.

"You're good at it, Dil, but it's bedtime."

"Will you be one or two hours?" Mark asks, not unsuspecting.

"I think in combination with an errand. See you later."

"Vague!" he cries.

And why?

Dil's bike is still inconspicuous behind the wall, and Nomi is exceedingly glad of that, as if it's irreplaceable.

She's off again but has to make up her mind at a junction: go for a workout first and then move on to 'the house' in the dusk or dark? She has no plan or strategy, only the weird wish to do this by herself, without any influence – for everyone's good. This urge is so strong that she doesn't need to gather much braveness anymore.

She lets the traffic lights decide: it's green for the turn left, toward the gym.

Of late she's trained hard there, with a variation of power and endurance, but tonight she can manage only twenty minutes, then she's too distracted for comfort. She takes a shower, checks out, and calls Mark to let him know where she's going.

"Oh well," he says, "at least you're not being stealthy about it."

"No, there's no need for that, is there?"

"But you prefer to go without me."

"Yes," Nomi says, "possibly this once, which is nothing to do with you, only in a positive sense. You know how thankful I am."

"There's no need for that either. Will you be careful?"

"Yes, darling Mark."

Why, though? she wonders.

"Keep your phone on, Nome!"

"OK, but don't call me, except if something is wrong with the kids."

"Or with me," Mark says.

"Of course. I love you."

I love you. See you next."

Boy, did all that sound like the goodbye for a long trip?

As the two-year sedation has worn off, her heart is thumping the minute she enters the street, knowing that she'll need to go further than last time.

She parks the car in about the same spot and turns the engine and radio off. As if she listened. Must have been classical music, or else it would have been disturbing her.

There are lights on in the house. That doesn't necessarily mean anything, but her guts tell her it does. She walks along the sidewalk on the opposite side of the street. From elsewhere, kids' voices come floating by, and above her a pigeon flutters wildly in the gutter. A single cyclist passes by, a car drives away, and a lawn is mown on the other end of the street, but the sounds of people are nothing compared to the passion of blackbirds in the dusk.

Most residents have turned lights on before the curtains are drawn. They may not realize that they're very visible from outside, or they don't mind.

Somebody calls a dog. Cooing away, the pigeon has landed in a budding tree. The house watched by Nomi has a spacious but ordinary and rural garden with wild flowers and laconic groups of primroses, violets, forget-me-nots.

Some of the kids' voices have become rough. Is there a sports field or a playground nearby?

Even on the sidewalk by the house she's not afraid to look inside, where Evan is walking to and fro. He picks up a magazine and sits at the table. What an advantage to know that he lives here, who she called 'the man' up till recently.

A red and white cat strolls by at utter leisure. Nomi wants to get more impressions unseen, so she stops behind a half-full box bush, but then she's ill at ease. The evening is growing humid, which makes her cough a little. The kind of trance that soothed her tension is gone, and she hurries to the door before doubt can strike all over.

Panting, she rings the bell at once, then reels back: with a shock she puts herself into his shoes. She's never been inside the house. Art was outside with Bernard, and they were all strangely polite, waiting until everything was clear and 'settled'.

"Excuse me," she calls out when Evan opens the door. "I beg your pardon."

They're staring with searching eyes, the past is breathing down their necks and he is in sudden despair, but both of them are either victims or co-responsible, now forced to defrost.

"You're the mother," he says.

"Nomi."

"Hi, I'm Evan, and it's me to beg your pardon to start with."

On Anne's behalf?

Without betraying her.

But how can this be, just like that?

They don't shake hands and couldn't say 'pleased to meet you'.

They didn't pay much attention to each other last time, when lives were hustled, only to Art, who left him and went with her in the end without crying or screaming, after the granddad intervened. All were trapped between the protocol and their instincts, longing for Art, caught between the knowing and feeling, police and family, interrogation and handing over. With Art in the middle, everybody was unbearably aware of the others, also aching to hold and kiss him and cuddle him to pulp, as far as he'd let them.

In order to limit the silent tumult, the men controled themselves and let Art be with Nomi. After all she was the one who lost him most. Self-conscious, she shielded Art as much as possible, not claiming him or keeping him out of sight, but with Hattum's approval. He had to be absolutely accurate. There was no hysterical muddle, no Salomon fight requiring a sword.

Evan had heard enough about the abduction, and Anne's behavior of the last hour spoke for itself yet. His resistance broke soon after hers. He fell ill but in a more physical way than she. It resembled food poisoning or gastroenteritis.

Those hours and days shrank to flashes that will have to grow back. Nomi has prepared herself, but a shiver runs through Evan as if the illness has also come back.

Mechanically he's retreated a step, and she goes in. They stop and stand again, as if expecting a third person – who arranged the contact? – or they need to wait for their brains to work again.

He shuffles past her to close the door, then he walks to the room, followed by her.

She doesn't look around in there, but as surprised as he is, she asks, "How is Anne?"

His eyes have drifted before he answers, lost in thought, "Good. She's more or less independent again. In my apartment. There's a lot going on right now."

Before the next question from her or himself, Evan swallows and nods and tries to look at her without feeling sick. He sits and asks, "How is he, your boy, Art?"

Nomi can see that his eyes are burning. She sits down too, not next to him or facing him, but at a ninety-degree angle. Neither of them leans forward or backward.

"He's well," she says. *Very well* is kept in. "It's a tricky age, but hey..." *That's part of it all and he is so worth it.*

"Headstrong?" Evan asks.

"Yes, at times that's putting it mildly."

A smile or grimace of him says: I noticed that in pleasant ways, but one thing is sure, he doesn't take after me.

"Is he at pre-school?"

"Yes, four mornings a week."

Did it take much adjusting at home at the time? Didn't he recognize you?

And Evan goes on. "Can he enjoy himself there?"

"Yes, he likes the bustle and action and change. Which is hard to dose."

In their positions they could easily avoid each other's eyes, but in the second instance Nomi does glance at him, asking, "I understand that you have looked after him too?"

"With heart and soul," Evan blurts out as if he couldn't wait. "The best weeks of my life!" He puts up a firm face and says, "That's because I'd just begun a new life, and Reg helped massively, I mean Art – after a bad phase. It sounds corny, but that chunk of time with him was an enormous gift to me."

"And then," says Nomi, "you had to start from scratch."

"Yes. Every day."

"In this house."

There are still toys in the pen, on the other side by the dining table, that was or is also Anne's worktable.

"Sorry," he says with a hand on his eyes. "I've never put his things away, after all this time. I can't bear seeing them, but I can't lose a thing either. Mostly for Anne's sake."

"I'm glad too," Nomi says.

She wants to go around the house and feel everything that was touched by Art, but she won't move. Simultaneously that impulse of hers makes room for something else.

She asks, "Has Anne been back here?"

"No. We're dreading that terribly, of course. Maybe I should clear the baby things first. It seems too hard on her to do that herself."

"Have you suggested it?"

He sighs. "I will. There appears to be a breakthrough in the air."

Nomi keeps boldly direct. "Would you stay and live here?"

"I think so, but that's like torment, isn't it? Yet it would also be hard to leave for good. The very idea that other people settle here... Well, as if anyone would buy it. You are an estate agent, so tell me honestly..."

After a heavy pause Nomi says, "It's a good house. Art was comfortable here and it was a long time ago. You've done a fine job with it."

Evan gets up and bumps about. "I can't even think of selling it! Sorry, your child was kidnapped – by my partner – and now you're helping us?"

"No no, I wouldn't dare. I thought it would be like harassment. I had no idea, just came here for my own sake."

"OK." He puffs a lot of air out. "I don't know what to do. Tell Anne about this? What is it: a miracle or catastrophe?"

Nomi is silent.

In the middle of the room, Evan stops, his arms dangling. "Do you want to see everything? His room?"

"Yes, I've always thought that had to be done. It's been on my mind all this time."

"That's logical, he's your boy, you're entitled, but can I talk with Anne first? We have no leg to stand on. It seems impossible to do that, before she's been back here again. Or would it be a good thing?"

He puts his hands on his head and turns around, his back toward Nomi.

"It's alright," she says. "No matter what. I'm sorry to have intruded like this."

"No, maybe it's just as well. But you know," he rubs his face, "this is also Reg's house. I never knew him and that was my fault. You see, many things were his too. So you can imagine what Anne will have to face."

"Yes, I can, and I'm sorry."

Making for the door, Nomi gives him a gentle, wide berth, and she holds the knob. "I came for my own good, but I hope it will help Anne too."

Wish her well on my behalf, could sound normal.

"Thanks," he says, without seeing her out.

And would you like her phone number? is often a regular question.

<>

Bernard sees a physician who gives him a B12 shot on the spot – the ampoule is 'borrowed' from another patient – and promptly Bernard feels better, smiling with a wink, "Here's the power of suggestiveness and wishfulness!"

"Yes, after a miracle or two of this evocative kind, people are canonized. Hordes fly to Rome for such ceremonies. But in earnest," the doctor says after more testing and measuring. "I think you've been undermined by a virus for years, dormant or stuck, gnawing away. I'll prescribe medication, but it went deep, so be patient."

Bernard is partially pleased that something concrete and treatable can be a scapegoat. But there's a heart murmur as well, and an appointment is made at the cardiologist's, which is all going fast – while he is in denial?

Days later, the heart film and echo show a formidable leak in a valve. A puff or cloud of something streams out somewhere, and he can't stand the thought of that, but if it doesn't get worse, major surgery won't be necessary now.

"We'll check it every year," says the cardiologist. "You'll be notified for the next appointment. And call us in case of rhythm disorder or water retention."

In the consternation Bernard fails to ask how it's come about, what exactly is leaking (oxygen?) and if it's bound to wear him down. He wants to ignore this immediately, and it's not the reason why he cancels a lecture and declines an invitation for more appearances.

He can't understand his colleagues who travel to one gig after another and write big blogs about them. When do they write their novels? Or colleagues, for that matter, who struggle with discipline and inspiration. If the work is a burden or it stagnates, go do something else and have a good time!

But they'll declare him a fool for writing pointless film scripts, and rightly so. He needs discipline to stop scribbling and do something useful! Since he's not hearing from filmmaker Debbie again (a year is nothing in that business?), it's time to be realistic for feasible projects and count his blessings.

Alright, when *And Walk* is finished, he'll get more active in the field of performances. "You'll find inspiration there too!" people tell him. But he hates that phrase, and he has novel material for years.

Sudden Depth has international reviews: "A wonderful book full of beautiful and colorful characters." Perhaps Debbie has read some. She's not stealing the story, is she? That's a notorious risk of sending material without legal protection; a conflict can be ugly and expensive. Even via renowned film agents the copyright issues are complicated. They made him sign lengthy statements once, which he hardly read. From the BBC he's received letters that might be a trifle fishy: "Very interesting indeed. However, we are developing a similar story right now."

But he doesn't want to be paranoid, and if he's too cautious, he'll get nowhere at all.

Ambition is a tyrant.

There are easy-going people who continually run into luck with grand results without a sweat, and how did they begin, in all modesty?

It does happen.

Somewhat recalcitrant, he googles local gardeners with the first name of the woman on website Amore (which may well be an alias) and behold! Here's the photo that he knows from the dating site!

Goodness, how active, successful, worldly, and charming she is. Well, Mr Bloomsdale, be wise and give it a rest. Save yourself from disappointment. She would not fancy a neurotic or heart patient, who thinks he needs to be two parents and two grandparents at the same time. Back to cliché basics, man: cook a tasty and healthy dinner to begin with! And tomorrow, relish a day at Green Lake again.

<>

When the window cleaner is at work where there's no balcony, it strikes Anne that she feared not only inquisitive looks from him and passers-by, but also the option to jump.

It's coming back to her: the cleaner outside the window where the baby was asleep.

What a paradox: she misses those days, although the sense of liberation makes her quiver. So different from the present! She doesn't pass Pat's plants to Evan but finds them a place out here. She loves arranging them, and she can look down into the deepness without a panic. It's no abyss!

The sense of moving on remains when Wil calls and says once more, "Do come and live here, to spare yourself and put an end to the rigmarole for good."

After about three visits from Wil at the clinic, Anne hasn't seen her mother again. And now she answers quietly, "Last time, you said your front door was blotted with nasty slogans about me."

"Well, yes, that was imagery, how it felt at first. And you don't need to move in with me, although that would save sums of money, which you can use now. That house of yours has become worthless!"

When Anne came to her senses during Grant's treatment and the supporting activities, she thought she could never blame people for anything anymore: after her own crime she lost the right to pass any kind of judgment. But these intentions were torpedoed by Wil.

"How does your mother survive in her own town?" Doctor Grant asked Anne.

"Oh, she has a charm button and a sad key and charity knob, operated cleverly."

"Are you the sole person she can try to destroy?"

"No," Anne duly explains, "But she's honestly willing to help. I'm indebted to her!"

"Or she kept you in her frenetic power. I've met her," Grant goes on. "With contrasting moods, breaking your self-esteem and stability."

"Oh, so my father was the sweet man?"

"Perhaps powerless?"

"Like me," Anne says.

"No, that was a temporary weakness. Your vulnerability has been a starting point for you now, giving access to suppressed moments. The rest of your life is ahead of you."

"Without her?"

"That's possible," says Grant. "But then you'd miss opportunities, to measure and show how you're healing, overcoming, forgiving..."

"Anne?" Wil resumes. "When you're up to it, I can come over for a week or so, even to tidy and clear the house – before you'll return there. I'll take a payable hotel."

"No, thanks, we're making plans for the house."

Renovate in every sense. Make it sustainable in the process. A very fresh paint inside and out. I'll be doing a lot myself. A nice form of community service! If I dare standing out there in full sight of passersby...

"Will Evan help?"

"And friends."

Have you got friends left?

"They know all about you?" Wil does ask.

"Yes."

Lorna and Cindy have offered support. Even doctor Mullan! Because he's retired?

"Anyhow, you're welcome here too, for a long or short while, for some distance from past events and a fresh view of things, to forget..."

Anne sighs and scratches her forehead. "I've got piles to do now, so..."

"Oh, sorry, off you go. Bye!"

A week after the lunch at C&D, Anne goes for groceries at the local market on her own, undisguised. She does and does not miss Lorna. She won't be a pain to Evan. He'll be in early today – for her sake? She'll treat him to a nice pie and sorbet ice-cream with rum.

On the streets it doesn't escape her when gazes dwell on her, but she seems to be getting used to that. There may be so many reasons! It will pass one day. She alternates the hat and glasses with more openness, depending on the weather and her state of mind. Her self-esteem returns, and next week her self-defense course begins. Just for confidence and strength in general, as Lorna states.

Nothing bad happens in the stores, and for minutes Anne forgets her past. The scars appear to shrink.

Last night she recorded episodes of *Abducted*, to study them with a sharp mind by day. It's a favorable aspect that Peter Mills is not on the actual TV shows himself; he'll add to *Time-In* all the more – should he consent.

Back at home, she makes the room extra homey with flowers, perky newly bought Vivaldi concertos and the dinner table with treats and pretty things.

Evan looks tired and admits, "I feel torn sometimes, between the apartment and the house. It's no fault of yours, obviously, we're alright and I want this myself, you know that, don't you?"

Suddenly she hears the humming of the oven louder than Vivaldi, and she turns the music off. Beware and keep an eye on the time: these turnover pies can blacken in a blink, and the broccoli could be over-cooked before you know it.

For ages she's known what's coming. Life has warned her repeatedly: you can't be sheltering in postponement forever; the time could be right before you think you're ready.

But maybe she should have eaten something first.

There's no need for her to ask, "Why now?"

Evan says, "I guess you'll never really be ready. In two- or five-years' time it can even be harder. And now the um... Art's mother has paid a visit."

What? He calls him Art and that's good. But in her house? No, it's their house, which helps, and she takes a moment to realize that Evan lives there with his warmth and sense of humor, good looks and handiness, his animosity, social ease, endeavor, patience. All these must do well there and do him justice, as she witnessed those weeks, when they were the three of them.

To affirm that they are alright, she checks the oven and takes a gulp of mineral water – mm, nice and cool.

Pulling herself together, she asks, "When was that?"

"Wednesday night."

She doesn't ask why, or: Why haven't you told me?

"Did she phone first?"

"No," Evan says. "She was on the doorstep out of the blue, and polite, never aggressive or hostile."

"What did you do?"

"Nothing, really."

"And she?"

"Not much either. Her name is Nomi."

As if that's never come up.

"How long did she stay?" Anne asks.

"Hm... Some twenty or thirty minutes, or shorter, it's hard to tell."

"What did she say?"

"That it's a good house. She's a kind person, and also concerned about you, wondering what it must be like for you, for us."

"Isn't she horribly furious?" Anne says.

"I didn't see anything like that."

"How can that be?"

"Well," Evan thinks. "Don't know."

She has enough reasons to be happy now. After the magic ending.

His voice drops. “She knows about Reg – dying. And she’s had some time to cope with her own horror.”

“So it’s my turn?”

“Anne, love, it’s incomparable.”

“But you brought it up, you mentioned her.”

“Yes. She’d like to see where Art lived. His room.”

The name pronounced by Evan – as if he’s used to it – keeps the situation understandable and safe, at a distance, for the little time being.

“What did you say?” Anne asks.

“That I’d square it with you, of course.”

“Thanks. Will she come back then?”

“We can’t stop her, can we? We don’t *want* to, we had her son in the house. It’s better this way, I promise. It’s extraordinary of her to come over!”

The plural ‘we’ is good again, but the heat of the oven hits her leg from behind at the kitchen table, and she turns it off, telling herself: you need to get a new oven, babe, that doesn’t do this, get hot and burn on the outside. Or are we going to move house?

It would be especially dangerous for toddler’s hands.

The possible bits of reintegration have been practised, visualized, but the reality of applying it all is looming like a mountain. She did climb some big ones with snowy slopes, worried about the way back, due to lack of time, past a slippery glacier with crevices. During one breath-taking pink sunset, she was watching it from a reassuring distance, profoundly grateful to be safe.

Some ground has been broken here, for a track or course of action, and she thinks: what can go wrong? I merely need to peel an onion as large as life.

Absently she says, “Let’s go.”

“What?”

"I can do it now."

"I see. But Annie, dinner is ready, and going on an empty stomach is a bad idea."

She gets a piece of pie from the oven and puts it on his plate. "I'm going to the bathroom to fix my face. You can eat, I'll drink something, and we'll bring food in the car."

"Wait, Anne, there's no rush."

"How can I wait? Would you prefer to go tomorrow? Would I get a wink of sleep?"

He takes a bite but says, "Prepare yourself, please, put yourself in the situation to come. What did Grant suggest? Look at the photos of Reg and Art. Or would you like to call Lorna? She said you always can."

He knows it's pointless and goes on eating, to arm himself or to gain time.

"Sorry," Anne smiles, "you don't need to gobble on my account, you can eat on our way there too. In the bathroom I'll start focusing. You're right. And we won't forget to blow the candles out."

He's never expected to find a pool of blood from a cut wrist, when she stays in the bathroom rather long. She would not abandon him. Grant knows damn well what he does and what's going on: "Anne is connected with her surroundings now, with her loved ones. She would not betray your trust."

But a brief moment he feels alone for two.

Stopping at a traffic light, people may be amused by the way she feeds him a crusty and crumbly pie, taking small bites herself. If she can taste that it's still hot and delicious, is it a self-defense diversion?

At funerals the food and drinks need to be good as well.

Evan often makes a fuss in traffic, behaving like an idiot, he admits, for example when a light is red "insanely long" – "Why can those people there go first?" – or when someone drives *under* the speed limit, or others fail to indicate direction and brake abruptly. But now he's subdued, without the usual inclination to hoot, which Anne frankly regards as his worst characteristic.

With the savory food she's grounding herself.

While they're looking straight in front of them, thoughts about their destination are not diverted by rush-hour. Anne keeps the names of Art and Nomi in her head. She'll be going through Art's things, whose mom has a request and does everyone a good turn with it.

For the first step into this huge future, Anne badly needs her glasses and hat, because of the neighbors and others in the street, even though there wasn't that much contact. As they're approaching, her brain clings to the practical things. Does she want Evan to pull over outside the house or further down the street? Will they walk to the front door or go around the back? It might be better for her to go alone and reduce the risk of a disgraceful melodrama for both of them, but she needs him by her side, like the other time, although she can't seem to remember or feel much. She knows the bare facts via Evan, who gave them to Grant in one numbed go.

She knows the word 'catatonic', but it doesn't touch and shake her yet, which could happen in frightening ways. Shouldn't Grant or Lorna be present now? What did they agree and decide again?

She's not asking Evan about it. Both have been quiet, until she says, "Please, try to park in our spot straightaway? With me on the curb side by the house. And will you act as if I'm a colleague of yours?"

He nods and slowly drives into the street. Here and there it's dinnertime, but several children are playing outside. Another car pulls over close by, which Anne is glad about.

She should have sat in the back, like in a taxi, to see and be seen less. She doesn't want to recognize anybody, but she won't close her eyes. Did it use to be this lively here? In what time of the year? A number of kids are now old enough to play out by themselves. A year or two can make an awesome difference.

There's no free parking spot right by the house. She gets out at once, but after Evan, and she makes herself walk normally, if possible, up to the front door, that's opened by him – not on the inside like then, as he had to report step by step in Grant's room, where the atmosphere was so neutral and clean that he did alright.

Too familiar coats and little jackets are on the pegs here, for several seasons. She's prepped herself for grotesque, teary, and dreary histrionics without end, in the living-room and upstairs and everywhere.

The fact that Evan takes part, keeps her going, but they leave some crying space between them. It's a trial as it is to feel and smell everything of Art or Reg – how to tell? – in his bathtub and the play pen. All images probe the thin skin of her body and soul.

After a long day of bumps and hiccups, the boy would lean languidly on her cheek, neck and chest. His fingers fidgeted and made curls in her hair, then he pulled at it so hard – a primal reflex? – that she gave a shriek unwillingly, which made him jump in his turn, but fortunately he was very consolable.

She can't believe that Art slept in Reg's cot. It's beyond her that she was responsible, and she needs to clutch Evan, with his salty face, or else she'd freeze all over again.

Art is alive, but he doesn't exist in her world anymore. Or something can be done to put an end to the lunacy of it. His mom was here and would like to come back, which is not impossible. Evan said her name, and it sounded sweet. Why not?

<>

When Art was one-and-a-half, he'd come slip-shuffling down the stairs in his sleeping bag at night, and like a dog, he'd lay on the landing outside the master bedroom.

At 5:45 a.m. today, Art switches on a big light in this room, hops into his parents' bed and says, "When I eat my bread neat, I don't need a diaper?"

"You mean in bed?" Nomi mutters half asleep. "I think when you're four or three."

"When am I three?"

"In a couple of months."

"How long is that?" Art wants to know.

"Over a hundred nights."

"Then I'm not a toddler anymore?"

"No, a bigger boy."

"And what's it called after that?" he asks.

"Hm... Maybe a school kid."

"No! I don't want that!"

He's bursting from sadness, which lands raw on Nomi's empty stomach.

"Can I call Granddad?"

"No, sweet, it's too early."

"But I know how."

"I mean that Granddad is asleep."

"But Granddad doesn't say 'give me some peace.'"

Art moves back and rolls over. He presses a thumb on the top of Mark's head and cries, "A hole!"

Mark shivers and cringes, yet Art whispers in his ear, "How come?"

The youthful, not excessively vain dad moans and sighs, knowing that only a sense-making answer may save the chance of some rest. "When we grow older, our hair gets thinner."

"Not mine?" Art checks.

"No."

"How old are you now?"

"Thirty-five."

"And Granddad?"

Mark thinks. "Not sure... Fifty-seven."

"And how old when you're dead?"

"Don't know."

"I know. More than a hundred!"

"OK, something like that. You can go and play, if you like... Your fleece top and slippers are downstairs."

"Or I'm going to sing."

He begins with "*Handy Pandy Beetle, it climbed on Daddy's neck. Down came the rain, but the sun is coming back.*" In order to mix the lyrics and reality, he says, "Look through the curtain! You go to work?"

Some days are an intermezzo, when time takes a breath. Spring is good for estate agents and all creatures. Nomi is still home a lot with the children, partly because that agrees with her, although the Art afternoons are harder to combine with work these days, mainly since his naps have become scarce.

As Mark often takes over, they enjoy the variation, freedom, and liveliness. He just dislikes the necessity of discipline and strictness for the kids, to which he's forced when Nomi is worn out.

Art loves to play outside, where he acts tough and seeks contact himself – without Dilli's flair – with others between two and eight years of age. Nomi sees how he tries to hold his own. Sometimes she lets him go with a pain in her stomach. She'd like to support and steer him continuously, shield him entirely from life in advance. How to prepare a child for the cruelty and powerlessness of man and nature: by taking away his innocence?

Nomi is a practical person who excels in order and efficiency, but these past years she's had spells of musings that are difficult to fit in.

Why didn't she ask Evan for a phone number? She doesn't know his last name and Anne Hoaver will not be listed anywhere. Not anymore.

She might ask Hattum, or Bernard could help via the publisher, if need be, but she'll try and wait for Evan to contact her. He did understand her intention, didn't he? He knows how to reach her, and she shouldn't disturb them there again. For the time being she won't leave for a midweek or weekend either.

<>

Due to a sore throat and a stubborn tickling cough, Bernard is having a bad night. At three a.m, sentences for *And Walk* pop up, that he writes down lying on his side, in the light of a lamp.

Then he nestles happily, but there's more to come and this happens a few times.

When he puts earplugs in, he can hear his heartbeats – only because he went down and up the stairs for the bathroom? Is he really "hearing" or rather feeling the thumping, due to defective pumping?

Bernard also wonders: have the neighbors turned up the bass's volume of their music in the dead of night? But in a daze filled with mockery he realizes that it's his own breathing, grinding by a blockage in the nose.

Have mercy, is my mind going too?

He capitulates and takes a tablet of codeine phosphate. *NB: this medicine can make you feel tired straightaway. It's used to suppress the cough reflex.*

At seven, he's downstairs in his bathrobe. He eats cottage cheese with fruit, and sips coffee, and keeps writing on the couch by the window, with just enough daylight.

He's floating between regions of the mind when the landline right beside him seems to ring at the top of its tone. At this hour he expects no salesperson, publisher, or journalist, only friends or family with bad news, but his parents are gone, his brother is young and jealous-making healthy, and Nomi has been through enough by now, hasn't she?

Or who'll be the judge of that?

Automatically he's answered before the caller's number

appears on the slow phone. "Hello?" And immediately they hang up.

Have hackers got me now?

His heart runs wild: what if Nomi or Dil or Art is lying at the bottom of the stairs and Mark is in the shower... God, let it please not be them! If they call from the hospital and that's why the signal is gone...

The phone rings again and once more he forgets to wait for the number. Now it's extra odd: he can hear that another number is speed-dialled, so the connection is cut again.

For the third time – as if it's meant to be biblical – he's hauled out of his atmosphere. He sees the number and can hear some breathing on the other end. "Art? Dil?"

They hang up. Must be Art, exploring the boundless world. Too bad that his doting or dotty granddad won't call back, scared to disturb the parents this early.

The *And Walk* manuscript is nearly finished and writing-urges need restrainment because of appointments and the lack of sleep. Even during breaks, ideas will be autonomous, also on his way to the dentist's and hairdresser's.

Being a writer is a peculiar and unsocial job that fatigues and feeds at the same time, or is it me?

Well, man, just do the two-day dishes, call the friends who've been in their new house for months now while you haven't been to admire, go and take flowers to Hannah's grave, prune bushes before they're uncontrollable, muck out the shed before you break a leg over the five-year spider webs, buy all the available medicine against the flu or sinusitis and heart ache, as a precaution – no luxury. Have yourself pampered with a lengthy massage, eat a plate of rolls, and run that fat off your hips again, don't check your watch and don't enter the bookshops where you'll get overwrought, send a postcard with colorful stamps instead of an email, go see neighbors who've crashed their car or have to close down their store.

Buy a fine pen and write a bright anti-depression book.

Page one:

Read a hundred social media a day and watch all the attached films, check the global glam news from lifestyle coaches and hairstyle celebs and wealthy influencers, then decide: who of these people or you or yours are of unsound mind? Finally come down with a snotty cold and blow all the crap out again.

His eye is caught by the codeine leaflet: *if you're troubled by side-effects, your pharmacist will also have noscapine. That is as good as codeine, with considerably fewer side-effects, but it's not covered by insurance.*

Will they spend their profits on cures for the side-effects? Who will write a column on the politics of insurance companies and the mental health department?

<>

For two days Anne has left a roll of toilet paper on the floor and fretted about the lime scale on the dish rack. She gets into a state when stars and such ("who is *not* on TV?") talk more and more trendy trash: "relax down!" Between the thousands of them they have one or two adjectives in their vocabularies, and when a third is used, the whole country will follow and drivel about nothing else.

So don't watch and listen, bitch, she tells herself.

But well, we need to stay in touch the least bit, don't we?

Ah, woman, remember what you've coped with of late. What would you do about the plane crash here and earthquake there: fly over and give a hand? We just gulp the footage.

Evan has taken two days off.

At night she wears earplugs again, a habit from the clinic era that she did break.

Around the rooms are notes with rules, tips, and tools, to find off and on, or Evan points them out unexpressly at the right moments, which is meekly appreciated.

Stick to regular meals.

Go to bed on time.

Skip dainties or sugary snacks.

Keep up with the chores and rhythmic motion.

Take one step and see what's next.

With tricky choices and doubts: take the middle course.

Don't sulk or complain but say and ask.

Determine: is this truly my problem?

Don't think long but find out and act.

On the third day, to end this crisis that had a concrete cause – only human and forgivable? – Anne goes and buys shampoo and lands by a shelf of eco baby-lotion, without perfume and not tested on animals. For a sec she wonders: why didn't they have this in her time? Or was it here unnoticed? As more things were.

She buys one flask for herself and one for Cindy's baby. She'll give it to her soon.

"For yourself?" Evan checks with decreasing concern.

"Yes, you see, it's wonderful care for the skin. You can use it too. Shall I do your back and bottom?"

In the afternoon she wants to go to her house again, that she almost calls *Reg's house* now, where he was born and briefly bred. What do experts keep telling us: the first six months of a life are the most important ones?

They also say: when you're thrown off a horse, get on it again at once.

Anne's head is clear enough to know that there's no golden mean this time, it's now or never. Grant has explained what should have been self-evident: once Art will truly and fully be back where he belongs, not lingering in her mind anymore, all space can be released for Reg, and she may heal.

"Do you want me to call Nomi?" Evan asks.

And a stranger would think that's a sister-in-law or a mutual friend.

"Yes, please."

"Would you like her to go first?"

"Well," Anne says, "there are things... that I bought for Art. Clothes he wore. And toys. I can imagine they'd like to have them."

Both parents.

Or to dump them and finish the madness forever.

"But Anne, only you can sort them out."

"Let me think..." She stutters with a thumb and finger on her eyelids, forcing herself, before the name comes out. "Nomi wanted to see what Art's place was like there. A sorted pile of objects in a box won't help. Will you ask her what she has in mind?"

In other circumstances Evan would say: 'you can do that yourself, if you wish.' And he seems to say this by mistake, "Maybe the two of you can go together?"

Anne gapes at him, and her goosebumps produce a visible shudder.

"Sorry, sorry," he hisses with reaching arms.

But watchfully he lets her be, and she heaves a deep sigh, as if she held her breath a long time.

She sits and says, "If you knew what I was hearing from Grant and staff and fellow... residents. For example: 'You're not as mad as you sound, or just as mad!' And that could also apply to you, but you might be less mad than you think."

Evan sinks down too and strokes his temples.

Neither of them laughs and there's no need to say, "Let's be serious now."

"What if it's feasible or beneficial, appropriate," Anne mumbles. "It would be up to her, of course. Would you call and ask her?"

"Now? You mean for plans later in the house?"

"Yes, please. I couldn't phone her myself."

"But I don't even have their number."

Anne stares at him, and he thinks out loud. "They're estate agents. Let's see."

Anne takes her folder with column notes, which can bring concentration and tranquility. By way of distraction.

She writes what comes up, to be developed later. "Taxes for homeopathic physicians equal consumption rates of synthetic perfumes and cosmetics, tobacco and liquor, but it's the doctors who need to cure the consumers of those products."

Her paper folder for *Time-In* is on the tall closet, in sight but out of reach as long as she's at the table. Holding a ballpoint pen, she takes care not to click the on and off tip constantly. It's an obnoxious sound for those who don't make it.

There's a rough draft on the laptop –

A training course on offer at the Lawyers Association begins as follows. *Name of the course: International Child Abduction.*

Then the absurdity of that is explained: this training will deal with the aims and practices of the International Child Abduction Treaty, as well as the role of advocacy in child abduction cases, with details on the activities of the Child Abduction Center. ...

If she was a lawyer, she would sign up. There's little embarrassment or secrecy left between Evan and Anne, and the marketing manager in him is not often lost for words. When he actually makes the call to Art's parents, there's a delicate instant, but he's not leaving the room for privacy, from shame or shyness.

"Good afternoon, this is Evan Bingham."

Mark answers with an open, calm and cheerful "Hello," presuming that Bingham is a potential client.

With dagger sharpness Evan realizes now that one of the children there might have answered the landline – if it's for both office and home? That happens when parents are busy or off to the bathroom. Or they teach the kids how to answer politely for practical purposes, for education!

What would he say to Art: not "Hello son. Is your mom or dad in? I was your acting dad for a while. We had a fabulous time. Remember our adventure by the pond? What a shame that you won't recall that or me for the rest of your life."

Unless...

Evan's voice is gone, and Mark repeats kindly, "Hello, this is Mark Meyer."

"I um... Is Nomi around?"

"No, on her mobile now."

There's another pause, until Evan says, "I'm sorry, Nomi and I have met, we talked about Art, and she expects my call. I'm Anne Hoaver's friend."

They did 'meet'.

Surely Mark knows about Nomi's visit, or has a tender nerve been stirred?

"Sorry," Mark says, "work and private stuff are mixed here. Nomi is at work, but if it's important, I mean, have you got her number?"

Mark waits. "On the site... OK?" he asks tensely. "Or can I take a message? Your number?"

"Um, yes, that's always handy."

A child's voice resonates through the house and phone – a boy or a girl? The age of about three? Close by and unrecognizable at the same time. Impatient or unafraid, it resounds timelessly, like ages ago, when the baby discovered his own voice and tested its volume and high tones – until it hurt Evan's ears. Now he might distinguish words coming from the same boy.

"Excuse me," Mark says. "There's a little man on the toilet here, and that's good news, but he doesn't know I'm on the phone. Apologies!"

"Better hurry then. Thanks."

Evan takes a breath and reviews Anne's situation, glad that he didn't stop to ponder beforehand.

Once more he opens the tasteful and adequate site of the estate agents, including Nomi's number. He dials right away, but it goes to voicemail. He doesn't want to leave a message, she has his number after all, but at the last second he realizes that she can't link it to a familiar name, so without a message from him she might never call back, or late.

Is that a hint or indication? It's not the right thing or time?

"This is Evan, also on behalf of Anne..." is the only thing he can utter, which seems an awful great deal to him, sucked into the voicemail.

Wobbly, he walks to the fridge, gets a can of beer and drinks half of it in one go. Then he sits at the table and sees a perspective or relativity of a year and day in a life's course. Dumbfounded by the common knowledge that 'it's all about now', he gulps the rest of his beer.

<>

With simple explanations Nomi often asks for a photo or video hour without the residents present. Fully in her element and the moment, she wanders around the large house of a couple who will retire and move nostalgically to an apartment in the town of their roots.

The grass has been mown, smelling as if it can feel the rain of later, and the windows have been cleaned.

Ruffled by this joy – can it be true or right? – she takes a break and checks her phone. Evan's message is between two others, one from Mark, that she answers first, as a way to regain herself.

It's another while before she answers Evan. "We can meet, the three or four of us. I'll confer at home."

After the kids' negotiations about watching television, the family meal is a bizarre interlude to Nomi, whose mind is elsewhere.

Dilli listens to conversations, she remembers and follows up, sometimes after days. Nomi has stopped being surprised. Art's memory has an ease about it: human existence looks as clear to him as it was to Kierkegaard: 'Life can only be understood backwards, but it must be lived forwards.'

In his photo book, two months will be missing – from an age when a great deal is going on. No doubt, Art and Dilli will view the album. The names of Evan and Anne can be mentioned out of kid-ear range, before Art will say: 'I want to meet these people.'

They must have photos too. We can't bring that up, can we?

"Will you come to their house?" Nomi asks Mark.

"Do you want me to?"

"Yes, but not for me, only if you care to yourself."

"Tonight?" Mark asks.

"Why not, before the storm, or tomorrow morning. I'll call him back in a minute."

"But will both of them be there? That would make me feel awkward, as if we are viewers. And if Evan comes by himself, I'd feel sorry for him if you and me are together."

"Oh well..." Nomi shakes her head.

And Mark asks, "Would you dare being with her in that house?"

Or anywhere.

"I think so, but let's leave it to Evan."

With Evan himself she feels little discomfort or sourness. He went through a doubleness of spectator and perpetrator, which few people will recognize.

"We could ask Bernard," Mark suggests, "I mean to come and babysit. But he's under the weather and very occupied... If you don't mind, I'd prefer to stay home tonight, for your sake in the broadest sense. You can finish what began with you and Art, which is nothing to do with guilt, or me finding an excuse."

Words can smart and burn, or clean.

She nods and shakes her head. Because of the children she takes her phone upstairs.

Evan and she agree to meet at seven that night.

Lost in complex thoughts, she walks down slowly, and in the hallway she asks Mark, "Should I bring photos to show them, of Art? As he is now?"

"Are you out of your mind? To rub salt in their wounds?"

Nomi is appalled. "Of course not!"

"But are you going for your own good or theirs?"

She squats on the lowest stair step and says, "I hope everyone's! Remember, I created the temptation. I left Art in a public space. I gave her the opportunity!"

Those moments are still there.

But don't drag them along!

"No, you left Art in good faith."

Fiercer than before, Mark goes on clearing the hall, with the coat rack and storage closet. "Better go," he adds, "and set things right, for yourself, once and for all and everybody. Please, remember at last: it ended well, you can leave the nasty guilt behind. I'll take Dilli to bed and put Art in the bath; he had an hour of sleep in the afternoon."

Nomi won't let her frame of mind be affected. "Alright, I'll bring photos just in case, and we'll see."

"You can't leave photos there!" Mark cries out. "Don't give any to them!"

As if Art would fall into their hands again.

"No," says Nomi, "I won't, but they don't do voodoo."

"OK, we know nothing about her, so we'll stay on guard."

With lots of benefits of doubts.

The adjacent room has been mouse-quiet, and on the threshold Dilli appears. "What can't Mom do? Where are you going?"

Nomi has never been good at lying, no matter how responsible or necessary it was to do so. Trying to sound casual, she says, "I'll be doing errands."

"Can I come?" Art asks. "I've done a sleep!"

"Sorry, not this time."

Nomi has been known to say, "If you won't nag for candy in the shops! You know what, we'll brush your teeth for the night first, to be free and easy later."

But no spontaneous adventure tonight.

<>

The sky is overcast, but for April it's exceptionally warm, and there's no wind. A thunderstorm would come against the wind direction, forever deceptive. It can lie low for hours and even dissolve into a void.

"That was no big deal," people may say then, who would have liked some sensation or a kind of discharge.

Nomi can't seem to tell if it's her third or fourth time at this house now, all in all. Each time it's been mistakably different. Deep down, this visit remains inevitable, and somehow she's getting used to it, including both the repulsion and sympathy. The tough days of your child's life can be forgotten, that's natural protection, but Art's away-days never passed by, or they passed her by and undermined. To him they may have been agreeable and harmonious. She needs to salvage a part of that period yet, for the sake of her own completeness.

Overcoming oneself can be fearfully similar to surrendering. Nomi shies from a step that will affect the fragile privacy of others. She failed to inquire if Anne would be present, because that can't be, can it? She'd neither invite nor stop her.

If she were Anne...

Now she needs to keep her head and focus on parking the car: not close to his or theirs in front of the house, but which one is it?

The curtains are open. Although she throws merely a swift look, it can't escape her that many lights are on, just like for a viewing, and there are two persons.

She rings the bell and warns herself: think of Art, yet stay in this present, because it's much bigger than the past and future. But that doesn't go for these people. Like a slap with a wet cloth, it strikes her that their current time is a minimum or an emptiness, unless something can be done about it.

The other doubt returns as well: should she have consulted the police? Or their therapist? It's too late to cancel, the door opens, there's nothing left but her feelings. She has initiated this.

She's the one who offers her hand without a word, which Anne shakes. Nomi discerns so much sorrow and apprehension and courage that she lets go to wipe her eyes, which don't know where to look then.

Until Anne says in half a voice, "I don't want to hide, but I'm terrified. Not by you, but of my own emotions, the vehemence."

Nomi's cheeks hurt, as if there's a lockjaw. She can't say: me too, and I'm ashamed, because my pain is much smaller now.

Am I an intruder?

If I'd simply skipped the third bike store, or brought Art inside with us, all distress of the past years would never have been. Or would it find an alternative route, if we have things coming as meant to be?

Anne says, "I've been prepared for this a long time, with confrontations and all, but not as brusque as today – even if it's been due. This is only my second time here since... In a profound way it seems less hard with you around. Because it's important. Forgive me."

Nomi says, "And me, please. It's also my second time inside."

When Anne looks her in the eye in total silence, Nomi adds, "Yes."

"I'll be in the garden," Anne says. "You'll feel free everywhere. You can ask us everything too, of course."

Anne withdraws.

Nomi doesn't want to pervade Reg's area, that would be a kind of violation, but it is what Art had to do, it's what happened to him and all his strong senses.

She goes upstairs, past the little gate, stubbornly redundant, and the door to the nursery is open, with the cot and sleeping bag, the dresser, changing cushion and requirements, like the toys for distraction at sore-bottom times.

She sees each object but won't touch them. It's a tall order as it is to think of Art, the way he must have been here, as lively as at home. He lived here a shorter time than Reg, but Nomi stays for as long as she can, where he crawled on all bare fours. Greatness between sitting and walking happened then.

<>

Anne doesn't mind the dark sky; it makes a spot in the garden less conspicuous, where a new fruit tree has not been planted. Not yet?

Evan is busy with weeds and molehills, cutting and raking, and he likes asking her for advice. The funny, good man has mown around the lady-smocks to leave them intact, the way he'd make a child happy. Now there's a lilac little island in a sea of green and white and yellow. But pruning the climbing roses he typically ignores her advice: he wears no gloves and sustains a couple of scratches.

Next time she'll give him a hand, although she wouldn't cut the grass from under his feet when he loves to be active.

She's brought a novel and notebook out, but in order to see the words she needs to sit close to a house window with lights on inside. As a local anesthetic for this evening, it's fine to write a sentence now and then.

Her eyes also follow the clouds, that stack until they topple, and the swallows as whimsical as the butterflies. It's no idyll, she has a headache and in the distance there's always a baby crying or crowing or calling out. Or could it be a lamb in the play farm?

Cindy sends a sisterly or best-friend email discussing regular babysitting after November – one morning or afternoon a week? – and she might dare saying yes, because cot death has no earthly cause, and it would not happen twice in her presence, would it? Let alone the stealing. She has learned her lessons, and fate is not that cruel or crazy?

They know all that, Cindy and her. Still, she will ask Doctor Grant again about extreme bad luck: are some people a magnet for things like that?

Nah, rubbish!

She'll also have to ask about the congenital aspect of her disposition, versus the results of insight, willpower, love, stamina, before

Evan may insist passionately on a terrific new beginning with a family, "Since the country won't be flooded", and there will be no more war or pandemic?

He must be right: rescue plans for the world are made by those who know a thing or two: politicians, engineers and physicians? A gigantic businessman? Or they're bluffing their ways to office during elections. Are there any eco-people with big, bold views and sufficient power?

Evan is already brave enough to say, "We share the death of Reg sort of double, because I wasn't there."

Does he mean that he could or should have prevented it?

Did Cindy lack the courage to ask the babysit question in her face? No, idiot, she sends emails about all things, and this is her thoughtful way of giving me time to reflect or be upset.

A young cat from nextdoor – born after her time here? – comes and licks drops from the outside tap. It brushes Anne's legs, crushes wild forget-me-nots, and beheads a field mouse on the pretty alehoof, that doesn't even blink.

Wil phones to say that she has a bad flu. "It's everywhere, so watch out."

But through the window Anne spots Nomi inside. She goes and tells her that the sleeping bag and cuddly toy were bought for Art. It's a relief to Nomi, even though she's felt that nothing horrible sticks to any of Reg's things. His death was probably a painless return or passage to something timeless. It must have been a profound and tender kind of fulfillment – almost something literal?

The house has never been 'haunted'.

"Will you have them?" Anne asks. "And some toys?"

"To be honest, I don't really know."

Should things be left for Mark to see? It's a pity that he's not been in here, but she keeps that to herself. Life doesn't need to be faultless or flawless, although that is an obstinate wish of hers.

Nomi asks, "What would *you* like?"

"Well, in a way they don't belong here." Anne wants to speak fast, but she swallows and looks outside. "Maybe, if they go with.... It could help me saying goodbye. Not sure."

Would it not help to have a 'souvenir', keepsake, memento? What's the damn word; *not* 'reminder'.

Nomi waits and says, "What's best for you?"

"Alright, despite myself... Shall I get them and put them in a bag?"

A nice and solid one, no plastic.

"Yes, please."

Going upstairs, Anne discovers how much more she can bear or face now. She will be able to return to the day when this flight of stairs was a slope of ice.

With sore hands she packs Art's things respectfully and takes them to Nomi downstairs.

Evan comes in puffing and sweating. "The garden can do with a downpour, but it wouldn't surprise me if it's a false alarm. Sorry, can't shake hands."

With a helpless gesture he shows Nomi some scratches and dirt on them.

"You've been very thorough," she says. And after a gaze into the garden she adds, "Thank you both. Please, have a good new life, including the past. I mean, there's no blame anymore."

Nomi leaves without hurrying or tarrying.

Evan sees her to the door, saying "Thank you so much," and he walks on to the shower.

<>

Dear Anne > Evan,

Is this email account still used? Otherwise, I'll think of something else. Or it would be confirmation that this whole idea is too baloney for words.

It stays hard for me to grasp that our collaboration came to such an abrupt and sad end, simultaneous to my wondrous reunion with Art, but I've heard that you and Nomi have been in contact, and that helps me coming to terms with it yet.

Am I correct to understand that you're considering moving back to your house? If so, I could write a letter to people in your street and explain 'how on earth you find the nerve, how it shows outstanding character and wisdom on everyone's part.' Or am I being a meddlesome and presumptuous fool? You could be better at it yourself, of course, but I happen to know all sides of the situation. It's no accomplishment.

My flu head is a brick of mucus, and the fever is doing a vexingly slow job, so perhaps this is part of a delirium or a narrowed consciousness. Let me mention this just in case, for the sake of completeness or open closure: should you and Evan ever wish to see Art again, if it's beneficial or necessary at some stage, it seems to me you can put it to Nomi and Mark, and if ever they agree, I might be of modest, practical use, for instance when Art is with me or we're clambering our hearts out at one of these adventure parks.

One day you may let me know whether the fever has affected my brain. Or tell me if that's what you think already. Now I'm off to the vitamin C, nose spray, cough syrup, oscillococcinum and more means of help, to cure the body and soul – I hope.

Best wishes, final or not,

Bernard.

. . .

After reading that several times in the course of three days, lost between opposite emotions, Anne imagines or fantasizes how Evan and she would take Art cycling one more time – even if he no longer fits in the handlebar or carrier seat. And who knows what that could lead to, how it might continue in one way or another, if she won't be certified again first. But what if a young and foolhardy power dog tears loose from a slender owner and shoots in front of the bike wheel! Madness happens before you can act, and they could have a bad fall: Art on his head...

It can happen to anybody, with or without someone else's child.

But no no no, can't be in reality! Let the image suffice and have effects.

She sends Bernard a word of deep appreciation. "I'll keep your email and will reply shortly, or when I can. Many thanks. Get well! Now I'm off to Reg's farewell, without palpable means of help. And without self-pity!"

<>

With a soft brush and breathing breaks, with professionals and Evan on standby, Anne digs through Art's time, to reach Reg again and distinguish them definitively. Their lives got entwined so much, they need to be disentangled, especially the interdependency of all three.

After that, she can picture Reg lifelike too, at various ages up till now and later, based on perceptions of her own surroundings, in combination with her evocative and realistic imagination, so that he will remain, although they didn't stay together.

Sometimes it's too lifelike for comfort.

When other moments are clearly unreal, they can be a touch of letting go –

He's built three firm towers in the colors of the flag, then he runs around the room like a soccer pro and cries, "We win!"

When he spills some sticky syrup on his best shirt, she quickly fishes a tissue out of his pocket and cleans up, to which he says, "Yes, you can borrow it."

After pinching candy from a mate, he's sent out sternly to stand in the hallway. Another time he discovers his own anger and says, "I'll go stand in the hall myself."

His social virtues grow tremendously, across bumps and fears. Waiting for a train to faraway, he takes a seat on a platform bench, gently between Anne and a shabby, elderly man, to whom he speaks meekly, "This is a bench for three?"

When the man smiles and nods, Reg takes a recent present out of his bag and shows it, not to boast but to share its beauty and his joy. "This is an R, for Reg. It's cardboard and that can break. So, I'm very careful. But we're also strong. I'm Reg."

The train trip is wonderful but quite long, and right before his destination, he falls asleep, half on his Legos, half on Anne's arm.

ABOUT RUNNING WILD PRESS

Running Wild Press publishes stories that cross genres with great stories and writing. RIZE publishes great genre stories written by people of color and by authors who identify with other marginalized groups. Our team consists of:

Lisa Diane Kastner, Founder and Executive Editor
Joelle Mitchell, Licensing and Strategy Lead
Cody Sisco, Acquisition Editor, RIZE
Benjamin White, Acquisition Editor, Running Wild
Peter A. Wright, Acquisition Editor, Running Wild
Resa Alboher, Editor
Angela Andrews, Editor
Sandra Bush, Editor
Ashley Crantas, Editor
Rebecca Dimyan, Editor
Abigail Efird, Editor
Aimee Hardy, Editor
Henry L. Herz, Editor
Cecilia Kennedy, Editor

Barbara Lockwood, Editor
AE Williams, Editor
Scott Schultz, Editor
Rod Gilley, Editor
Kelly Ottiano, Editor
Carolyn Banks, Editor
Brittany Bell, Editor

Evangeline Estropia, Product Manager
Pulp Art Studios, Cover Design
Standout Books, Interior Design
Polgarus Studios, Interior Design

Learn more about us and our stories at www.runningwildpublishing.com

Loved this story and want more? Follow us at www.runningwildpublishing.com, www.facebook.com/runningwildpress, on Twitter @lisadkastner @RunWildBooks